Advance Praise for *The Eye of the Tigress*

"Take a cartel Queen Pin, two dueling fed law agencies who hate each other and you, judges who would love to see you at the end of a rope, clients who don't pay, and sicarios locked and loaded with full magazines of bullets with your name on them—and it's just another day at the office for Cash McCahill, defense lawyer extraordinaire and the bane of prosecutors, judges, cops, G-Men, G-Women, and the Dallas Bar Association.

Former U.S. Attorney-turned-novelist Paul Coggins has provided us with the second installment of Cash McCahill's misadventures as he is thrust into a maelstrom of warring drug cartels in *The Eye of the Tigress*—a kick-ass tale with more twists and turns than a high mountain road, and stunning characters that are marginally fictional—is the perfect antidote for those long days and nights of lockdown at home. The only downside is we now have to wait for book #3!"

—Payne Harrison, *New York Times*
Bestselling Author of *Storming Intrepid*

"Paul Coggins has done it again, another hard-to-put-down crime thriller featuring criminal defense attorney Cash McCahill. With a plot that sizzles and an unforgettable cast of characters, *The Eye of the Tigress* takes you on a wild ride that you'll remember long after you turn the final page. Buy a copy today!"

—Harry Hunsicker, Former Executive Vice President of the Mystery Writers of America and the author of *Texas Sicario*

"Author Paul Coggins' tenure as a defense attorney again serves him well for Cash McCahill's newest adventure delving into the criminal underworld. The story's narrative engulfs you with sharp characterizations, then keeps you buckled up tight for the ride to follow. Himself a blend of snarky wit and derring-do, McCahill remains the attorney you want and need for your next dustup with the cartel...or perhaps for his own, tiger included. Fast-paced and simply wonderful, here is a worthy sequel you won't put down."

—Brent Jones, Author of *Days of Steel Rain*

Also by Paul Coggins

Sting Like A Butterfly

A Cash McCahill Novel

THE EYE
OF THE
TIGRESS

PAUL COGGINS

SAVIO
REPVBLIC

A SAVIO REPUBLIC BOOK
An Imprint of Post Hill Press
ISBN: 978-1-64293-896-8
ISBN (eBook): 978-1-64293-897-5

The Eye of the Tigress
© 2021 by Paul Coggins
All Rights Reserved

Cover Design by Cody Corcoran

posthillpress.com
New York • Nashville
Published in the United States of America

1 2 3 4 5 6 7 8 9 10

To Becky, Gina, and Jess
A Trio of Tigresses, Burning Bright

A ZEN STORY

A man walking across a field encountered a tiger. Fearing for his life, the man fled, but the tiger gave chase. The man reached the edge of a cliff, and just as he thought the tiger would get him, he spotted a vine growing over the edge of the cliff. Grabbing it, he swung himself over the edge to safety.

The tiger snarled at him from above. While precariously hanging in midair, the man saw another tiger growling at him from below. Trembling, he clutched the thin vine that was saving him from serving as dinner for the tigers. *What could be worse than this?* he wondered.

Then two mice appeared and began gnawing at the vine. As they chewed and the man pondered his fate, he saw a plump strawberry on a ledge next to him. Grasping the vine with one hand, he plucked the strawberry with the other.

Ah, how sweet it tasted!

CHAPTER ONE

Before Cash woke in hell, the last thing he remembered was the hypodermic needle that sent him there.

A death rattle greeted his return to the real world. Well, a rattle anyway.

He lay on his back on the cold, concrete floor of a dimly lit building that smelled like a barn. Six feet away, a diamondback rattlesnake coiled for a strike.

An inch of reinforced glass separated the lawyer and the rattler. That and the whim of *La Tigra* looming over him.

Cash catalogued the damage through his reflection in the glass. A black eye and a busted lip. Three days of stubble. Brown hair, a matted mess. But on the bright side, still boyishly handsome for his mid-forties.

From Cash's vantage, *La Tigra* looked ten feet tall, roughly twice her true height. This was his first brush with her in the flesh, though he'd seen plenty of photos. For two decades, she had made the FBI's most wanted list. Ditto for the DEA and ICE.

An incredible run for a cartel kingpin. Unprecedented for a queenpin.

Had he not known her true age, he would've undershot by a decade and pegged her as late thirties or early forties, based

1

on her hard body and mocha complexion. Her only visible ding—a tiny white scar—bisected her upper lip. The curl of a cruel smile swallowed the scar.

Cash rolled onto his stomach and climbed slowly to his feet, woozy from whatever drugs jacked with his system and senses. "Where am I?"

"In the world's sixth largest zoo," *La Tigra* said, "and the largest private one."

Her English was good. Far better than Cash's Spanish.

He turned full circle to take in the hive of glass enclosures housing snakes of all sizes, stripes, and colors. Hundreds of them were on display, not counting the armed guards at the exit.

"I began your tour with the reptiles," *La Tigra* said, "where you should feel most at home."

His full-body shiver said otherwise. It wasn't the first time he'd been called a snake. Or compared to one.

Nor did it calm his nerves when a miniature crane whirred into action, remotely controlled by an acne-scarred soldier who looked all of seventeen. The kid should be home playing video games and surfing porn sites.

The crane lifted a cage containing a hyperactive white mouse and swung the cage up and over the rattler's terrarium. The mouse froze. The floor of the cage opened, and dinner fell into the snake's lair.

Cash turned away from the sacrifice.

La Tigra didn't. "Your last stop will be my pride and joy."

Cash shuddered. *Last stop* sounded ominous. Two guards dragged him outside the reptile building and into the merciless heat. It took seconds for his eyes to adjust to daylight. The natural habitat preserve extended in all directions—far as the eye could see.

La Tigra took a frayed straw hat from a groundskeeper and pulled it low down her forehead, shading her face. The hat clashed with her black, leather outfit.

He had a sinking sense there was a shot clock on his life. Score soon or time would expire.

The straw hat held the key to his survival. Not the hat so much as what it said about *La Tigra*. A reminder that she had a keen sense of self-preservation and a practical streak a mile long.

From all he had read and heard, she had wiped out hundreds, perhaps thousands, to become the apex predator of the human zoo. To remain on top had called for even more sacrifices.

A drug czar had to be ruthless. A drug czarina, ruthless squared.

What he didn't know was whether she killed for sport, pleasure, or amusement. If for any or all of those reasons, it was the end of the line for him.

Perhaps, however, she eliminated an impediment only after running the cold calculus and concluding that the downside of letting someone live outweighed the upside of keeping another pawn on the board.

Another snake in the pit.

Soldiers shoved Cash onto a golf cart. *La Tigra* sat next to him. A caravan of carts carried the odd couple and a dozen armed goons down a twisty, paved path. Past galloping giraffes on the right, lazy lions to the left, elephants huddled under shade trees ahead, and in the far distance, a herd of hippos wading in a lake.

"It was brave of you to sacrifice yourself to save the FBI bitch," *La Tigra* said during the ride. "Brave or stupid."

"I've been told they're not mutually exclusive." Cash's voice barely rose above a whisper.

"Either way, it was beyond stupid of Hector to trade the beautiful agent for you. Unforgivable." Her last word was spoken more to herself than to Cash.

Poor Hector.

The carts stopped outside the domain of a white tiger, who emerged from a condo-sized shelter and approached the ten-foot glass fence, drooling at the prospect of feeding time.

Cash backed away from the fence. The tiger held its ground.

"He's beautiful," Cash said.

"*She* is magnificent." *La Tigra* sounded like a proud mother. "One of only five in existence."

"You might want to check your math on that," Cash said. "I saw one like her in Vegas, as well as in every zoo I've visited the past thirty years."

She shook her head. "Not like her. Bianca is a white Siberian, born and bred in the wild. What you have seen are crossbreeds, born in tiger mills and raised in captivity."

Cash would've bet his law license that Bianca was the only purebred in the hands of a private collector. Not that he still had a license.

Mesmerized by the beauty of the beast, Cash was slow to notice the crane truck rolling down the path. It stopped at the fence, facing the tiger. Big-ass crane this time. Had to be thirty feet tall, with a scoop large enough to lift a man.

Didn't take long to figure out how this would end. Cash's life—like that of the late white mouse—dangled by a thread. A sinner in the hands of an angry goddess.

He was down to his final appeal. "Killing me would be a bad deal for you. Worse than Hector's tradeoff." His voice cracked.

"You have nothing to bargain with," she said, "and no time left."

"Do you know who I am?"

She nodded.

"And what I do for a living?"

"You're a fucking lawyer. I own a hundred just like you, on both sides of the border."

It was his turn to shake his head. "Not like me. Not with my trial record." He forced himself to slow the pitch. Kept his voice steady, more or less. "Call Mariposa Benanti. She'll vouch for me."

La Tigra laughed. "Who do you think told me about you? She has a final message for you. Said she would see you in hell."

"What's it worth to have a guaranteed win in an American court?" Despite his best efforts, he rushed the pitch. "A get-out-of-jail-free card...one you can play any time...any place you choose."

"Hmmm, you said free?" She sounded skeptical but interested.

"I waive my trial fee. You pay only expenses."

She nodded to the crane operator. The crane revved up. The scoop yawned.

"Okay," he shouted, "I'll cover the expenses."

She smiled, and both the crane and the tiger went away hungry.

CHAPTER TWO

Three months and one regained law license later....

Cash McCahill stared into the killer's eyes. Not for the first time. Probably for the last.

This was far from his first visit to the women's prison in the sticks of west Texas. Hell, he could hold a reunion of ex-clients here at CCI Big Spring—the latest and largest facility fattening the wallets of prison profiteers.

Officially, CCI stood for "Contracted Correctional Institution." Unofficially, for "Cash Cow Inmates." Prisoners locked up and milked dry by the American Corrections Enterprise, or ACE for short.

Cash entered the visiting room and sat across the table from Mariposa Benanti. The windowless room stank of sweat and cheap perfume, and the peeling, puke-green paint job gave it all the personality of a cardboard box. Regs required the space set aside for lawyer visits to be soundproof and bug-free, but Cash harbored doubts on both counts.

Despite the familiar setting, today provided Cash with one first—a chance to study Mariposa in captivity, to gauge the toll taken by her lockup pending trial.

Pushing fifty, she seemed smaller than he remembered. Swapping stilettos for slippers had shaved three inches. Her lips had deflated—he guessed going cold turkey on Botox would do that. Crow's feet were taking root. Gray swaths streaked her dark hair. Cruel lighting bleached out an olive complexion, and orange was definitely not her color.

At the sight of Cash, her dark eyes flickered to life, but the jolt of seeing a familiar face fizzled as quickly as it had flared. While seconds silently ticked by, her eyes sank deep into their recesses.

No smile greeted him. Then again, she had rarely smiled on the outside. Not a good look for her, and she knew it.

Cash had expected to find Mariposa in even worse shape, given her self-exile to the isolation wing. Fifty-three days in solitary behind her and twenty-seven to go before the bell rang for round one with the federal prosecutors.

At Seagoville Federal Correctional Institution—where Cash had done his time for jury tampering—he had spent only a week in solitary. Six days and seven nights alone had left scars on his psyche. Every fortnight or so, the cold sweats struck.

He had landed in isolation as punishment for a smart mouth. Mariposa sought refuge in solitary in a desperate bid to stay alive, or at least to last longer there than she would in gen pop.

Given the change in their circumstances, it was damn unfair that she could still jump-start his juices. Heaven help the prosecutors if her defense lawyer managed to pack the jury with straight males.

"About time you showed." Mariposa's voice hadn't changed. Still the same toxic blend of brittle and badass. Equal parts hurtful and haughty. "You playing hard to get?"

"You haven't got me." Cash delivered the line straight, as if he actually believed it.

"Yet," she said.

He shed his ex-lover skin and slipped into lawyer mode. Legal Ethics 101: set the ground rules for the meeting at the outset and stick to them. "I don't and can't represent you."

Not that I'd want to.

He went on. "That means whatever you say to me will not be privileged and confidential. Also means the feds can bug this room. Keep that in mind before you decide to bare your soul."

Her eyes narrowed. "Why can't you represent me?" It came off more like an accusation than a question.

"For starters, the government has put me on its witness list to testify at your trial next month. Ethical rules don't allow me to be a lawyer and a witness in the same case."

"You weren't always so keen on following the rules—certainly not while you were representing my husband by day and screwing me by night."

Damn. Cash would hate for that statement to be picked up on tape. The last thing he needed was another beef with the bar.

"It was never clear back then who was screwing whom," he said. "Either way, I never lost a case for Larry."

"Was that to save his skin or yours?"

"Your late husband made it painfully clear on many occasions that either we both won or both lost." The defensiveness drained from his voice. "Even if I could represent you and you could afford to hire me—"

She cut him off. "I'm a very rich woman."

"You *were* a rich woman. But since the feds froze your assets, you couldn't afford to hire my paralegal."

"So you really think the government found all my assets?" Her tone said *not a chance.*

Two ways to interpret her allusion to offshore accounts in tax havens, given the likely presence of a bug in the room. Either a slip of the tongue by her, or a warning shot at him.

Much as Cash hoped for the former, he steeled himself for the latter. "Remember what I said. Our conversation isn't privileged, and this room could be wired."

Her tone turned hard. "If I go down, it won't be alone."

Nope, not a slip. Of the legal fees paid by the Benantis over the past decade, Cash wondered how much had been dirty money, laundered to look and smell clean. He came up with a rough calculation: *all of it.*

"As I was saying before being interrupted, even if I could represent you and you could afford me, there'd still be one tiny technicality that would prevent me from taking your case. You tried to have me killed."

"Well, if you're going to hold that against me." She laughed.

He didn't.

"For what it's worth," she said, "I had no choice. It was either you or me."

"So you did have a choice."

"Yes, and I made the same call you would've in the circumstances."

"Then I'll make the same decision now that you would if our roles were reversed." He rubbed his chin. "Come to think of it, our roles have been reversed. When I was doing time and

you were on the outside, I don't recall a single visit from you."
He stood. "That's my cue to exit."

"You won't walk away from me."

"Why the hell not?"

"Because you are who you are. You may not be *my* lawyer,
but you're still *a* lawyer. Even worse, the kind who got in the
racket for all the wrong reasons."

"As if you'd know the right ones."

Her stab at a smile fell short. "Money, prestige, power. But
mostly money."

He didn't ask about her list of the wrong reasons for doing
what he did. "Stop dancing around and get down to business.
What am I doing here?"

"You have to convince *La Tigra* to spare my life."

It was Cash's turn to laugh. "And while I'm at it, why don't
I get the feds to issue you a formal apology?"

"I'm dead serious," she said.

You're half-right anyway.

"I'm in no position to ask our mutual friend to the south
for a favor. Other way around, I owe her a big one," he said.

A roach the size of a rat skittered across the floor. Good
timing. Reminded Cash of a lawyer he and Mariposa knew all
too well. "Besides, this sounds like a job for your trial counsel,
Rhoden."

She stiffened in her seat. "We both know who hired Rocket
and what he was hired to do."

"Puh-leeze," Cash said, "that publicity whore calls himself
Rocket, but no one else does." He didn't dispute her read of
the fix she was in. Higher-ups had hired Rhoden to make sure
Mariposa didn't flip.

"I don't give a shit what anyone calls him," she said, "but we both know what he is."

"Then I'll give you the same advice I'd give my best friend if she were in trouble, free of charge." Cash almost choked on the last three words. He hated to fall into the habit of handing out freebies. Downright unprofessional of him. "If you don't trust your lawyer, get a new one."

"Not an option," Mariposa said.

Cash shook his head slowly. "You can't go to trial with a lawyer you—"

She cut him off again. "We both know that I won't make it to trial, not unless you help me."

He didn't challenge that either. "Don't get your hopes up, but I'll make a call."

"You have to ask her face-to-face, and by ask, I mean beg." Her eyes misted. Not the first time she had used that weapon on him.

It worked every time. He pushed away from the table but couldn't escape the look in her eyes. "If you think I'd voluntarily return to Mexico, you're delusional. The last time I went down there, I almost ended up as tiger food."

"The point being," she said, "that you talked your way out of a jam back then. You can do the same for me now."

"If the goal of this conversation is to tee up your insanity defense, put me on your witness list. I'll testify you're certifiable."

"We meant something to each other once," she said.

"I hate to keep harping on this, but that was before you gave the green light to kill me."

"Can we get past that?" Her voice broke. "You're my only hope."

"There is another way." Bug or no bug, he owed her his best advice. "Witness protection."

She shook her head. "Your FBI squeeze has already dangled that poison apple. Problem is, the feds have a lousy track record of keeping their witnesses alive."

He rummaged for a Plan C but came up empty. "Exactly what am I supposed to tell *La Tigra?*"

"If she lets me be, I'll cop to all counts of the indictment. No deal. No cooperation. Spend the rest of my days inside, doing whatever the fuck this place does to turn a profit."

"Would you buy that if you were in her shoes?"

"Only if you sold it."

"I'll think about it," he said, "but I start a short trial tomorrow. Have to wrap that up before I could go anywhere."

She reached across the table, grabbed his hands, and squeezed. "I'm hanging on day to day here." Her voice swelled. "So are you."

No need for the second warning that she had the goods on him. The first shot had done the trick. He broke the grip and stood.

A crunch underfoot meant one roach down. One to go.

CHAPTER THREE

Cash couldn't leave the women's unit at Big Spring without checking on a client. He had Wanda Walters—a.k.a. "Wacky Wanda"—pulled from the prison gym and brought to the visiting room.

Good thing she came alone, because he couldn't have picked her from a lineup. That's how much she had changed.

She had gone from being a punching bag to actually punching a bag, transforming her body from whippet thin to wiry taut. Four hours a day in the weight room will do that, boosted by a regular 'roid supply.

Three years ago, Wanda—a mousy bank teller—had fallen under the spell of a con artist and dipped into the till to buy the expensive toys that kept him around and aroused.

He testified against the lovestruck teller and got a walk. She took the fall.

Today, her ego had ballooned, along with her pecs, biceps, and triceps. She could pump more iron than men half her age and twice her size and outwrestle all comers, Cash included.

Determined to prove her dominance, she rolled up the sleeve of her orange jumpsuit, past the elbow and the fresh dragon tattoo encircling her bicep. By prison standards, her tatt rocked. Low bar.

"Let's arm wrestle." She assumed the position. Right elbow anchored on the metal table. Hand in the air. Eyes daring Cash to accept the challenge.

He leaned back in the chair. "Let's not and just say we did."

"Chicken?" Wanda's voice registered lower and more masculine with each visit.

"Guilty as charged," he said. "In the interest of self-preservation, I subscribe to my own personal philosophy. I call it the four Cs: Cash's Code of Constructive Cowardice. Saves my fragile ego and my more fragile body from many a bruise."

Her twitching fingers taunted him. "Man up and grow a pair. We can make this contest interesting. I win, and you represent me gratis. If you pull off the upset, I double your fee."

Cash started to point out that she hadn't paid him a penny since he'd pried her file from the grubby fingers of Tony Dial—a.k.a. "Terrible Negotiator Tony." T.N.T for short. That waddling case of malpractice had bamboozled her into copping to five counts of embezzlement, with no cap on the sentence and no credit for restitution.

Cash shelved the nonpayment issue, allowing Wanda to save face. "Don't make me regret asking to see you while I was in the neighborhood," he said.

"Yeah, I hear you're representing the new bitch on the block, the stuck-up hottie hiding out in stir."

"You heard wrong on two counts. I'm not representing her, and she's not stuck-up. Just suffers from a strong interest in staying alive."

"If that dumb bitch thinks she's safer in stir than gen pop, she's nuts. In stir, no one can hear you scream."

Cash rubbed his chin. Maybe an insanity defense had legs for Mariposa. For Wacky Wanda too.

With the test of strength taken off the table, Wanda lowered her forearm. "How's my appeal coming?"

"Technically, you don't have a right to appeal." Not the first time he'd told her that. "You bargained that away when—"

She cut him off. "That fool Tony did that."

"Okay, he cut the deal, but you signed off on it. So now you're limited to a habeas petition, with ineffective assistance of counsel being the sole ground left open to us."

"Tony was as fucking useless as tits on a bull dyke."

Cash couldn't argue with that. "I plan to file your petition next week, and we'll see how it goes. In the meantime, do me a solid and keep an eye on your new BFF in solitary."

"Are you trying to protect her from us," she said, "or us from her?"

Cash smiled. "We'll see how it goes."

* * *

The back-to-back meetings with Mariposa and Wanda behind him, Cash pushed the intercom button. With a trial starting tomorrow at nine, he needed to return to the office. That meant having a guard escort him from the visiting room to the front gate. From there to the parking lot, he'd be on his own.

No guard showed. He pressed the button again. And again.

The lights in the windowless room dimmed and then died. Stewing alone in the dark transported Cash to another pitch-black room thirty-five years ago and to the nightmare of his mother's disappearance.

The walls crept closer. The temperature spiked, along with Cash's heart rate.

He smelled an ambush. Wouldn't be his first prison beating. Might be his last.

The door banged open. Light flooded the room, temporarily blinding him. His heart skipped several beats before racing like mad.

Two angels emerged from the light and invited themselves in. On closer look, not angels but agents. FBI Special Agent Maggie Burns—a.k.a. "MagDoll"—followed by Marty Shafer of the IRS's Criminal Investigation Division. CID for short.

Make that, one angel. The jury was still out on Shafer's final destination.

"Well, if it isn't Beauty and the Beast," Cash said.

"Fuck you too," Shafer said.

"Settle down, Marty." Leave it to Maggie to defuse the situation. "McCahill might've been referring to you as the beauty."

Riiiiight.

From the age of six through her days at Ole Miss, Maggie had racked up enough beauty titles to own the crown. Auburn hair. Hazel eyes. A willowy frame only half-hidden by the G-woman getup. Blue Blazer, stiff white shirt, skirt to the knees, black pumps.

Calling Shafer a beast rang less true. Not that anyone would mistake him for Ryan Gosling, but he wasn't exactly Quasimodo either. More like an unremarkable mosaic of forgettable features, divided by deep wrinkles into jigsaw pieces. The whole somehow less than the sum of the parts.

Maggie and Cash took the only seats in the visiting room separated by a metal table, forcing Shafer to stand.

"What are you doing here?" she said.

"Funny," Cash said, "I was about to ask you the same thing."

Shafer slapped both palms on the table. "I know why the prick's here." He leaned over, invading Cash's space. "He came to warn Benanti to clam up...not to play ball with us. That counts as obstruction in my book."

Cash rocketed to his feet, going nose-to-nose with Shafer. "Don't flatter yourself. You don't own a book and wouldn't know what to do with one if you did."

Maggie pounded the table. "Sit down, McCahill. Whether or not Marty could make an obstruction charge stick, if he can provoke you into slugging him, you'll do the full nickel."

Cash sat. "You here to offer Mariposa a deal?"

Maggie shot Shafer a keep-your-trap-shut look and turned back to Cash. "If you weren't hired to sit on Benanti, why are you here?"

"Last time I checked, there's no law against visiting an old friend who's fallen on hard times."

Shafer leaned over the table. A deeper invasion of Cash's space. "Dollars to donuts, this slimeball's trying to poach the case from Rhoden."

Maggie put her hand on Shafer's forearm. It was enough to reel him away from Cash.

"You feds took that play off the table when you put me on your witness list," Cash said. "I can't testify for the government and also cross-examine myself. The law's funny that way."

"If you were truly her friend," Maggie said, "you'd convince her there's only one way to avoid the needle."

"Isn't that a conversation you should have with Mariposa's lawyer?" Cash said.

Shafer snorted. "That dirtbag's slimier than you, hard as that is to believe."

A knock on the door interrupted Cash's comeback. The door opened, and the devil appeared in the flesh.

"Speak of the devil." Leave it to Shafer to resort to the obvious line, as Rob "Rocket" Rhoden swaggered into the visiting room, sporting a shit-eating grin and aviator sunglasses.

The shark wore sunglasses everywhere, except court. Claimed to have super-sensitive eyes. If true, that'd be the only thing sensitive about him. Also the only true tale he'd ever told.

Rocket pretended to count heads. "Quarters are a bit cramped." The accent betrayed his Boston roots. That, along with the red hair and ruddy complexion.

He hadn't hailed from a Brahmin upbringing in a Beacon Hill brownstone, with stops at Choate and Harvard to meet and mingle with the right people. Instead, his background had been a hardscrabble slog through the mean streets of Southie, capped by long nights at Suffolk Law School.

"I see the problem," Rhoden said. "We have one lawyer too many."

Cash made a show of looking around the room. "The way I see it, there's only one real lawyer here."

"Bail now," Rhoden said to Cash, "and I won't report you to the bar for talking to my client behind my back."

Cash laughed. "You! Snitching to the state bar. That'd be a switch."

"We'll see how the bar feels about your attempt to poach my client."

"Again, that's rich coming from a bottom feeder like you. The way I remember it, you couldn't wait to tell Goldberg's clients that he was knocking on death's door."

"That was true then," Rhoden said, "and truer now."

"You followed up that lie with the bigger whopper that I was headed back to prison."

"Only a matter of time." Rhoden pointed to the agents. "You'd be back behind bars already, if these two so-called *special agents* would get off their asses and do their jobs."

Maggie stepped between the attorneys. "Much as the world would be a better place if the bar flushed both of you, I don't have time to measure your micropenises today. Marty and I need to talk to Benanti, and unfortunately, we can't do that without her lawyer being present."

She turned to Cash. "McCahill, that's your cue to leave."

Cash stood and turned to Maggie. "Here's a simple tip on how to tell when Rhoden's lying. His lips will be moving." He slapped a business card onto the table. "Remember, Rhoden, every lie to a fed is a five-year felony. Keep my card handy. You're going to need a good lawyer."

Rocket swept the card off the table and onto the floor. "Are you going to refer me to one?"

"You wouldn't recognize a real lawyer if he hit you upside your head," Cash said.

"Don't do it, Cash," Maggie said.

Shafer groaned. "Oh, Maggie, you're spoiling my fun. I would like nothing better than watching a dustup between these two dirtbags."

Cash withdrew from the field of battle but consoled himself with one thought. He had denied Shafer his ultimate pleasure.

CHAPTER FOUR

The watering hole at the Westin Galleria in North Dallas had the typical hotel bar setup. Tables out in the open for those with nothing to hide. Booths for the cheaters.

The motif of the month was tropical escape, which translated into plastic tiki torches, Gauguin prints, waitresses in tight Tommy Bahama blouses and short khaki skirts, and rainbow-colored drinks with tiny umbrella stir sticks.

Cash sat at the bar, where he downed two mai tais, deleted four frantic messages from his assistant Eva, and turned down a two-for-the-price-of-one happy hour special from a pair of working girls.

Or wannabes anyway.

Cash let the rookies down easy. Amber and Zooey—surely stage names—bookended him at the bar. Amber—the taller and more talkative—kicked off the pitch by claiming to be an SMU senior and introducing Zooey as her sorority sister.

Long ago Cash had lost count of the hookers who formed the backbone of his client base, the vast majority touting college degrees and sorority affiliations. Sweethearts of Ramma Jamma Slamma.

While Amber rambled on nervously, Zooey kept her mouth shut and her dark eyes fixed on her drink. With an olive complexion and an exotic air, Zooey could pass as a precious import from a host of hot climate countries.

"You girls are a long way from campus," Cash said. "What are you studying?"

"Economics." Amber struggled to make her alleged major sound sexy.

Cash turned to Zooey. "And you?"

"Same." A south-of-the-border inflection spiced up her accent.

"Then I assume you're looking for a capital investment from me." Cash patted the wallet in his breast pocket. "How much are we talking about?"

Negotiations ground to a halt as the girls looked at each other. An awkward silence underscored their confusion.

Amber recovered first. "Two thousand for the best night of your life." Came off closer to a question than a proposition.

Cash could've countered with two hundred, and they would've jumped at it. Instead, he let out a low whistle.

Amber looked flustered. "But because we like you and for one time only, we'll make it an even thousand."

Rookie mistake to bid against herself. Amber wasn't cut out for the profession. Not the one she was flirting with anyway. Nor the one Cash had mastered.

He considered which version of the "scared straight" speech had the best shot at success. Not a good shot. Just the best one.

He cleared his throat. "Free advice from someone who also bills by the hour. When you price your product, factor in two intangibles. First, the rapid depreciation of diminishing assets, the chief one being your youth. Second, the hidden costs of occupational hazards, like hospital bills, bail bonds, and legal fees."

He handed each a business card. "You girls are very attractive, but I don't hire pros. However, they often hire me. Don't take this personally or as a rejection. This time it really is me and not you."

End of the lecture. "Keep my card handy. You're going to need it."

And sooner than you think.

As if on cue, FBI Agent Maggie Burns showed up. She stopped short of the bar. Best case for Cash, she held back while her eyes adjusted to the subdued lighting. Worst case, she was having second thoughts about meeting him for a drink.

Whatever her bullshit reason for running late, it hadn't been to change into something sexier. She wore the same Bureau-sanctioned, boner-killer outfit she'd had on at the women's prison earlier today. She couldn't have stuck out more in the pickup zone if *FED* were written on her forehead.

She steamed to the bar and performed her trademark magic trick. The one where she flicked open the lapel of her blazer, wide enough to flash the badge. The shiny, gold one that made denizens of the dark disappear.

Sure enough, the counterfeit coeds fled like roaches from the light. Joining a stampede of more seasoned pros, who knew a narc when they saw one. Maggie's arrival shot to hell the male-to-female ratio at the bar.

She mounted the stool next to Cash's—the one vacated by Amber—and draped her arm across his shoulders. "I can't leave a walking hard-on like you alone for five minutes." Her tone, only half-playful.

"Oh, those two? They were selling Girl Scout cookies."

"And lord knows you do have a sweet tooth."

"What took you so long to get here?" He was more irritated than curious. "We were on the same flight from Lubbock."

"Yeah, but you were in first class," Maggie said.

"And deplaning from coach took an hour?"

"No, but swinging by my apartment complex to swap cars did."

He swiveled to face her. "Let me get this straight. The Westin is midway between the airport and your apartment, but instead of driving straight here from DFW, you went all the way home to trade cars, before backtracking to the Galleria."

"Of course I did." Not a hint of defensiveness in her voice. "The rules on government-issued vehicles are—"

He cut her off. "Spare me the lecture on G-cars. I was a fed once." The wise course would've been to drop the subject, but he couldn't resist busting her bureaucratic balls. "So, you're telling me that...." He shook his head in disbelief and started over. "Let's say you work late into the night and need to pick up dinner. There's a Chinese restaurant on your way home. But instead of stopping at the restaurant, you'll drive all the way home, swap cars, go to the restaurant, and then return home."

She nodded.

"You're the only tool in the Bureau who would do that."

"Pardon me if I don't take career advice from someone who surrendered his badge to avoid being fired."

Ouch. At least she had the decency not to bring up his status as a felon, another ground for blowing off his counsel.

"Badge of honor to bail from that office." He caught himself talking too loud and lowered his voice. "Means I was doing my job."

Again, it would've been better to move on, but he couldn't. "The U.S. Attorney and I butted heads. Moore wanted to deep-six a righteous public corruption investigation. I didn't. End of the investigation, along with my career in public service."

"You could've handled it more diplomatically," she said.

"Like how?"

"For starters, by not calling the U.S. Attorney a 'cocksucking chickenshit' in front of a roomful of agents and prosecutors. Did I get the quote right?"

Cash smiled. "Close enough." Past time to leave ancient history behind. "How did your meeting with Mariposa go?"

Her eyes clouded. "Like you'd expect. With Rhoden blocking us all the way, it went nowhere fast."

"She won't make it to trial, will she?"

"I don't see how," the agent said. "She can buy a little time by hiding out in isolation, but sooner or later, the cartel will get to her."

Maggie ordered a Diet 7UP. A good soldier following another silly rule by the folks who put the *Bureau* in *bureaucracy*. No consumption of alcohol while armed. The bulge in her blazer showed she was strapped.

She slid her hand atop his. "You have to convince her to trust us."

He signaled for a third mai tai. "That's a bridge too far. Best you can hope for is to persuade her that she has a longer life expectancy under your wing than outside it."

"Then sell her on that," she said.

"Tough sale, given the Bureau's lousy record of keeping snitches alive." He slipped his hand from under hers and reached for his wallet. "I'll settle up here and get us a room, where you can spend the next couple of hours convincing me to convince her."

"That's not in the cards tonight." She gave him a brush-off kiss on the cheek. "On my way here, Eva texted me. Said you were dodging her calls and told me to send you straight to the office. If I cross her, my life expectancy will be shorter than Mariposa's. Yours will be too."

"That *bruja* doesn't run my life," Cash said.

"Guess again."

Cash knew when to fold a losing hand. Five minutes later, he hit eighty on the tollway, headed downtown to the office. A call came over the car phone, interrupting "Jungleland" during The Big Man's sax solo.

A capital offense.

The caller's number was blocked. A fed thing. Had to be Maggie, already regretting her decision to part for the night.

He took the call, his heart outracing the Carrera. "About time you came to your senses."

Static and labored breathing on the line.

"Maggie, is that you?"

More heavy breathing before the call died, and the Boss came back on with a lament for the wounded and the dead. The song triggered a fear that had followed Cash since childhood. A premonition that he would wind up wounded but not dead.

CHAPTER FIVE

ash smelled an ambush. That and a half-century of cigar smoke.

A permanent haze filtered the framed newspaper clips and courtroom sketches on the walls of Gary "Goldy" Goldberg's office. The room had the musty odor of a third-rate museum, the oldest relic being the dinosaur behind the desk: Goldberg.

Since last year's stroke, Goldy seemed like a shadow of his old self. More faltering. Less firebrand. The head had always been too large for the body, but lately the imbalance had grown more pronounced. Made Cash wonder how he stayed upright.

Cash looked from Goldy to Eva before pointing to the stranger in the room. "Who's he?"

"Meet our client," Goldberg said.

"Like hell he is."

The stranger stood and offered a French-manicured hand to Cash. "Chris Campos, and we have met before." The throaty voice straddled the sexes.

Cash took the hand and made the connection. Familiar facial features left him 90 percent certain of the identity. Green-gray eyes cinched it.

"What happened to Cristina Campos a.k.a. 'Tina'?" Cash said.

"Mister Goldberg told me to shove her back into the closet," Campos said, "until the trial's over."

Cash kept his temper in check and his voice steady. "Eva, please take Tina...uh...Chris to the conference room and wait for me there. Mister Goldberg and I need to confer."

After Eva and the client left, Cash unloaded on the old man. "What the hell were you thinking?"

"Our client needs to man up before we introduce him to a jury of religious nuts, rednecks, and retirees." Goldberg met and raised Cash's decibel level. Though his body was withering, his voice remained as strong as ever.

"*Our* client? Try *my* client."

Eva returned and closed the door behind her, ignoring Cash's order to babysit Campos in the conference room. Not that her first insubordination of the day took him by surprise.

She wore a pantsuit with a floral blouse that hung loosely, hiding her gym-hardened body. Experience had taught Cash that the petite frame packed a wallop. The yellow daffodils populating the top brought out a mocha complexion that matched the shade of Cash's coffee. Her dark, frizzy hair corkscrewed wildly. She was going through a boho phase.

"Keep your voices down," she whispered. "It is so not the time to air this shit. We can't have the client witnessing his dream team at each other's throats, not on the eve of trial. He's already freaking out."

The *bruja* had a point. Cash turned toward her. "Tell this old fool not to make any more dumbass decisions, without running them by me first."

She snapped at Cash. "He was here for the client, while you were off chasing tail."

Dammit. Just like her to follow up one solid point with another.

Goldberg spoke to Eva. "Tell the whippersnapper that this old war horse has forgotten more about winning trials than he ever knew."

Eva rolled her eyes. "I've died and gone back to grade school."

Cash cut out the middle-woman and faced his mentor. "In all the years I've worked for you, I did manage to pick up one or two valuable lessons. You always said that when a storm is brewing, never try to fly around it. Instead, sail straight into its teeth."

"Eva, you've got twelve hours to turn Chris back into Tina," Cash said. "Doll her up. Make her as drop-dead gorgeous as she was on the night of her arrest." He handed her the firm platinum AmEx card. "Make her look young."

"She is young," Eva said.

"Make her look younger."

She pocketed the card. "Sounds like a job for the incredible Doctor Katz."

"Whatever it takes," Cash said.

Goldberg pushed a typed document across the desk. "But we've drafted a dynamite motion in *limine*, barring the prosecutors from referring to Campos as a crossdresser, tranny, fairy, shemale, ladyboy, femboy, sissy, whatever."

Cash tore up the motion. "Let's protect our client from sticks and stones and not worry over whether words will hurt him...uh...her."

* * *

The brush with Tina Campos brought back a ghost from Cash's past. Martin Biddle had been a crossdresser like Tina, but at the same time, not like Tina at all.

For six months, Biddle and Cash had shared a cell at FCI Seagoville. A cell hadn't been all they'd shared. Both had taken the fall for the real guilty parties.

Both had survived in prison by submitting to the third cellmate, Marcus Allen DuPree—a.k.a. "Big Black." Cash served as his personal jailhouse lawyer. Martin Biddle, as his prison punk.

One big difference between the two. Cash had made it out alive. Biddle hadn't, despite Cash's frequent assurance to him that "I've never lost a client, and I'm not about to start with you."

Time after time, he had talked Biddle off the ledge. Cash had been his cellmate and his counselor. Until the end came, and Cash had been twenty miles from Seagoville. Still Biddle's counselor. No longer his cellmate.

On the way to Southlake, he called Bettina Biddle from the car, giving the new widow a chance to veto his visit or prepare for his arrival. The "For Sale" sign on the front lawn touted a "reduced price" for the Spanish-style house. His first notice of the offer to sell.

Bettina greeted him at the door, looking tired but happy to see him. Her dark hair and dark eyes contrasted nicely with the pale, flawless skin. Always petite, she seemed to have shrunk since his last visit.

She wore black workout clothes. The Equinox Club logo probably doubled the price of the gear.

She invited him in and settled onto the living room couch, tucking her bare feet under her thighs, lotus-style. He took the chair farthest from the couch. He trusted the widow to exercise control. Himself, not so much.

The house was suspiciously quiet. "The little angels must be asleep," he said.

"One little angel down. A little devil, still stirring."

"Which is which?"

She smiled. "Depends on the day, the hour, and the minute."

"I see you've put the house on the market." He worried about upending the girls so soon after they'd lost a father.

She looked past him. "With Marty gone, we don't need this much house."

He didn't call her on the bullshit reason. "Is everything okay?"

She was slow to respond. "Everything's fine."

"You need to work on that line," he said, "if you want me to buy it."

"I hired you for one task, to look into my husband's death, to prove he didn't commit suicide." She took several deep breaths before going on. "I can't afford to ask you to do more."

"Such as?"

"The prosecutors have a forfeiture order against Marty for two million dollars. I don't have that kind of money lying around, so the house has to go. Though mortgaged to the hilt, it's still the biggest asset left to liquidate. Won't pay off the debt, but it's a start."

Cash sensed that she had more to unload. "What else is keeping you awake at night?"

"The insurance company won't pay a penny on Marty's death."

"Because of the suicide ruling?"

She nodded.

"If you're not using me to battle the Justice Department and the insurance company, tell me you've hired a junkyard dog to go up against the bastards."

She kept nodding.

He committed the litigator's cardinal sin of asking one question too many. "Who's your lawyer on those two fronts?"

"Tony Dial. Do you know him?"

The air rushed from his lungs. "Yeah, we call him T.N.T. Short for 'Terrible Negotiator Tony.' I wouldn't hire that hack to handle a traffic ticket."

CHAPTER SIX

"Tina Campos is a tranny and a hooker." So began Cash's opening statement to the jury, starting with a slur that made his client squirm. "Pardon me. I meant to say she's transgender and a sex worker. I'm trying to be more politically correct these days."

Cash let the lie sink in before resuming, "As Shakespeare succinctly put it, 'A rose by any other name.' Transgender, tranny, crossdresser, sissy, t-gurl, femboi, ladyboy. Tina has suffered the sting of all those words and worse. Your job as jurors is to get past the labels. We won't ask you to understand her lifestyle, much less accept it. Just put your prejudices on hold for the limited duration of this trial."

The jurors' expressions ran the gamut from disgust to distrust. Seven women, five men. Six white, four brown, two black. No LGBTQ. At least none who copped to it. Not the best panel he'd ever drawn, but far from the worst.

The same went for Judge Anna Tapia. Neither the best nor the worst draw for Cash and his client. Sure, she favored the feds, but what judge didn't? At least she knew the strike zone and called balls and strikes more fairly than most.

Cash walked behind the defendant and placed a hand on her shoulder. Eva had worked her magic, giving Tina a head-to-toe makeover and turning her into a knockout. She would turn heads not only in a dark bar but also under the harsh lights of a courtroom.

"My client is not charged with being transgender, which is not a crime at all. She's not even charged with prostitution, which is a state offense and not one for you to consider. Instead, she's accused of assaulting a federal officer, who was acting in the line of duty."

Cash moved toward the jury box, standing as close to the twelve as the judge would allow. "An honest, hard-working agent will take that seat." He pointed to the empty witness stand. "And he will swear under oath that my client, Tina Campos, struck him with her handbag. Not once, not twice, but three times."

Cash paused for effect. "And here's the surprise twist in the trial. We're going to agree with the agent one hundred percent. What he will say happened did in fact happen."

The jurors did a collective double take. One or two gasped, but not loud enough to drown out the groans from the defense table.

* * *

At the midafternoon break, Cash sat alone in the hallway on a wooden bench. The trial had moved faster than expected. The government had wrapped up the direct examination of ICE Agent Sam Dobbs. After the break Cash would take him on cross.

During two decades in the trenches, Cash had crossed scores of agents. Good ones. Bad eggs. The vast bulk, mediocre and muddling toward retirement. He'd encountered truthful witnesses, lying sacks of shit, and every shade in between.

Generally, the shorter the cross of an agent, the better. Score a few quick points and get the fed off the stand before the defense lawyer tripped a land mine.

The trial had boiled down to a half-hour or so of cross-examination, followed by whatever time it took to convince Tina not to testify. With forty-five minutes of closing arguments for each side, the case could go to the jury by late afternoon, tomorrow morning at the latest. This would prove as close as Cash had ever come to a so-called stipulated trial—one where both sides agreed on the facts.

Skyler Patterson blew past Cash in the hallway. Without a word. Not even slowing for a drive-by insult. So not like her.

Even at the speed of flight, she seemed grounded. A workhorse with a low center of gravity, thin through the torso, thick from the waist down. A single, self-contained woman who flew under the radar and the gaydar. Equally immune to the charms of Cash and Eva, she kept her head in the weeds, not the clouds.

He caught up to her at the elevator bank. "What gives? You were supposed to cover my trial."

"Sorry." Skyler didn't sound sorry at all. Her blue eyes never settled on him but continually swept the horizon, always searching for someone higher on the food chain. It wasn't personal. She treated everyone and everything as a bump on the road to a bigger story.

"My editor pulled me off your trial to cover the fireworks in Judge Ferguson's court."

Cash slumped. Rocket's latest headline-grabber had drawn a gaggle of reporters, meaning the media whore had scooped Cash again. What's worse, he couldn't blame the reporters for bailing on him.

Rocket's radioactive client, Toby Fine, ranked about a hundred rungs higher on the buzz-o-meter than Tina Campos. The internet mogul had created the *Backdoor*—a fast-exploding website for sex ads. Even Tina advertised on it.

Both Fine and the site stood accused of aiding and abetting the sex trafficking of minors. Fine had drawn heat as the owner on paper of a Delaware company, whose sole asset was the *Backdoor*. The real owner was no doubt safely out of the country and outside the reach of the law.

"Sorry, Cash. Gotta run." Skyler boarded the elevator. "Four o'clock deadline."

With the door closing fast, Cash said, "How'd it go for Fine?"

"Rocket crashed and burned."

The news lifted Cash's spirits.

No sooner had the elevator swallowed Skyler than the crowd from Ferguson's courtroom flooded the hallway. A scrum of mangy media types surrounded Fine and Rocket, shouting out questions.

Blades of red hair bobbed above the churning press of bodies, a painful reminder that despite Rocket's dismal results in court today, he still commanded the center of attention.

In contrast, Fine all but disappeared into the crowd. Cash caught only glimpses of the bald, doughy defendant, who couldn't have looked less like a mastermind or more like a bean counter.

Rocket lifted both hands to still the crowd. "Ladies and gentlemen, much as I would love to bestow upon you the precious gift of a sound bite or two, Judge Ferguson—in his infinite wisdom—has slapped a gag order on the parties and their counsel. As a result, I cannot speak with you until after Mister Fine is acquitted of these bogus charges and fully vindicated."

Cash smiled. While the gag order prevented Rocket during the trial from speaking to the press *on the record*, he would leak like a sieve until then.

Rocket oozed smugness. Despite rough sledding in court and Ferguson's shut-the-fuck-up order, he had planted his name in every story for the next two to three news cycles.

Fine turned even paler than usual. He looked scared. Spooked to the point of second-guessing his choice of counsel.

Cash had seen that look before, and it didn't bode well for Rocket.

* * *

After the break, Eva and Cash beat Goldberg and the client back to the defense table. On a cane since the stroke, Goldberg had slowed down, physically and mentally. His frequent trips to the bathroom tested the limits of the breaks and the judge's patience.

Eva whispered to Cash, "You need to give Goldy a bigger role in the trial. His feelings are hurt."

Cash tensed. Like he needed more shit to deal with on the brink of the make-or-break cross of the agent. "I've got to do what's best for the client." His words came out harsher than intended.

"I'll remind you of that in a few years," she said, "when you're Goldy's age."

"In the classic words of the Who," Cash said, "I hope to die before I get old."

"It'll get here in a blink."

Goldy and Tina returned to the courtroom. Goldy doffed his trademark black Stetson at the door, revealing a comb-over as translucent as cotton candy. He tucked the cane under his arm, as if it were there for show, not support.

With no time to debate Eva, he settled for shooting her a steely glare. She shrugged it off and gave back in kind.

ICE Agent Sam Dobbs retook the stand. He must've spent the break fixing his hair, which had been teased to new heights. The sweeping pompadour added an inch to his six-four frame.

Judge Tapia reminded Dobbs that he was still under oath. Tapia's fine features, delicate and soft in her youth, had become striking and aristocratic in her mid-fifties. She came from old money, had married into megabucks, and it showed. The black robe hid a body that would be the envy of women half her age.

The agent's eyes locked on Cash, until the jurors returned to the box. At which point Dobbs' focus shifted to the twelve. Hours of agency training on the fine art of testifying hadn't been wasted on him.

On direct examination, the agent had laid out the elements of the crime. He testified that—while acting in the scope of his duty—he had apprised the defendant of who and what he was. After which, she had pummeled him with her purse. He pointed to Tina as his attacker and identified photos of the defensive bruises on his arms.

To make matters worse, Dobbs came off like the Eagle Scout he had been and would always be. Brave, honest, trustworthy, with liberty and justice for all. Any attempt to bloody him on the stand would surely backfire. The jury couldn't love the witness more if he were made of Blue Bell Mint Chocolate Chip ice cream.

Cash took a different tack. "Agent Dobbs, when you approached the defendant, did you know she was transgender?"

The witness blushed and said no.

"Did you even suspect her of being transgender?"

Dobbs' blush deepened. "N-n-no." He sounded less certain. Good chance the prosecutor hadn't prepped him for this line of questioning. Probably assumed Cash would steer clear of the defendant's sexual orientation.

"Would you have approached Miss Campos differently if you had known or even suspected her of being transgender?"

The prosecutor raised a relevance objection. Judge Tapia frowned. "Mister McCahill," she said, "I'm not sure where this is headed."

"Permit me a few more questions, Your Honor," Cash said, "and I'll tie it all together."

"See that you do," the judge said.

The witness claimed he wouldn't have acted differently had he known the defendant's orientation. Probably even believed it, as did the jurors.

"Will you tell the ladies and gentlemen of the jury what Operation Doubtfire is?"

Dobbs went white. "That undercover investigation has nothing to do with this case." He sounded rattled, confirming Cash's suspicion that the prosecutor hadn't prepped him for this.

"Move to strike as nonresponsive, Your Honor," Cash said.

The pimply-faced prosecutor stood. "That operation is ongoing and, therefore, confidential."

Judge Tapia rolled her eyes. "Not any longer." She turned to the witness. "Answer the question."

"We have a task force working with the FBI and the Dallas Police Department to apprehend a serial killer," Dobbs said.

"A killer who is believed to impersonate an ICE agent, right?"

The witness looked to the judge before answering. "Y-y-yes."

"A killer who specifically targets trans women, correct?"

Dobbs spoke so softly that Tapia made him repeat the answer, louder the second time. Another yes.

"So it would be perfectly understandable if my client feared for her life when approached by someone claiming to be an ICE agent."

The judge upheld the prosecutor's compound objection. Argumentative and calls for speculation. No matter. Cash had planted the seed of doubt in the jurors' minds.

"Isn't it true that your own agency has spent considerable time and money warning the LGBTQ community of a serial killer, possibly disguised as a federal agent?"

Another soft, affirmative answer, followed by the judge's admonition to the witness to speak up.

"What date did your encounter with Tina Campos occur?"

"August ninth of this year," the agent said.

"And prior to August ninth of this year, what date did the serial killer last strike in Dallas, Texas?"

"August sixth."

"So three days before you stopped Miss Campos, a trans woman had been killed by someone possibly impersonating an ICE agent, right?"

The witness nodded, caught himself, and answered verbally.

"Agent Dobbs, will you tell the jury what this serial killer, who is still at large, does to his victims?"

Cash thought he heard the prosecutor's head explode. Instead, it was the judge's gavel coming down hard. "You've made your point, Mister McCahill," the judge said. "Let's move on."

Mission accomplished. Cash released the witness.

He would rather lose a finger than give up a minute of the time allotted for the closing argument. Nonetheless, to placate Eva, he gave Goldberg half of their time for summation. To Cash, this was roughly the equivalent of losing all his fingers and toes.

Goldy rose to the occasion. "On the fifteenth day of July, in the year of our Lord 2021," he began the closing. By the time he reached the third "in the year of our Lord," the two black jurors were smiling and nodding.

The old man was giving the choir some of that good old time religion.

Eva flashed an I-told-you-so smile to Cash. His turn to shrug it off.

* * *

Early in day two of the jury's deliberation, Judge Tapia called the lawyers and the defendant back into court. "This is dragging on too long," she said. "I'm considering giving the jurors an *Allen* charge, in an attempt to break the deadlock. Any objection?"

"None from the government." The prosecutor no doubt banked on the odds—the government won about 90 percent of its trials, so anything to hasten a verdict probably redounded to its favor.

"No need for a dynamite charge," Cash said. "We'll have a verdict any minute now." He had a premonition that the jurors had reached consensus yesterday afternoon, but wanted to sleep on their decision.

"How can you possibly know that?" the judge said.

Before Cash could respond, the bailiff entered the courtroom. "Your Honor, we have a verdict."

Tapia turned back to Cash. "Lucky guess, Mister McCahill?"

Goldberg patted Cash on the back and said, "They don't call my co-counsel the jury whisperer for nothing."

* * *

Flush with victory, Cash rounded the corner on the fifteenth floor of the courthouse and came upon the sore losers. The pimply-faced prosecutor pretended to walk with an invisible cane, while his asshole supervisor laughed and clapped. Pimples said in a shaky voice, "In the year of our Lord."

Cash kept his temper in check, barely. "That old man has forgotten more about trials than you two will ever know. You're not worthy of carrying his briefcase, so treat him with the respect he deserves."

"Look who's talking," Asshole said. "You two fought like an old married couple throughout the trial."

"We're family," Cash said. "That's what families do."

"Fucked-up families maybe," Asshole replied.

Cash stopped at the elevator. "Is there any other kind?"

He pushed the down button and turned back to the prosecutors. "Besides, the old man played—"

The elevator arrived with a ping. Cash swallowed the rest of his sentence. Smarter not to taunt the prosecutors with the news that Goldy could get by without a cane, which served simply as a prop to generate jury sympathy. The old man might go there again.

Cash entered the compartment, and the door closed behind him. Besides, he might be in the market for a cane himself.

CHAPTER SEVEN

ob "Rocket" Rhoden prided himself on his prize pecs and awesome abs. Thursday night meant a ninety-minute training session at the Equinox Club on Cedar Springs, followed by a dinner of steak and potatoes at Eddie V's next door.

Cash worked out at the same health club at 6:00 a.m. on weekdays, mostly because he was a morning person, but partly to avoid running into Rhoden. Bad enough to keep bumping into the windbag at the courthouse.

Tonight, however, Cash went looking for Rhoden and found him face down on a padded table. Based upon his moaning, he was enjoying the cool down stretch a little too much. Sweat speckled his gym shorts and muscle shirt.

State-of-the-heart exercise equipment, tons of free weights, and scores of cardio machines surrounded five massage tables in the center of the high-end club. Outside the island of tranquility, dozens of trainers in black uniforms barked orders to clients, who paid dearly for the abuse.

No surprise that Rhoden had hired the hottest trainer in the gym: Julie something. An All-American swimmer who had recently graduated from the University of Texas. A decade younger than Rhoden, two decades younger than Cash.

She kneaded her client's shoulders, while he purred like a pervert on a playground. Cash would bet his Porsche that Rhoden had popped a boner.

"After you finish the rubdown," Cash said to Julie, "better wash your hands. Then wash them again."

Rhoden turned his face toward Cash. His eyes blinked open. His complexion, ruddier than usual. "And here I thought they kept out the riffraff at night." Rhoden rolled onto his back. Erection confirmed.

Julie must've noticed it too. She rolled her eyes.

"I certainly understand why you need a massage," Cash said, "after getting your ass kicked in court all afternoon."

"Who said I got my ass kicked?" Rhoden sounded groggy.

"Only every reporter who witnessed you flame out."

"Ah, that's right." Rhoden smacked his lips. "Today the press showed up in full force for me, but not for you. Here's a riddle for you, McCahill. When your cases crash in court, but there's no reporter there to hear it, do they make a sound?"

Good question.

Rhoden yawned. "Why are you disturbing my peace?"

Another good question. Deserved a good answer. Instead, Cash gave him a straight one. "I need to see *La Tigra*."

Rhoden perked up. His moment of zen over, he slithered off the table and onto his feet. Patted Julie on the rump before leading Cash to the dark, deserted spin room. Packed with stationary bikes, the soundproof room reeked of sweat.

"Why?" Rhoden said.

"I've been asked by our mutual friend to intercede on her behalf."

"Does this mutual friend happen to be *my* client?" Asked as if Rhoden already knew the answer. "And if so, why didn't she come to me?"

Cash gave him a get real look.

Rhoden didn't insult Cash's intelligence by claiming the moral high ground or denying the obvious. Though technically Rocket's client, Mariposa Benanti didn't pay the bills or command his loyalty. He prospered by protecting her boss and his *patrona* at all costs.

That also kept him alive.

"*La Tigra* will never cross the border," Rhoden said, "so you'd have to go to Mexico to see her."

"I know that."

"I assume you know where she lives. The location of her compound in Sinaloa is hardly a secret."

"One woman's compound," Cash said, "is another's fortress. She's not someone you can drop in on uninvited. I need you to clear the visit for me."

"What's in it for me?"

The obvious questions kept coming, as did the obvious answers. "For starters, if I'm successful in my mission, you won't have to explain to the feds why another one of your clients met a tragic end while awaiting trial. You're getting a reputation as the 'Typhoid Mary' of the trial bar."

"That's easy to explain." Rhoden mounted a bike. "Shit happens." He pedaled slowly. "Or how about this one? Sometimes bad things happen to bad people. If you want my help, you'll have to do better than that."

"If I go to Mexico, there's a good chance I don't come back. Be an opportunity for you to remove a competitor."

Rhoden pedaled faster. The wheels were turning, on the bike and in his head. "Not that you're any real competition, but it would be nice to...." He let the sentence hang and hopped off the bike. "How do I know you won't try to steal my client while you're in Mexico?"

"If you're talking about Mariposa, I can't represent her because I'm on the government's witness list. I'm barred by this pesky thing called legal ethics. I'll introduce you to the concept someday." Cash went on. "If you're worried about losing *La Tigra*, I won't go after her business because, unlike you, I don't have a death wish."

"Could've fooled me," Rhoden said.

CHAPTER EIGHT

R hoden called Cash the next day. *La Tigra* would see him, but not make it easy.

Easy would've been for her to send a jet to whisk him straight to a private landing strip at the compound. A couple of hours in the air savoring champagne and caviar, his every need served by a former Miss Sinaloa. Followed by a five-minute limo ride to the mansion. The red-carpet treatment.

Instead, he flew commercial on his own dime. Aeromexico had a daily flight to Culiacán Airport, with a stop in Mexico City. Burned a full day in transit, thanks to the four-hour layover.

Cash's friends from the FBI almost made him miss the flight. After clearing security at DFW Airport, he spotted Maggie Burns beneath a massive electronic arrival/departure board.

What's she doing here, and how the hell did she know I'd be here?

He waved to her. She didn't wave back.

The reason for her chilly reception loomed at her side. Bill Graves—general counsel of the Dallas FBI and her office rabbi—glared at Cash. An ex-marine and ex-cop, Graves had attended night law school while on the force. He learned the law of the streets by day, book law by night.

Night or day, he breathed Bureau.

Not that Cash's relationship with Maggie was a big secret. Still, she didn't flaunt it in front of her colleagues, especially not a father figure like Graves.

Maggie's presence at the airport tripped Cash's internal alarm. Adding Graves to the mix triggered an all-out warning.

With Maggie frozen on the spot, Graves approached Cash and gripped his arm. "We need to talk." Tall, black, and gray at the temples, Graves had that whole voice-of-god thing going. A deep, rolling timbre that would've cowed 99 percent of the population into complying without question.

Cash fell into the one percent: The Great Uncowed. "Some other time, Graves. I have a flight to catch."

"You'll make the flight," Graves said, "unless you come to your senses after hearing us out."

The agents took Cash to a windowless conference room with barely enough space for three chairs and a metal table. A calendar courtesy of American Airlines clung to the wall. It featured a photo of Southfork Ranch, along with the wrong month and the wrong year.

Only Maggie sat. Graves and Cash retreated to opposite corners, like boxers between rounds.

"Do you have anything you want to tell us about your travel plans?" Graves had a way of turning a question into a command.

"No." Cash waited several seconds before heading toward the door.

"Sit down." Graves also had a habit of making a command sound like it came from on high.

Cash looked at Maggie. She nodded. He sat.

"If you're determined to go to Sinaloa and get yourself killed," Graves said, "no sweat off my balls. You were never one of my favorite people."

Classic understatement by the hard-ass.

"And here I thought we'd buried the hatchet," Cash said.

"You thought wrong," Graves said. "You were a pain-in-the-ass prosecutor before you went to the dark side and became a total prick. I put up with you when I had to. Now I don't."

Graves and Cash had a history of butting heads. Graves' job as general counsel cast him as the referee between agents eager for a quick indictment and prosecutors who held out for more evidence.

While at the DOJ, Cash followed a cardinal rule: get all the evidence up front. The agents played by their own set of rules. No indictment, no stat. No stats, no stripes.

In a past life, standoffs between Cash and an FBI agent had led to closed door meetings with Graves that usually ended in angry words and occasionally in threats to go over the other's head.

Once or twice, they had come close to blows, but Cash had always held back, hinky about hitting someone old enough to be his father. That, and pretty sure the granite tough Graves could knock him into next week.

"I don't give a shit what happens to you," Graves said, "but for some inexplicable reason, my partner does." He cocked his head toward Maggie.

"I'm not exactly sure why I do." Maggie's words exploded with a rush of pent-up anger. "Since you didn't bother telling me where you were going...or why."

All of which underscored something that had been gnawing at Cash since encountering the agents at the airport. How did the feds know about his trip to Mexico? He hadn't told anyone, other than Rhoden.

Not Maggie. Certainly not Goldberg or Eva, both of whom would've blown a gasket.

"Bad enough that Agent Burns wastes her time on scum like you," Graves said. "Puts her in a terrible light with the brass. But if she sticks by someone who carries water for the cartel, she'll be dead to us."

"Not that Cash gives a shit about my career." Maggie's well of anger ran deep.

Whoa there, girl.

Granted, it wouldn't break Cash's heart if she bailed from the Bureau. In a move to the private sector, maybe the stick would slip from her ass. Still, he had never asked her to turn in her badge. Never even broached the subject with her.

Not yet anyway. Still waiting for the right time.

"I don't tell you everything I'm doing," Cash said to her, "like you don't tell me all that you're up to. Case in point, care to enlighten me on how you discovered my travel plans?" Maggie looked to Graves. Without a word, without the twitch of a muscle, he ordered her to leave Cash's question dangling.

"I didn't think so," Cash said.

Not that the feds' ambush at the airport was a complete mystery. They must've picked up chatter about his trip to Mexico on a wire. The question dogging Cash was whether he was the target of the tap, or collateral damage.

Cash headed toward the door. "Sorry to run, but I have a plane to catch."

CHAPTER NINE

ash didn't make it outside Culiacán Airport before four of *La Tigra's* goons intercepted him. Three looked like extras from a bad narco movie, sporting black attire, a ton of bling, and expressions that ran the gamut from bored to bored stiff.

The fourth and shortest member of the welcoming crew wore a LeBron jersey. Cash was surprised they came in extra-small. *They* being both the jersey and its owner.

He recognized Number Twenty-Three from his past visit to Sinaloa. The one he'd sworn would be his last trip south of the border.

Another vow broken.

Cash extended his hand, but Twenty-Three didn't shake. Nor speak. Instead, he frisked Cash, lifting a wallet and cell phone before rummaging through his overnight bag.

They led Cash to a black Escalade parked in a tow away zone. An airport security officer leaned against the Cadillac. Didn't write a ticket or order the men to move the vehicle. Just stood guard until Twenty-Three slipped him a bill.

The goons shoved Cash onto the backseat and lowered a black bag over his head. The bag was still wet from the last victim's drool. Or tears.

A drawstring on the bag tightened around Cash's neck. "Is this really necessary?" His tone stayed steady. His ticker, not so much.

"Only if you plan on using your return ticket." Delivered as if Twenty-Three had used the line before.

La Tigra's men didn't bother tying Cash's hands. Given the circumstances, there was no need to.

The Escalade gunned away from the curb, pinning Cash against the seat. It weaved wildly through airport traffic. Horns blared. Curses flew to and from the SUV. Everything was *puta* this and *puta* that. The horns and vocal cords finally took a breather, but only after the vehicle broke free of congestion and sailed onto a smooth surface.

Cash lost track of time and direction. Ordinarily he could've used the radio to calibrate the distance traveled. Allot roughly three minutes a song and estimate an average speed of seventy-five miles an hour. The hitch today, everything on the station's playlist blended into a nonstop pounding that scrambled Cash's senses.

His migraine reached stage three before the vehicle veered off the highway and started climbing. As the roads turned rougher, the SUV shuddered through the shifting of gears.

Queasy from inhaling the stench inside the bag, Cash feared the onset of a panic attack. His heart raced ahead of the radio's pulsating beat.

Riding blind, Cash figured there had to be a thousand places to bury a body along the stretch of nowhere and almost as many reasons to dispose of his. Not that the flunkies needed a reason. If *La Tigra* ordered his execution, done.

Cash caught a break that nipped his welling panic. The radio crackled with static before going silent. His heartbeat slowed.

The climb steepened, which came as no surprise. *La Tigra* had built her fortress into the side of a mountain. Only one way in and one way out. Except for her, of course, since she usually traveled by helicopter.

Cash had gleaned most of the intel from a PBS documentary on the new wave of female cartel bosses. *La Tigra* had been the featured czarina on a segment titled *The Eye of The Tigress*.

On the ascent, the SUV stopped twice for brief conversations in Spanish between the driver and an outside party. Cash picked up the words *gringo abogado* in both exchanges. Each time the driver made it sound like a bad thing.

The stops had to be checkpoints, clearing traffic to and from the compound. The PBS documentary had warned that armed guards, sensors, attack dogs, and drones policed the perimeter of *La Tigra's* property and that she had a mean territorial streak.

On the third stop, the bag remained in place as Cash was pulled from the Escalade and dragged across a lawn that smelled freshly cut. The goons let go, and Cash dropped to his knees.

He picked up the scent of perfume. A familiar fragrance. Same thousand-dollar-an-ounce brand favored by Mariposa, back when she and her late husband had F.U. money.

He turned toward the scent. "*La Tigra?*"

Silence.

He stood, expecting to go down again. "You didn't have to send your men to rough me up. It was my idea to come here."

"They were not there to rough you up." Definitely *La Tigra's* voice. "But to protect you."

"They had a funny way of showing it."

"Unfortunately, mine is not the only organization in Mexico. Sadly, not even the only one in Sinaloa. Not yet anyway. If my competitors learn that you are working for me, they will try to take you out."

Cash started to protest that he wasn't working for her. He owed her a single case. One and done. The deal he had cut under duress, to save his skin.

He held his tongue. Might be safe to lie to himself about his future, but not to her.

"Can I remove the bag?" he said.

"Not yet."

Thwack!

The sound sent a shiver through Cash. He tensed for a blow that never came. Relieved not to have cried out. Shocked that no one else had.

Thwack!

Cash processed the distinctive sound. Figured out the type of club at hand.

Thwack!

The bag came off. Temporarily blinded by the sun, Cash blinked the scene into focus. *La Tigra* on the backswing, silver-shafted driver in hand, eyes fixed on a golf ball. Her follow through sent the ball flying two hundred yards down the fairway.

Scores of golf balls littered the driving range. To the right of the range, stretched an eighteen-hole golf course, replete with sand traps and water hazards. To the left, stood a white mansion with an orange tile roof. An infinity pool overlooked the vineyards.

A caddie teed up a fresh ball, as white as *La Tigra's* shorts and knit shirt. Her mocha complexion seemed a shade darker than he remembered. She had the lean, smooth legs of a dancer.

First time Cash had seen her bare legs. He could spend hours exploring every inch of them. Even manage to get lost between them for a night or two.

On her next drive, a slice sent the ball into the rough. She tossed the club to the caddie and turned to Cash. "Do you play?"

He shook his head. "I subscribe to Mark Twain's theory that golf is a good walk spoiled."

"A pity," she said, "because Nancy Ochoa designed my private course."

The name didn't mean anything to Cash. He kept that to himself.

The caddie handed her a putter. "I thought the golf course was where you lawyers found your clients," she said.

He followed her to a practice putting green, adjacent to and roughly the size of the helipad. "There are two kinds of lawyers," he said. "The underwhelming majority who hustle clients at golf courses and the few of us who don't have to."

She putted on the green for about ten minutes. Cash followed the caddie's advice and remained still and silent while she stroked from different directions and distances, sinking more than she missed.

After nailing a twenty-footer, she gave the club to the caddie and sent him away. She led Cash to a poolside table, where a maid in a white uniform poured each a glass of red wine.

"Hope you know more about wine than you do about golf," she said, "because I have found there are two kinds of men. Those who enjoy wine and those who do not enjoy life."

He savored the aroma before taking a sip. "A nice cab but not your best vintage. Aged two, maybe three years in an oak barrel. Is that a hint of black cherry?" He didn't expect an answer and didn't get one. "Tastes a tad thin, for what should be a full-bodied blend. Probably means there was too much rain during the harvest season."

She nodded. "From my Napa vineyard. And yes, we had more rain than normal three years ago."

She raised her glass for a toast. "To lawyers who win cases."

Clink.

"To clients with deep pockets," he said.

She didn't drink to his toast. "I hope you did not come all this way to beg to be paid for a service you promised to perform for free. I let you live. That should be worth something."

"I'm definitely not here to renegotiate our deal." The thought had crossed his mind that she might offer to fork over a little something. If not full freight, maybe a small token of her appreciation. Guess not. "I came to plead for the life of another."

"Who is the lucky client?"

"The unlucky non-client is Mariposa."

La Tigra's dark eyes narrowed. The tiny scar on her upper lip hid behind a frown. "Rhoden said you might raise this subject with me, but I had my doubts. After all, she was willing to throw you to the wolves." She took a sip. "Or in your case, to the tiger. You must have a short memory."

"Or a forgiving heart," he said.

"Perhaps she holds something over your head."

La Tigra hadn't risen to the top of the drug world by being dumb. Nor by believing in the inherent goodness of men.

"Regardless of my motive for coming," Cash said, "I can assure you that Mariposa has made peace with doing life. She's willing to plead guilty to the full indictment. No deal. No cooperation. Live out her remaining days behind bars."

La Tigra leaned forward. Her magnetism pulled Cash closer. The intoxicating perfume overwhelmed the aroma of the wine.

"Are you willing to bet your life that she can do the time without breaking?" she said.

Cash hesitated.

La Tigra smiled. "I didn't think so."

"Yes, I'll bet my life that she will not turn on you."

"You understand that you would literally be staking your life on that."

Cash nodded.

La Tigra leaned back. "I will take the matter under advisement. Is that not what your judges always say in the movies?"

"Yes, that's what they say."

When they don't have the balls to say no to my face.

The maid returned with a full bottle, but Cash put his hand over the glass. "Thanks, but no more wine for me."

The maid nodded and put down the bottle. She sprinkled a line of white powder and lay a small straw on Cash's plate.

"Again," Cash said, "thanks, but those days are behind me."

"You cannot afford to insult my product," *La Tigra* said, "or me."

"You can't afford to have a lawyer who's too fucked up."

"Nor do I want one who is too clean."

"Hey, if it's clean you're worried about, I can provide plenty of affidavits from judges, prosecutors, and agents, who will swear that I'm anything but."

Her stare hardened, warning Cash that he was down to his final appeal. "This is a test, right? You don't really expect me to do a line."

"Only if you plan to use your return ticket."

Cash picked up the straw but hesitated. He had run out of stalls. He lowered the straw to the powder and his nose to the straw. Balked again.

"What are you thinking?" she said.

"I was wondering how a woman like you survives in a man's world."

"The same way a man like you survives in a woman's world."

CHAPTER TEN

Desperate to drain the snake after a bumpy flight, Cash hurried off the plane at DFW Airport. FBI agents grabbed him at the gate and hustled him to the windowless conference room where he had been hot-boxed two days ago.

They passed three restrooms on the way to the interrogation site. Cruel but usual punishment. In exchange for a piss stop, Cash would've copped to the assassinations of MLK, JFK, and Lincoln.

Seated at a metal desk, Cash stared at FBI general counsel Bill Graves, who looked as if he hadn't cracked a smile in the past forty-eight hours.

Or ever.

No Maggie today to improve the scenery and perhaps soften the blows. Instead, Supervisory Special Agent Stanley Bowers loomed in a corner. The Bureau always hunted in pairs and never allowed itself to be outnumbered. Bowers would play the role of straight man to Graves' ramrod straight man.

A pale, pudgy C.P.A. and J.D., Bowers had lobbied for years to make "Stan the Man" his affectionate nickname with the troops. It never stuck. Not the nickname. Nor any affection.

Bowers had earned a rep as a bureaucratic infighter, positioned to inherit the post of general counsel upon Graves' retirement in two years. Perhaps sooner if he could nudge Graves out the door early.

G.C. was only the first rung of the ladder. Bowers made no secret of his plan to become the Special Agent in Charge of North Texas within five years. Next stop, the mother ship in D.C.

Cash pushed away from the table and stood. "This game is getting old."

Graves shoved him back down. "Much as you may not enjoy spending time with us, it makes me sick to breathe the same air as you. So let's cut the shit and get this over with."

Bowers placed two pages and a pen on the table. Cash skimmed the headings of the documents. No need to read further. He knew both by heart. The longer one, an advice of rights form. The shorter, a waiver of counsel.

Must be an intelligence test. To see if I've completely lost mine.

Cash shoved the pages away. "You're delusional if you think I'll sign either."

No response.

"Am I a subject or target of an investigation?"

More silence.

"If so, what's the alleged crime?"

Cash knew the tricks of the interrogation trade, the silent game being the oldest and most effective tool for breaking a holdout. Nine out of ten people suffered from a compulsion to fill a pause in a conversation, and agents preyed on that weakness.

Cash employed a counter-strategy called shut-the-fuck-up. The silence stretched to the two-minute mark before he declared a tie. "Been a long couple of days, gents. I'm going home." He stood.

"Sit down," Graves said.

Cash remained standing but didn't leave. He kept his smartass comeback to himself.

"Where did you go and who did you meet with in Mexico?" Graves asked as if he already knew.

"You don't really expect an answer, do you?"

"I've known you long enough," Graves said, "to never expect you to do the right thing. Besides, we already know where you went and who you saw. We just need to fill in the blanks on what you and *La Tigra* talked about."

No surprise that law enforcement on both sides of the border tracked who entered and left *La Tigra's* territory, fully aware that more went in than came out.

"We talked golf," Cash said. "I'm considering taking up the sport, and she gave me pointers."

Bowers slapped the table with both palms. "You can mouth off to us, wise guy, but you're not helping your girlfriend."

"I haven't had a girlfriend since the ninth grade," Cash said, "and I have no idea what you're talking about."

"Whatever you call your sick relationship with Maggie," Bowers said, "one thing's for sure. It's killing her career."

Cash's spine stiffened. "What's she got to do with any of this?" The silence began to take a toll. "Is she in some kind of trouble?"

Graves' granite expression slacked. Not a lot, but enough to signal that the mention of Maggie had hit a nerve with him as well.

"We can't comment on personnel matters beyond saying...." Graves glanced at Bowers and clammed up. A slip of the tongue would give the asshole more leverage to oust him from the agency.

Graves locked eyes with Cash. "If you care about Maggie at all, walk away from her and lose her number. Every second she spends with you, she digs herself a deeper hole at work. You'll be doing yourself a favor as well. Come nut-cutting season, she'll choose the Bureau over you every time."

Cash started to protest but held his tongue. Not the time or place to push back. Besides, Graves had known her longer and probably better. He was saying what Cash suspected.

Bowers planted both palms on the table and leaned forward, casting a shadow over Cash. "It's career suicide for an agent to hang around scum like you. A felon and a shyster. I can't decide which is worse."

Okay, still not the right time or place, but Cash had to push back. Though the agents might be exaggerating Maggie's peril, he couldn't run the risk they weren't. "Ease off, fellas. I've got my life back on track." He pulled the bar card from his wallet and dropped it on the table. "Regained my license and working on a pardon to clear my record."

"Once a felon, always a felon," Bowers said. "Plus, I wasn't talking about your prior felony, but the one you're committing now."

"Which is?" Cash tried not to sound concerned.

"Conspiracy to murder a government witness," Graves said.

"Who is?" Concern rippled through Cash's voice.

Graves dropped a folder onto the table. A stack of blowups slid out. Shots from all directions and angles of Mariposa Benanti, hanging in her cell. Belt wrapped around her neck and tied to a rafter. Eyes bugged out. Bare feet dangling inches above a pool of piss and shit on the floor.

Cash lowered himself into the chair, not trusting his balance. An endless loop of death shots circled his reeling mind.

Images of Mariposa mixed with those of Martin Biddle, until the two merged into a single cross-gender corpse.

"When was her body discovered?" Cash's voice cracked.

Bowers scooped the pictures back into the folder. "About two hours after you left *La Tigra*'s compound."

The jury of one had come back sooner than he expected. The speed of the verdict surprised Cash. The death part didn't.

"You can't really believe I had anything to do with this."

Bowers snorted. "Yeah, why would we possibly suspect you of wanting to kill the woman who set you up to take a fall for jury tampering, and later gave the green light to have you snuffed? You have the mother of all motives, and the timeline nails shut your coffin. You visit Mariposa in prison for an F.U. farewell. A couple of days later, you crawl on your belly to *La Tigra*. Hours after you kiss the ring, Mariposa winds up dead. We can put two and two together."

Cash stood nose to nose with Bowers. "Only if you count with your fingers." He turned to Graves. "How can you be sure Mariposa didn't commit suicide?"

"Her tongue," Graves said, "or more accurately, the missing one."

Cash winced.

Graves pulled a photo from the deck and placed it on the table. What looked at first glance like a lousy lipstick job turned out to be blood—caked and purplish.

"Someone cut out her tongue and kept it as a souvenir," Graves said.

Cash turned the photo face down but couldn't unsee the scene. He looked up at Graves. "My money's on a guard."

Neither agent took the bet. Their silence told Cash that he hadn't been the first to suspect an inside job.

CHAPTER ELEVEN

"You won't believe who waltzed in without an appointment and demands to see you ASAP." Eva's voice crackled over the intercom. "The last person on the planet who should show his face here."

With a Fifth Circuit brief due tomorrow, Cash had no time for drop-ins or guessing games. Chained to his desk by the filing deadline, he was going more stir crazy by the minute. Not a sit-down lawyer by nature, he suffered in the eighth circle of hell: the rewrite stage.

He pressed the intercom button. "Just tell me who it is."

"You need a break. Get off your ass and come see for yourself."

It turned out to be the next-to-last person he would expect to find at his door. The very last would be *La Tigra*, who couldn't afford to set foot in the United States.

Rob "Rocket" Rhoden hovered over Eva at the reception desk. All that separated them were three feet of mahogany and her good taste.

Rhoden hadn't bothered to shave or suit up. He wore his trademark aviator sunglasses, flip-flops, faded cutoffs, and a t-shirt that read: *My Pen Is Huge.*

Classy.

A role reversal on the wardrobe front. Sharp-tongued and sharper-dressed, Rhoden practically lived in tailored suits, while Cash usually went casual on non-court days. Today, however, Cash sported a Canali double-breasted silk jacket, Italian-cut and a bargain at two thou.

Cash interrupted Rhoden's doomed efforts to wheedle Eva's cell number. The fool's gaydar must be on the blink. Then again, even had the blowhard known her sexual preference, he would've persisted in making a jackass of himself. In his twisted mind, he could convert any lesbian by the power of his huge pen.

"Whatever you're selling," Cash said to Rhoden, "we're not buying."

"We need to talk privately." Without waiting for an invitation, Rhoden barged into Cash's office and took the chair closest to the desk.

Cash followed him into the office, closed the door, and sat behind the desk. He parted stacks of papers for a clear view of the competitor. "By all means, make yourself at home." Spoken with all the insincerity he could muster.

Rhoden scanned walls decorated with framed courtroom sketches and newspaper articles of Cash's trial wins. Not as impressive as Goldy's collection but not bad for a twenty-year lawyer, with a timeout of two years for bad behavior.

"What do I have to do to persuade your hot secretary to have dinner with me?" Rhoden said.

Cash smiled. "You're not her type, and she's not yours."

"In what respect?"

"She has a brain. Look, I've got an appellate brief due tomorrow, and I don't—"

Rhoden cut him off. "Win your cases, and you don't have to mess with appeals. Now fill me in on your meeting with *La Tigra*."

Cash winced, haunted by his failure to convince *La Tigra* to spare Mariposa. "You know the ending. Shouldn't be hard to guess the rest."

"What did *La Tigra* say about me?" An undercurrent of fear crept into Rhoden's voice.

Classic Rocket. Convinced that every exchange revolved around him. "*Nada*," Cash said. "Hard as this will be for you to wrap your head around, you never came up."

"That can't be right." Rhoden fidgeted on the hot seat. "Don't B.S. me."

Cash toyed with the idea of jacking with the prick, but the unfinished brief beckoned. "You weren't a topic of conversation. It was all about Mariposa."

"You sure did a bang-up job for her," Rhoden said.

Thanks, asshole, I really needed reminding of that.

Cash had a comeback locked and loaded but didn't fire it off. Not now. Not with Rhoden on the ropes. Despite the bravado in his voice, the spark had left his eyes.

Cash had seen the look before, mostly among lifers in prison. "I'm confused. Are you troubled or relieved that your name didn't come up in my visit with *La Tigra*?"

"Both." Rhoden slumped, like a boxer too weak to answer the bell.

Against Cash's better judgment, he felt sorry for his nemesis. Well, sorry enough that he took a shot at lifting his spirits. Not too much, merely nudging the needle from suicidal to scared shitless, where it belonged.

"We'd both be better off if *La Tigra* never knew our names," Cash said.

"Too late for that."

"Oh, I don't know. Maybe a new lawyer will come along, and she'll forget all about the two of us."

"*La Tigra* forgets nothing," Rhoden said.

Cash couldn't argue with that. He saw a different side of Rhoden. An almost human one. More vulnerable than vulture. "It's not like you to wallow in self-doubt."

And even less like you to show it to me.

Rhoden stood and walked slowly to the window. The third-floor office had a panoramic view of the outdoor parking lot behind the federal courthouse. He faced the lot as he spoke. "That fucking ingrate Toby Fine is threatening to dump me. He's pissed that I haven't killed his case."

Cash perked up. Wow. The hearing in Judge Ferguson's court must've gone completely off the rails. The needle had swung back to suicidal.

"Hey," Cash said, "I've been fired by more clients than I can count. More often than not, the basket cases came crawling back in the wet ass hour."

Rhoden turned toward Cash. "I couldn't give a flying fuck about Fine. Far as I'm concerned, that perv can burn in hell or Houston, whichever's hotter. What's got me spooked is whether *La Tigra* told him to shit-can me."

Cash got it. If *La Tigra* had lost confidence in Rhoden, that means she doesn't need him anymore. If she doesn't need him....

Cash leaned back in the chair. He'd go only so far to bolster the competition. "Surely you don't expect me to return to Mexico to plead for you."

"Hell no," Rhoden said, "not after what happened to Mariposa."

Again, thanks for bringing that up, asshole.

"Then I'm not clear on why you're here." Cash's tone took a hard turn. "What do you want from me?"

"*La Tigra* must've said something about her plans for me."

Cash replayed in his mind the meeting in Mexico. What was said and what was left unsaid.

On the said part, something came back to him. "Okay, she did mention you once. She asked why I was there on Mariposa's behalf and not you."

"What'd you say?" Rhoden's voice got shrill.

"I didn't say anything. Just gave her a 'get real' look. She knows the score. Mariposa did too."

Rhoden fell into a silent funk. Broke out of it by muttering to himself. Didn't take a lip reader to know he wasn't praying. Cursing the fates perhaps, but not praying.

Cash let him stew for a minute before saying, "Time for you to shove off. I have something to finish and then someplace to be."

"So you're too busy to help a brother of the bar?"

Oh, so now we're brothers.

"Not sure what you expect me to do."

"For one thing, keep your eyes and ears open," Rhoden said. "If someone has the knives out for me, I need to know."

Be quicker to list those who don't.

"You're being paranoid," Cash said. "If *La Tigra* has a beef with you, you'll know it."

Rhoden shuddered. "My dog got killed yesterday." His voice shook.

So that's what spooked him into coming.

"Look," Cash said, "dogs get run over all the time."

"How often do dogs hang themselves?"

Cash rocked forward in the chair. The news of another hanging reminded him of unfinished business. This was the third suspicious death connected to Rhoden, the "Typhoid Mary" of trial lawyers. First, Martin Biddle. Next, Mariposa Benanti. Now, the dog.

"I've got to finish this brief," Cash said, "but then we have to talk about a client of yours, one who also died at the end of a rope."

"Mariposa?"

Cash shook his head. "The other one. Martin Biddle."

Rhoden went pale. "I've got nothing to say about that punk." He fled, as if chased by a ghost. So unnerved was the narcissist that he left without laying another line on Eva.

Cash could've spared Rhoden the effort. If there's one thing he had learned from life, it was this: you can run from a ghost, but you can't outrun one.

* * *

The gold-plated casket dominated a strippers' stage surrounded on three sides by floor-to-ceiling mirrors. Endless reflections made it look as if gold bars stretched to infinity.

The open casket invited a viewing of the deceased, but Cash couldn't summon the will to walk twenty feet for a last look. Perhaps a last kiss.

Mariposa's memorial service presented Cash with a string of firsts. For starters, he'd never heard Rick James' "Super Freak" played at a funeral before. And at the request of the deceased.

Second, the venue was certainly unique. Past references to services performed at the gentlemen's club carried an entirely different meaning.

However, it was fitting to send off Mariposa at Metamorphosis in North Dallas—the crown jewel of a chain of high-end strip clubs that had cornered the market for prime flesh in the southwest. The chain had been a multibillion-dollar enterprise run by the Benantis during their lifetime and now by whoever *La Tigra* had tapped to take over.

Selecting six strippers in black G-strings and stiletto heels to serve as pallbearers seemed a tad over the top, but Cash had never enjoyed a funeral quite so much, down to the three-minute eulogy delivered by the club D.J., in the form of another song on Mariposa's request list. "Dust in the Wind" kicked off the deceased's setlist.

Cash attributed the sparse turnout to the presence of feds—undercover and uninvited. He made out a dozen FBI and DEA agents, who were trying too hard to blend in. The off-the-rack suits a size too small gave them away. That and the fact they were the only ones in the club not drinking.

Another reason for the spotty attendance—the feds had collared most of the Benanti crew. Word spread on the street that the underlings were willing to roll over in return for reduced sentences. Bad news for wannabe snitches. With both Benantis dead and the higher-ups out of reach, they found themselves locked up and shit out of luck.

FBI Agent Maggie Burns joined Cash at his table. Finally, a fed who looked like she belonged here, ready to command center stage. Though she wore a conservative black dress, he couldn't shake an image of her in a G-string. After all, he had seen her in less.

He picked up an open bottle of Korbel Brut, but she placed her hand over her glass. On duty and carrying, she wasn't about to violate the regs. Not in front of so many witnesses anyway. Especially with the snake Stanley Bowers in the house.

"What are you doing here?" Cash said.

Her eyes swept the room. "You never know who'll show up at an occasion like this."

"You don't really expect *La Tigra* to be here, do you?"

Her eyes settled on him. "You tell me."

"Okay, she's not here. She won't ever be here. She didn't get where she is by being stupid or careless."

Maggie surveyed the room again, slower this time. "Know who else isn't here?"

"You tell me," he said.

"The Rocket."

"Puh-leeze," Cash said, "don't humor that showboat by using the nickname he gave himself."

"Thought he'd have the decency to attend his client's funeral."

"Not unless he could bill the time."

As the last strains of Kansas' ode to oblivion faded, the pallbearers strutted from the stage. The tallest of the troop stopped at Cash's table and said, "Any chance you two are game for a three-way?"

Maggie signaled for her to keep walking and turned to Cash. "Don't even think about it."

Too late.

CHAPTER TWELVE

"**A** businessman has to spend money to make money." Goldberg pounded his desk. The liver spots on his hand seemed to have spread overnight.

Cash braced for bad news on the financial front. Not the first time the fool had floated his cockamamie theory of economics, which boiled down to a time-tested recipe for disaster: for every dollar taken in, piss away two. The trade imbalance explained how the top criminal defense lawyer of his day—a magnet in his prime for seven-figure retainers—now teetered on the brink of bankruptcy.

Hence, the title of Skyler Patterson's hit job in last Sunday's *Dallas Morning News*: "How the Bantam Rooster of the Courthouse Plucked Himself."

"So I sprang for a full-page ad in the *Dallas Business Journal*," Goldberg said, "showing the world that we're back and badass as ever."

Cash groaned. Skyler's piece must've spooked the old man into a dumbass move doomed to backfire. His motive for the expenditure was as thin and transparent as the comb over that failed to hide his growing bald spot.

Buying an ad the firm couldn't afford further proved the reporter's point that Goldberg had been bleeding cash for years, leaving behind a trail of angry creditors, pissed ex-spouses, uncollected judgments, and contempt orders.

To make matters worse, Cash was pretty damn sure the world didn't subscribe to the *DBJ*. At least not their world of prostitutes, petty thieves, pervs, and perps with the bad judgment to steal something small.

He fought the urge to lash out at a seventy-year-old who had cheated death last year. With Goldy, the time for teachable moments had long since passed. Not much time left for any kind of moments.

Cash turned to Eva, seated at his side on the couch. She had ditched the boho look and entered a goth phase. Black boots, jeans, belt, and shirt. Black lipstick and nail polish as well. If this was meant to make her look edgy and dangerous, it wasn't working.

"How could you let this happen?" he said to her.

"Me?" Eva did a decent job of feigning outrage. "You two are the partners here. I'm just a lowly assistant."

"Someone has to babysit him," Cash said.

Goldy clapped loudly. "Hey, I'm right here, and I can hear you two."

Eva rose and walked behind Goldy, still seated at his desk. His head swiveled to track her movements.

She massaged his shoulders while leaning down to speak in his good ear. "Given the hole we're in, we can't afford to have you spend your precious time on marketing or bookkeeping. You need to focus one hundred percent of your energy on attracting clients and winning cases."

Goldy's eyes closed. His sigh heralded a smile.

As her left hand continued to knead his shoulder, her right lifted the checkbook from his coat pocket. A skill she had honed on the streets of Juárez as a runaway teen.

"Hey!" Goldy grabbed for the checkbook. A beat too late. "What do you think you're doing?" He sounded indignant but slowly settled back into the chair.

Eva picked up the intensity of the massage. "Freeing you to do what God put you on the planet to do. A great lawyer shouldn't waste his time with bills, creditors, and the humdrum of running an office."

The massage melted Goldy into his seat. He surrendered to her touch. "Great idea. Cash, why didn't you think of that?"

Cash rolled his eyes. Took all his strength not to respond and risk breaking Eva's spell over the old man.

"While I pull us out of the ditch we're in," Goldy said, "Eva will take over the firm's finances. This is strictly a short-term measure. Once we're back in the black, we revert to the way things were."

"Of course," she said.

Goldy's eyes remained closed. His shoulders slumped. His breathing slowed and slipped into a snore.

Eva motioned for Cash to step outside. They walked silently to his office. He sat behind the desk. She, in a client chair.

"That was a slick move," Cash said, "the way you conned Goldy into giving up his checkbook."

"Step one, complete. Step two is striking him as a signatory on our bank accounts, and step three, suspending his corporate credit card."

"All the while making him think he came up with the idea. I hope you treat me with kid gloves like that, when I'm his age."

"Consider it done," she said. "I'm taking your checkbook and credit card as well."

"Wait a goddam second! What makes you think I would cede control of the finances?"

"My track record." She walked to his coat on a hanger and took his checkbook. "I pay all my bills on time and send money to my mother in Mexico, all on the pittance you pay me."

Before Cash could protest, his cell phone chirped. Kent Michaels from Channel 5 is calling.

Seconds later Eva's phone vibrated. "It's Channel 8," she said.

The landline rang, making it a trifecta.

A cacophony of calls flooded the room. With no credible defense to Eva's power play, Cash welcomed the interruption.

Michaels from Channel 5 followed up his call with a text message, requesting an on-camera interview. The reporter would rush to Cash's office. The sooner, the better, for a segment to air on the noon broadcast.

Cash read the text twice but couldn't respond right away, stunned by the breaking news of Rhoden's death.

Turned out there was one interruption he didn't welcome.

CHAPTER THIRTEEN

H it hard by Rhoden's death, Cash balked at the requests for interviews before reminding himself that life would go on. Well, his life anyway.

He taped segments for Channels 4, 5, 8, 11, and 13, delivering a fresh sound bite on each clip and proving again that the most dangerous spot in Dallas was between a TV camera and him.

He drew the line with Skyler Patterson of the *Dallas Morning News*, denying her a precious quote as punishment for not covering Tina Campos' trial. Her snub had kept Cash's latest courtroom triumph under the radar.

The silent treatment with Skyler lasted all of twenty minutes. After which, Cash gave her a killer quote. Bull crap about Rhoden being a pillar of the defense bar. A champion of the underdog. A voice for the voiceless. With liberty and justice for all. Until death do us part.

At least the death line in the eulogy rang true.

Cash polished his favorite gem of the day and gifted it to the *News*: "The Rocket never coasted in the courtroom but went full throttle all the way."

He liked the line so much that he recycled it two days later at Rhoden's funeral, which made it two memorial services in one week for him. One more would set a personal record.

The two funerals differed in most respects. The chief differences were venue and viewing. Mariposa's send-off featured an open casket and six strippers in G-strings as pallbearers at an upscale gentlemen's club. In contrast, Rhoden went out with a closed casket at the smallest chapel at Restland Funeral Home.

Closing the casket was a no-brainer, given the hailstorm of bullets that had blown away Rhoden's face and severed three of four limbs. The holdout, a right leg that clung to the hip by a tendon. The remains more closely resembled a puzzle of bloody parts than an actual body.

Assassins wearing Charlie Sheen masks and carrying AK-47s had gunned down Rhoden in the parking lot of the Galleria Shopping Center. Fitting, since there were two-and-a-half hitmen. Twin hulks and a pint-sizer.

It had taken less than two minutes for a black Mercedes SUV with tinted windows to whisk the gunmen in and out of the lot. A hit meant to carry a message, with the cartel's fingerprints smeared all over the job.

What happened south of the border never stayed south of the border.

The murders of a criminal lawyer and his client within days of each other raised red flags and even scored a couple of news cycles, before fading into the oblivion of old news. Not that the cops or feds would lose much sleep over the deaths of a trafficker and her mouthpiece.

Nor did the departed duo leave behind many mourners. Certainly not judging by the sparse turnout at both funerals, which were depressingly alike in certain respects. Few butts in the seats. Not a wet eye in the house.

At Rhoden's funeral, the first two rows—typically reserved for family—remained empty. Cash had the third row to himself. He recognized the blonde across the aisle and one row back as Rhoden's assistant, Sami something. He had no idea who the elderly couple behind her were.

An ancient organist with henna-hued hair played "There'll Be Peace in the Valley."

Fat chance.

Skyler Patterson showed up late and sat next to Cash, ensuring there would be no peace at the service. Not for him anyway.

She had made a halfhearted effort to look funereal, with a black dress too short for the occasion and a hit-and-miss makeup job, but the red jogging shoes undercut the effect.

"I hear you're taking over Toby Fine's defense," she whispered to Cash.

"You heard wrong," he whispered back.

"Never known you to turn down a high-profile case, certainly not with a wealthy defendant in the dock."

She had a point. He assessed prospective clients on three criteria: whether taking the case would fatten the firm's bank account, generate publicity, and/or further a righteous cause.

Not necessarily in that order.

He generally subscribed to Meat Loaf's rule of thumb that *Two Out of Three Ain't Bad*, and Fine scored off the charts as a media magnet and a money maker.

The cause, however, not so noble.

One big problem—Cash had promised Eva no more cartel work. Well, except for the freebie he owed *La Tigra*. After that, the firm would cater strictly to white-collar clients.

"Probably better that you pass on the case anyway," Skyler said, "at least as far as Fine is concerned."

Cash turned to her. "What's that supposed to mean?"

"You're gaining quite a reputation, along with a new nickname."

"What nickname?" Cash caught himself mid-sentence and lowered his voice. She had a knack for getting under his skin.

"The *Angel of Death*. Not quite as crisp as Cash, but it has a certain ring to it."

"Bullshit, no one calls me that. By the way, Cash isn't my nickname. It's my name."

"It'll take time for the new handle to catch on, but it's off to a good start. You were working on Martin Biddle's appeal when he killed himself. Last week you visited Mariposa Benanti in prison, and she died three days later. The day after your meeting with Rocket, he catches enough lead to build a battleship. Are you noticing a pattern here? A reason for Fine to keep his distance?"

The organist segued into "Rock of Ages," padding the service with hymns to compensate for the dearth of testimonials.

Cash knew better than to engage with Skyler, who had a talent for twisting words and facts to fit her story, but he couldn't help himself. "Two people with ties to a cartel get killed. That's dog-bites-man material."

He didn't bring up Biddle, who had no cartel connection. At least as far as Cash knew.

"Good quote," she said. "I'll be sure to include that in my Sunday piece."

"Do you know what they say about cops?" Cash didn't wait for a response. "They're never around when you need one, but always show up when you don't." He rose. "Same goes in spades for reporters."

Cash left the service with mixed feelings. Buoyed by the promise his name would appear in print this weekend. Bummed by the threat that Skyler's hit job could be bad for business. Her story would test his theory that for a defense lawyer, there was no such thing as bad publicity.

From across the parking lot, it looked as if cops had ticketed Cash's Porsche. The ticket turned out to be a note tucked under the windshield wiper:

Limpia tu calendario.

He crumpled and tossed the note. Not signed, but it didn't need to be to get *La Tigra's* message across.

"Consider it done," he said to himself. "Calendar cleared."

His conscience, not so much.

CHAPTER FOURTEEN

kyler Patterson's article in Sunday's *Dallas Morning News* presented Cash with a classic good news/bad news situation. The good—his name appeared on the front page above the fold. The bad—his name appeared on the front page above the fold.

The hit job carried the too-cute-to-be-Skyler's-idea headline: "Cashing In and Checking Out: The Ups and Downs of an Embattled Lawyer." Most attorneys would've bristled at the tone of the piece and cringed at the new nickname: Angel of Death, credited to anonymous sources.

The nickname probably was Skyler's idea.

Cash pushed past the negative slant and drive-by insults. Instead, he fixated on the reporter's burial on the back page of Campos' acquittal. Skyler had reduced Cash's courtroom triumph to little more than a footnote.

A rapidly shrinking pool of readers subscribed to the *News*, online or off. Of the dying breed of readers, only a few pushed past the first few paragraphs of a story outside the sports section.

The muckraker had devoted four paragraphs to Cash's conviction for jury tampering, his hard time at Seagoville, and his release on a "technicality." She hadn't bothered to explain that the technicality turned on his innocence, at least of the sole charge on his rap sheet.

Sunday morning, Cash fell into a funk. He failed to answer repeated calls from the media, clamoring for comment on Skyler's story. He even ignored the ringing doorbell at his Lakewood house. It took a pounding on the door to rouse him from the couch.

He opened the door to face what could only be more bad news. Paula Marshall had surely come to deliver a kick to the balls, not a pat on the back. The big shot lawyer from Stewart Powell's megafirm had sunk her hooks into Eva, in a desperate attempt to pry her loose from Cash.

Without waiting for an invitation, she charged into the house, armed with a copy of the *News*. Even on the weekend, she dressed the part of a corporate attorney. The navy-blue pinstripe suit accentuated her broad shoulders and narrow waist. Blonde and big-boned, she cut an imposing figure. Her cold, gray eyes sent a chill through Cash.

One thing's for sure, Paula wasn't on her way to or from a church service. The closest she came to bowing to a deity was worshipping the currency that carried the warning: *In God We Trust.*

If Paula had swung by a church this morning, it had been to drop off Eva at the ten o'clock mass at St. Rita's.

Light a candle for me, mijita.

Paula slammed the newspaper onto the kitchen table. "I won't waste time asking if you've seen the lead story. Media whore that you are, I'm sure it's framed and hanging on the wall by now."

"Look, Paula, if you're here to kick me while I'm down, take a number and get in line."

"For the record, I've never waited until you were down before kicking the shit out of you."

Good point.

"I'll go out on a limb," he said, "and guess that you're not here to console me or express outrage at the libelous article." Her silence confirmed his hunch. "So why did you come?"

"I came for Eva's sake."

He sighed loudly. Not this again. Every month or so, Paula harassed him with the same request that escalated into a demand and hardened into a threat. She would start calm and civil, urging him to release Eva from his Manson-like spell. Soon the gloves would come off, and she'd vow to liberate her girlfriend.

Over his dead body, if necessary.

Neither Paula nor Cash bothered to deal Eva into the raging debate over her future. Mainly because she could match and raise their decibel level. Plus, she had made her position clear, laying the exact same odds of leaving Cash's side or Paula's bed.

Less than zero.

"I love her," Paula said.

"I don't doubt that you do, but Eva and I have been together for almost fifteen years. She was a sixteen-year-old street kid from Mexico when I took her in. I'm like a father figure to her."

Paula snickered. "More like a problem child, one who can't cut the cord. Besides, all that is ancient history, long before my time. Also before people around you started falling like dominoes."

"Bit of an exaggeration, don't you think?"

"Two victims in one week," Paula said. "I don't want Eva to make it a trifecta."

Damn, the bitch had a talent for hitting his rawest nerve. Plus, if Biddle were counted, Cash had already scored the hat trick. Easy to see how Paula had fast-tracked onto the management committee of her law firm, leapfrogging scores of bigwigs with more seniority.

Cash didn't need a scoreboard to know he was losing. Not only the debate with Paula but also the internal one. He resorted to his last line of defense. "What would she do?" The *without me* was silent.

"Work for my firm as a corporate paralegal, which would mean more money, more prestige, and here's the kicker, less chance of winding up dead."

"She'd be bored stiff."

"It's called growing up. The time in your life when you start eating vegetables and flossing daily."

Floss you, lady.

Cash hit back with all he had in the tank. "Eva is loyal to a fault. She'll never quit me."

"Which is why you have to fire her."

"For what?"

"For cause...or no cause...for talking back...laughing too loud. You're a clever boy. You'll come up with a reason."

"None that she wouldn't see through," he said.

She shoved her copy of the *News* across the table, toward him. "I'll leave this behind. Extra copy for friends and family, assuming you have any left. Maybe rereading the article will motivate you to let Eva go. 'Angel of Death.' It has a ring to it."

He returned the paper to her. "I have no intention of reading Skyler's flight of fiction again, and Eva is my best friend and my family."

"I'm counting on that," she said on her way out.

Paula hadn't waited for his formal surrender, no doubt knowing she didn't need to. Hours after her departure, he stopped lying to himself and concentrated on lying to Eva.

The hard part would be concocting some bullshit ground for canning her.

The harder part, selling it.

Light a second candle for me, mijita.

CHAPTER FIFTEEN

Monday morning, Cash arrived late at the office, still steamed over Skyler's smear. He placed a latte with half-and-half and two Splendas on the reception desk. Depending on how the day went, the coffee could be a peace offering or a parting gift.

Eva wore an expression that curdled cream. "Say it ain't so."

Her tone backed Cash away from the desk. "What now?" he said.

"I read in the *News* that you're taking over Toby Fine's defense." An undercurrent of anger amped her voice. "Would've been nice to give me a heads up. Even nicer if you had kept your word."

Eva paused, giving him a chance to fess up. He remained silent.

She went on. "What part of *no cartel work* do you not understand?"

"Don't believe everything you read, and where Skyler's concerned, don't believe anything you read. Case in point, I'm not defending Fine. He hasn't contacted me, and it wouldn't make a difference if he had."

"Guess again." She pointed to the closed door to Goldberg's office. "Your new client is in there with Goldy."

"What?" It was Cash's turn to raise his voice. "You left the old man alone with Fine? What were you thinking?"

"I'm not his babysitter."

"Like hell you're not."

As Cash blew past her, she scored the last word. "A babysitter would be paid more."

Cash rushed into Goldberg's office and slammed the door behind him. The old man looked relaxed. He leaned back in his chair, almost horizontal. Close to corpse pose. Boots on the desk. Eyes shut. Grinning like he'd pulled one over on Johnny Law.

In Goldy's zen-like presence, Toby Fine seemed like a new man. Cash had last seen him outside the courtroom, overshadowed by the showboat Rhoden and surrounded by a scrum of bloodsucking reporters. Fine had looked like a trapped animal. Almost a sympathetic figure.

Today, Fine garnered no sympathy—not from Cash anyway. A closer look revealed the predator behind the civilized façade. Hooded eyes and bloodless lips offset his flaccid features.

Fine stood and reached out a hand that had never done a day's honest labor. Cash was slow to shake hands and quick to break the grip, repulsed by the clammy flesh.

Goldberg opened his eyes and rocked forward. "About time you showed up. Toby here finds himself in the market for new counsel."

"We're booked for the year." Cash didn't try to sell the lie. "For next year too."

Fine sat, a sign he wasn't taking no for an answer. "In my experience, nothing clears a lawyer's calendar faster than a seven-figure retainer."

"Sorry, still booked solid," Cash said, "but I'll be happy to refer you to another firm."

Fine wrote out a check and handed it to Goldberg. "Talk it over between yourselves. I expect to hear back from you by noon tomorrow."

No sooner had Fine left Goldberg's office than Eva invited herself in. A welcome addition, given that Cash had her vote in the bag.

Goldberg took his best shot at winning her over. Not with words. Instead, he held the check to her eyes, counting on the string of zeros to rope her in.

She didn't blink. "Cartel money's not real, because you never live long enough to spend it. So it wouldn't matter if the check was for a hundred million dollars."

That's my girl.

"Even if our fee wasn't coming from a cartel," Cash said, "we don't represent pimps. Working girls, sure. But not their fucking pimps."

Goldberg shook his head. "This is an important First Amendment issue. Besides, Fine's not a pimp."

"You're right," Cash said. "He's worse than a pimp. Instead of working the streets like any self-respecting parasite, he parks his fat ass in a penthouse suite, while his website peddles underage flesh to any perv with a PC. The lower the kid's age, the higher the price."

"Since when do we swallow the government's allegations in an indictment whole-hog?" Goldberg said.

Eva leaned over Goldberg's desk, getting in the old man's face. "I don't give a damn whether the charges against Fine are true or false. We don't take cartel money. Period. End of debate."

"Time to vote," Cash said. "All in favor of taking on Fine as a client, raise your hand."

Goldberg raised the hand clutching the check and waved it in the air. It fell limp, like a flag of surrender.

"All opposed."

Eva and Cash raised their hands.

"The nays have it," Cash said.

Eva snatched the check from Goldberg and looked to Cash. He nodded. She tore it up.

Good thing too. Cash lacked the strength to do it.

* * *

The image of a million-dollar check in shreds haunted Cash all the way home.

Beat, broke, and bummed out, he dragged himself to the living room and flipped on a light. Froze. Ten feet away sat a man on the couch. Hard to tell his height, but he appeared to be slim. Close to Cash's build. Maybe a few pounds heavier.

Cash blinked the stranger into focus. He looked battle tested and boot tough. A crewcut that would pass military inspection. Lined, leathery face. Dead eyes that warned the world not to cross him.

Cash wouldn't risk it, not even if the intruder hadn't brought along a sidekick: a Glock.

"Turn off the light," the Glockster said.

Cash hit the switch. "How did you get in?"

"Wrong question." The intruder sounded as if he didn't give a shit how the night played out. "The right one is whether you'll leave the house tomorrow morning on your own two feet or in a body bag."

"I'm definitely interested in the answer to that one as well." Cash kept his voice steady, more or less. "And I'm totally in favor of walking out of here on my own power."

"My boss was very disappointed in your disrespect of Mister Fine this morning."

"Your boss being—?"

Glockster cut him off. "Being your boss, too."

"Ah, so she's cashing in her chit for Fine."

"Appears to be the case."

"Why didn't she make that clear before Fine came to see me?"

"She's a businesswoman. No sense burning a marker unless she has to. Most lawyers would've sold their mothers for a fraction of what Fine offered you up front."

"If she had made it clear that—"

Glockster racked the slide of the pistol. That shut Cash up.

"Is it clear now?"

"Crystal," Cash said.

"Just so there's no danger of confusion, you will take Fine's case and win it. If you don't, I'll be back to see you. But only after I make calls on everyone you care about, starting with your dog."

"Joke's on you," Cash said. "I don't have a dog."

"The sign on the lawn says to beware of the dog."

Cash shrugged. "Poor man's burglar alarm."

* * *

At 4:10 a.m., the doorbell woke Cash from a fitful sleep. Groggy, he trudged to the door and peered through the peephole.

No one on the porch. Nothing to see.

A scratching on the door prompted him to open it. A black Labrador puppy greeted him with a whimper. He patted the pup and removed the note tied to the collar:

DON'T GET TOO ATTACHED.

CHAPTER SIXTEEN

hen Bettina Biddle suggested meeting at noon at Nordstrom's in the Northpark Shopping Center, Cash assumed it was for a lunch that would break up her hard day of shopping, sandwiched between Pilates class and picking up the kids from school. Instead, he found her at the Chanel perfume counter, spritzing passersby with Scarlett—a new brand named for the film star.

Cash stopped outside her range. "Do you have a license for that weapon?"

She nodded. "Double O Seven here, with a license to shill."

"In my book," he said, "you're a ten."

She looked different today. Just as beautiful but younger, freer. Her brunette hair flowed halfway down her back, the bangs brushing her eyebrows.

"Perfect timing for my lunch break." She even sounded younger.

He took her to a back booth at Seasons 52, on the far side of the mall. Fearful of a crying jag or worse, he held his questions until wine arrived. "When did you start working at Nordstrom's?"

"Last week. Technically I'm a trainee for six weeks." She blushed. "The girls are back in school, so there's no one home."

There had to be more to the story, but Cash didn't push. The strategy paid off.

"Besides," she said, "we can use the money. I've come full circle. I used to have a personal shopper at Nordstrom's, and now I'm training to be one. Ah, the benefit of an arts degree from TCU."

"Did you and Marty meet in college?"

She nodded. "He was a scholarship student with a finance major and a night job at 7-Eleven, while I divided my time between the sorority house and the art department. I concentrated on Spanish painters of the Nineteenth Century, which gave me a good excuse to take a junior year abroad in Madrid."

"Guess it's true," Cash said, "about opposites attracting."

She checked her watch. "I get forty-five minutes for lunch, so I'll get right to the point of why I asked to meet. Have you found out any more about Marty's death?"

Cash sipped the Syrah, stalling. Though he knew the question would come up, he had no ready response. "I'm finding more questions than answers. The first big one, how and why did your late husband hire Rhoden to defend him in the criminal case?" His tone left no doubt as to his thoughts on the choice.

She winced. He had hit a nerve. "Marty's company recommended him and offered to pay all the legal bills. We had just bought a new house, and the girls were in private school. We were still paying off college debts. The legal fees would've put us underwater. At the time it seemed like a great idea."

"And now?" Cash said.

"He and Marty fought throughout the trial."

"Over what?" Cash said.

"Over everything. Whether Marty should testify. Whether Rhoden needed to cross-examine government witnesses and call witnesses for our side. By the time the case went to the jury, Marty didn't trust him."

"And you?"

"He was a pig." As she lifted the glass to her lips, her hand shook. Cash chalked it up to anger, not nerves. "He hit on me during the trial and even came on to me while Marty was in prison."

"Did you tell your husband?"

She shook her head. "He had too much to deal with, and I could handle Rhoden on my own."

"Rhoden's no longer a problem," Cash said. "I assume you know he was gunned down."

"I saw it on the news." She didn't sound sorry.

Cash didn't blame her. Rhoden's bad boy behavior came as no surprise. It would've been out of character for him not to have made a move on Bettina. In one respect, however, Rhoden's conduct had been unprecedented. Cash had never known him to lay off the government's witnesses completely.

Push his client to clam up and plead guilty, sure. That was Marty's M.O. But to play dead at trial—that had been new.

Rhoden lived to destroy people on the stand, but Marty's trial hadn't played out that way. To prepare Biddle's appellate brief, Cash had pored over the transcript. For long stretches of the trial, Rhoden had gone mute, becoming little more than a potted plant, while the prosecutors piled on evidence.

At first, Cash had given the defense counsel the benefit of the doubt. The critical decisions not to put the client on the stand nor to call witnesses could've turned on Rhoden's belief their testimony would've made things worse. Now Cash wasn't so sure.

"Besides testifying himself," Cash said, "who did Marty want to call to the stand?"

"Marty gave Rhoden a list of co-workers who had helped put together the financial statements that went to the banks. The prosecutors made it seem as if Marty had prepared the documents all by himself." Her voice picked up pace and heat. "That wasn't true. A team compiled them, and they were approved by supervisors before going out the door."

By the time the entrees arrived—a club sandwich for him and a kale salad for her—Cash had lost his appetite. Bettina's claim didn't get her husband off the hook, but it did raise a new question. If others had their prints all over the false financial statements provided to the banks, why didn't the prosecutors charge them with conspiracy to defraud? Why had they gone after Marty alone?

After all, conspiracy is the feds' favorite charge. With a bird's nest on the ground, why settle for breaking only one bad egg?

"You said that Marty's company picked up Rhoden's legal tab," Cash said, "but who actually recommended him to your husband?"

"Marty's boss, as well as the outside lawyers for the company."

"What are their names?"

"Marty's boss is Lou Watson, and the lawyers were Mister Powell and...." She tapped a forefinger on her lower lip. "Marsha something. No, something Marsha." She stopped tapping. "Marshall."

Cash's voice jumped an octave. "Paula Marshall?"

"Yeah, that's the name. Do you know her?"

"Too well."

"We screwed up big time by putting our trust in Rhoden." She pushed away the plate, the salad untouched. "We should've sold the house, borrowed what we could, and hired you to defend Marty."

"Don't beat yourself up over that. Two things would've kept you from hiring me. One, I didn't have a law license at the time. Two, I was behind bars."

"But hiring Rhoden," she said, "cost Marty his life."

Cash couldn't bail her out there. Rhoden would sacrifice his mother for an extra buck. "What I can't fathom," he said, "is why Powell and Paula would risk their reputations by recommending a cockroach like Rhoden. They're corner office partners at a white-shoe firm. What are they doing in bed with Rhoden?"

She stared at the table. "While we're on the subject of lawyers and their bills, I hired you to look into Marty's death, and I will pay you for your time. But right now things are a little tight. The prosecutors have frozen my accounts until we reach an agreement on Marty's restitution. I put the house up for sale and got a decent offer. When the sale closes in a month or so, the feds will take the lion's share, and I'll pay you from what's left."

He shook his head. "I've got a counteroffer. You take my bedmate off my hands, and we call it even."

"Your bedmate?"

He dropped a photo of Nuisance on the table. The pup, asleep on Cash's bed, looked more like a plush toy than a pet. "Your daughters could use a new friend."

She picked up the photo. "Just what we need. Another mouth to feed. You know that if I show this picture to my girls, I'm sunk."

He smiled.

Bettina checked her watch again. "Sorry to eat and run." She stopped. "Well, to not eat and run, but my break's almost over."

"Go back to making the world a sweeter smelling place, and I'll settle up here."

She put the photo in her purse. "Someday I'll get back at you for this."

He counted on it. After she left, he ordered another glass of wine. Saying goodbye to Nuisance would be tough, but a snap compared to his next move.

Getting rid of Eva.

CHAPTER SEVENTEEN

The pup whirled around and around in Cash's bed, robbing him of sleep for the second straight night. The *sicario*'s gift earned the name Cash had given him: Nuisance. Even in those rare moments when the black Lab calmed down, he stirred up unsettling childhood memories.

On their last day together, Cash's mother had brought him an early birthday gift: Max. A mutt rescued from the pound to keep her eight-year-old son company while locked in his room.

The lockdowns occurred at least daily and sometimes two or three times a day, whenever a visitor called on his mother. The men came rain or shine, day or night. Strangers and regulars without regard to race, color, age, shape, or smell. They stayed anywhere from a few minutes to all night.

To the silent boy hidden away in the bedroom, minutes had seemed like hours. Hours, like days.

The two dogs in Cash's life—Max and Nuisance—were different in every way: breed, size, color, disposition, and sex. No matter. Nuisance still triggered memories of the worst day of Cash's life.

That is, until today threatened to sink even lower. Cash was on the cusp of losing Eva. He'd lived with his mother for eight years. With Eva, fifteen. No one else had come close.

He could no longer confide in Eva. Not about the *sicario* anyway. Not with the bombshell about to be dropped on her. If things went as planned today, he might never confide in her again.

Over a breakfast of wheat toast and black coffee, Cash devised a four-stage strategy for surviving the fallout from Operation Adios. Step one: inform Toby Fine that Cash would take his case.

On the way to Goldy's apartment, Cash called Fine with the news. The new client didn't act surprised, relieved, or the slightest bit grateful. Instead, he asked what had taken Cash so long to come around. Sounded cocksure of himself. More depressing, certain of Cash as well. One more strike against the perv.

Step one, check.

Step two: break the news about their representation of Fine to Goldy. It might take the two of them, plus a small army, to handle Eva. Cash ambushed the old man at his apartment, interrupting a breakfast of last night's leftovers: chicken flautas, refried beans, and warm beer.

The ambience proved more depressing than the morning fare. At this point in his marital merry-go-round, Goldy had bought four houses in Highland Park—an affluent suburb carved from the heart of Dallas. Highland Park had done everything but build a moat to keep out the barbarians.

Goldy had lost all four mansions to exes in bitter divorces, each time landing in an apartment that was grungier than its predecessors. The current digs came with chipped furniture, shag carpet, peeling paint, and the stench of cigarette smoke.

Goldy more than made up for Fine's underwhelming reaction. "Hot damn, I knew you'd come to your senses. The money is too good to pass up."

"About the money...." Cash feared the old man's ticker couldn't take the shock of the next sentence. "We're handling this one *pro bono*."

Goldy looked as if he'd been gut-punched. His lips moved, but no words emerged.

"It's a freebie," Cash said, "the one I promised *La Tigra* to get out of Mexico alive."

"Is it too late to change my vote?" Goldy said.

"On what? Whether we take Fine's case or whether I get out alive?"

"Both."

Step two, check.

Now for the dicey move. Blindside Eva with the news. Send her reeling away from the firm and Cash's circle of hell.

He started the day the same way he planned to end it. As a certified grade A asshole. On the way to work, he picked up a latte for him, none for Eva. He blew past her at the reception desk without a word.

"Hey," she said, "where's mine?"

He stopped and stared at her. "In case you've forgotten the roles here, I'm the boss, and you're what we refer to in Texas as an employee at will. That means it's your job to fetch coffee for me, not the other way around."

"Yes sir." She snapped off a salute.

"The next time you're in my office, take a close look at the diplomas on the wall, especially the one that reads *Juris Doctor*. The J.D. behind my name stands for Just Desserts. I busted my ass in law school, so that now I get to savor the good things in life." He sipped the latte and smacked his lips.

"And here I thought the J.D. stood for Justa Dipshit." She smiled.

He didn't.

"Besides," she went on, "before you rewrite the history of your law school days, remember that your classmates voted you the student most likely not only to *be* a top criminal defense lawyer but also the one most likely to *need* a top criminal defense lawyer. Bullseye on both counts."

"Allow me to remind you, Miss G.E.D., that you never set foot in a college, much less a law school." Hitting her where it hurt.

"Prick," she said under her breath.

"I heard that."

"I made sure you did."

He entered his office and slammed the door behind him. Sat behind the desk to calm down.

The latte tasted bitter, reminding him how much he hated frou-frou coffees. In his book, a latte was a good brew spoiled.

* * *

Bunkered behind his boomerang-shaped desk, Goldberg shuffled papers. Cash could always tell when the old man was trying to look too busy to bog down in one of Cash's crackpot conspiracies.

"Have you told Eva?" Goldy spoke without looking up.

Seated across the desk, Cash deleted messages on his iPhone. Two could play the too-busy-to-be-bothered game. "I thought we'd break the news to her together."

"Should've known you'd put me in the line of fire." Goldy stopped shuffling and looked up. "You going to tell her about the late-night visit from the *sicario*?"

Cash shook his head.

"Then what reason will you give for changing your mind about taking Fine's case?"

"*We* will keep it short and simple. The firm takes cases for three reasons: money, publicity, and principle."

Goldy snorted in disgust. "You kissed the money goodbye."

"Right, but the case is high profile, and as you pointed out yesterday, there's a First Amendment issue at play. In the immortal words of Meat Loaf, 'Two out of three ain't bad.'"

"Hellfire," Goldy said, "I was bullshitting about the principle to get my hands on the dough. Fine's nothing but a high-tech pimp."

"Then we'd better wring a ton of publicity out of this sucker, cause that's all we've got left."

* * *

Cash waited until five o'clock to summon Eva into Goldy's office. On the way in, she fired the first shot. "Want me to *fetch* you a latte, Mister McCahill?"

"Make it a scotch and soda instead," Cash said.

She flashed a "you've-got-to-be-kidding" look before detouring to the bar.

"The good stuff's on the bottom shelf," he said, "hidden behind the cheap brands."

She muttered while mixing the drink and walking to Cash. Plopped the glass on the desk, hard enough to slosh some over the side.

"Better fix yourself a stiff one too," Goldy said to Eva.

"I'll take the bad news straight," she said.

Cash stared into his drink. "How do you know that it's bad news?"

"Two sure signs: First, you stalled until quitting time to lay it on me. Second, neither of you has the balls to do this alone."

Excellent points. "Some would consider landing a new client good news." Cash's voice trailed off.

"Spit it out," she said.

So much for blindsiding Eva. The *bruja* could smell a storm a mile away and Cash's B.S. from two miles.

"We're taking Fine's case," Cash said.

No hair-trigger explosion from her. Instead, a slow burn built into a seethe. "I'll have that drink now." She poured herself a vodka, killed the shot, and turned to Cash. "No, we're not. We voted two-to-one—"

Cash cut her off. "I changed my vote."

"You want to explain why?" It sounded more like a command than a question.

Goldy went back to shuffling papers, eyes glued to the desk. Cash offered the best bad excuse he had. "We need the publicity."

She pointed to Cash. "You're lying." Then turned on Goldy. "And by letting him spout this bullshit, you're just as bad. Something has changed since we voted against taking the case. What happened?"

"We came to our senses," Cash said in his most patronizing tone, "and realized there are only two votes here, not three. From now on, the office runs on a simple rule: one lawyer, one vote."

"You've been acting like a dick all day." The angrier she grew, the stronger her accent. "What gives?"

"This is not up for debate," Cash said. "Take it or leave it. That's how the new world order works."

"When you two *gentlemen* decide to give women the vote, call me and I'll come back." She slammed the office door on her way out.

The next explosion was the slamming of the door to the outside world.

Goldberg turned ashen. "What the hell are you doing? I agreed to try the case with you, but not at the cost of losing Eva. Run after her and apologize."

"She owes me an apology." Said without an ounce of conviction.

Goldberg snorted. "She's as stubborn as you are. That's not going to happen."

"Then we soldier on without her."

The color flooded back into Goldy's face, now red and ruddy. "We can't make it without her."

"No one is indispensable, old man, not even you. Fall in line or follow her out the door."

"But's it my goddam firm!" Goldy shouted.

Cash poured himself another shot. Straight scotch this time. "Before you go there, better consider who brings in all the work these days." His voice remained steadier than the hand that held the drink.

"I'm not going to dignify that with a response." Goldy stood and walked stiffly from the office. No goodbye. No slamming of the door.

No turning back now.

Cash raised the shot glass and toasted himself on a job well done. The drink tasted bitter. Bitter as a latte.

Steps three and four of Operation Adios, double check.

CHAPTER EIGHTEEN

While waiting for a table, Cash leaned in for a kiss. Maggie stiff-armed him, as her eyes swept across the packed restaurant. "Not here." Her outfit shouted hands off. Baggy jeans and a loose-fitting shirt buttoned to the chin.

Rise catered to a quiche-and-quinoa crowd that skewed female, white, well-off, and welded to their seats for hours. Today proved no exception.

Definitely not Cash's pick for a place to chow down. Nor had it ever before been Maggie's first choice, or even her hundredth.

Cash couldn't shake a sense of bad news brewing. Maggie, a lover of the big three "T"s in Texas (Tequila, Tex-Mex, and Tortillas), had steered him to a French bistro.

At Maggie's request, they scored the most secluded table in the back. Her tradeoff became clear. She was willing to sacrifice salsa for the certainty of not seeing a colleague. They were officially on the down low.

Cash mustered the courage to ask, "Are you breaking up with me?"

"Are you representing Toby Fine?"

"That's what I call a T-I-T," he said. "Typical investigator trick. Answering a question with a question."

"Whereas what you just did is a T-A-T. A typical attorney trick. Refusing to give a straight, yes-or-no answer."

"So I guess that it's tit for tat. Or in this case, tat for tit." He smiled.

She didn't. "Are you Fine's new lawyer?" More fire in her voice the second time.

"Guilty as charged," he said.

"I hope that will be your client's plea at his re-arraignment."

"Don't bet on it."

Disappointment clouded her eyes, or perhaps it was pain. "You know damn well that I'm the case agent on Fine."

"So?"

"You have to choose: Fine or me?"

The waitress returned, giving Cash a reprieve while she took their orders. His, eggs benedict, turkey bacon, and wheat toast with orange marmalade. Hers, a small Caesar salad and a crab soufflé. Iced tea for both.

The orders in, he turned back to Maggie. "I don't have a choice. You know the deal I cut to get out of Mexico alive. *La Tigra* called in the chit. I have to represent Fine and get him off."

"Even if it tanks *my* career?"

"This is *La Tigra* we're talking about." His voice rose several decibels before he caught himself. "I so much as balk at her command, and she kills me and everyone I care about. That includes Eva, Goldy, and lord knows who else. Everybody but you."

"How can you be sure I'm off limits?" she said.

"Two words: Kiki Camarena. The cartels learned a hard lesson after Quintero's thugs tortured and killed Kiki. They could murder with impunity Mexican police, prosecutors, judges, priests, and reporters. From time to time, they could even get away with snuffing a U.S. citizen or two. But kill one DEA agent...."

He stopped cold, haunted by photos that had crossed his desk during his stint as a federal prosecutor. Graphic shots of Kiki's charred and mutilated corpse. Cash hadn't known the deceased but had worked with DEA agents who did. Those agents spent the better part of their careers and spilled buckets of blood to bring the killers to justice.

Or what passed for it in this world.

Sixteen years after surrendering his DOJ credentials, Cash still couldn't flush the images from his memory. He went on. "Kill one agent, and the feds will rain down on the cartels their full fire and fury for decades. That's too much heat, even for Satan."

Maggie probed her salad with a fork. "You know how this will look to my bosses."

"I get that the brass don't trust me," Cash said, "but they should have a little faith in you. You've never crossed the line with me and never would."

"None of that matters. The appearance of impropriety does. It will look like I'm in bed with you because...well, because I *am* in bed with you. And God forbid we lose this one." She shuddered. "I'll be the scapegoat, with the scarlet letter stamped on my forehead. The dreaded 'A' for acquittal."

He needed something stronger than iced tea. "What is it you want me to do?"

Her shoulders slumped. "Nothing. Do absolutely nothing but what you always do. Defend the indefensible. If the choice boils down to career suicide for me or certain death for you, it's a no-brainer. Come Monday, I'll tell Bill Graves to take me off the case."

"Probably just as well, since I have to win this one."

"Win? No, you don't get off the hook that easy." Maggie reached into her purse and pulled out a photo. Placed it on the table between them. "You may score a not guilty verdict for the scumbag, but it won't be a victory. At least you won't feel like celebrating."

Cash stared at the shot of a dark-haired, brown-skinned girl tied spread-eagle to a bed. Wearing nothing but a blindfold, a ball gag, and a leather collar around her neck. Burn marks dotted her small breasts.

She was very thin. Very young. And very dead.

"Helen—that was her American name—was smuggled to Dallas from Cambodia, via Mexico." Maggie sounded hoarse. "Her dirt-poor family paid the equivalent of seventy-five dollars to a trafficker, who promised that their little girl would become a nurse over here. Work as a maid for a rich family by day. Attend nursing school at night. In no time, she'd be sending money back home. That was the sales pitch anyway."

She paused to compose herself. "Instead, the people you're working for brought her to Dallas and placed a fetish ad in the *Backdoor*, alerting the pervs that there was a new girl in town. A virgin up for anything, from mild to wild."

Another pause before she went on. "No telling how much she made for *La Tigra* and Fine during her ten months in hell."

"How old was she?" Cash immediately regretted asking. What the hell did it matter whether she was sixteen, thirty-six, or sixty-six? No one deserved to die like that.

Check that. Cash could think of one person who deserved it.

"Fifteen," she said. "But small as she was, she passed for younger. Made her that much more valuable to your client."

By the time the entrees arrived, Cash had lost his appetite for anything but a stiff drink. Doubted that one would do the trick.

Maggie had brought the picture to try to dissuade him from representing Fine. She ended up using it to make him feel like shit for doing so.

For Maggie, backup mission accomplished.

For Cash, another unshakeable image on the endless loop inside his head.

Helen, meet Kiki.

CHAPTER NINETEEN

"**I** see the circus is back in town." Bailiff Carlos Mendoza recycled the line whenever Cash dared enter Judge Ferguson's courtroom—a.k.a., "Fergatory."

Mendoza had a stooped posture and long arms that almost literally made him a knuckle-dragger. The sloping forehead pegged him as the prime candidate for the missing link.

Cash resorted to his standard comeback. "Said the clown to the magician."

"If you're a magician," Mendoza said, "do me a favor and make yourself disappear."

Paula Marshall led a small army into the courtroom, interrupting the banter between the bailiff and Cash. The presence of a deal lawyer like Paula in court could mean only one thing. A deep pocket client of Powell, Ingram & Gardner had money on the line.

A shit ton of it.

Eva brought up the rear. Though she and Cash had parted ways only two weeks ago, she seemed different. More polished. Goth phase gone.

A tight bun tamed her wild hair, and her wardrobe had undergone a serious upgrade. She and Paula must be shopping at the same place. Both wore tailored St. John suits.

He waved to Eva, who didn't wave back. No doubt still pissed about the breakup of the firm. Someday she'd thank him for that.

Or so he assured himself.

Lawyers and litigants packed the wooden benches. Ah, the beauty of docket day. The great leveler of the bar. The first Monday of the month at 9:00 a.m. sharp brought together all the parties on Ferguson's dance card for the next four weeks.

Clients and counsel decked out in everything from Goodwill to Gucci. Solo shysters rubbed shoulders with big firm Brahmin. Drug mules breathed the same stale air as *Fortune* 500 titans. Con men cooled their heels alongside CEOs.

As if there was a difference.

With seating space scarce, Cash led Toby Fine to the defense table, a bold move designed to prompt the court to call his matter first.

FUFO. First up, first out.

Puffy and pale in the best of times, Fine turned bulky and bluish in the worst. Like now. He had a pained look.

The bailiff banged the gavel and announced the arrival of the judge. In lumbered the Honorable Samuel Clemens Ferguson III. Called Fergy behind his back.

With his square jaw and barrel chest, Fergy would have been an imposing figure in the flesh. The black robe exaggerated the effect of an almighty being, before whom mere mortals quaked.

Everyone stood. Cash was the last up and first down.

Fergy cleared his throat. "Mister McCahill, it has been a good while since you last graced my courtroom. I see you managed to regain your license in time to appear as Mister Fine's new counsel of record." His tone dripped with equal parts condescension and contempt.

Cash stood. "I trust that Your Honor is as excited to have me back, as I am to be here."

The judge's frown said otherwise. "While you're in my courtroom, I strongly suggest that you avoid your trademark theatrics and focus on retaining that precious license."

"I accept the challenge, Your Honor." Cash added a bounce to his voice. "But I always thought of it as *our* courtroom."

The judge harrumphed. "Therein lies the crux of your problem. That and your brash assumption I would call your case first this morning."

Fine quaked. Cash didn't.

"Yes," Cash said. "I assume you'll want to have us on our way sooner, rather than later."

"'Tis a pity for both of us that you're dead last on today's docket. Vacate the defense table, before I have my bailiff remove you."

Mendoza rose from his chair and took a step toward Cash. The move would've been more intimidating if the Neanderthal hadn't knocked over his coffee cup while rising. He sopped up the spill with the docket sheet.

The judge glared at the bailiff, then at Cash. "Find a place on the bench, Mister McCahill, and wait your turn. It will likely be late afternoon before I deal with your matter."

To smiles and titters from the crowd, Cash and his client packed up and schlepped toward the back. As Cash passed Paula on the front row, she slipped him a note:

CAN WE TALK AT THE BREAK?

He nodded and kept walking. Good. He had a bone to pick with her. Eager to find out why she and Stewart Powell had foisted Rhoden on Marty Biddle. Why would anyone recommend that dirtbag to anybody for anything?

Fine found a landing place on the left. Cash broke right and squeezed between Eva and a baby faced associate on Team Powell. Eva's eyes remained riveted on the judge.

Cash leaned toward her and whispered, "How's life in the big leagues?"

"Couldn't be better. So much nicer to work at a firm where the lawyers don't have rap sheets."

"Sounds kind of boring."

She pointed to Fine across the aisle. "Shouldn't you sit with your new BFF? No one else seems to want to."

Sure enough, despite butt-to-butt parking on the pews, space had opened around Fine. A pariah among pariahs.

"He's my client, not my friend. You know me better than that."

She turned toward him and waited until their eyes locked. "I know you better than you know yourself." Her voice rose above a whisper. "You've earned a rep of never backing down, even when you're in the wrong. Especially when you're wrong."

He didn't have a ready defense. Nor did he come up with one before a hush fell over the courtroom. Cash wheeled around to catch the second coming of an almighty presence.

Stewart Powell stood in the entrance and surveyed the packed pews. Cash half-expected everyone to rise in tribute, including the judge.

Everyone but Cash, of course.

Instead, only the minions at Powell's firm jumped to their feet and jockeyed for the privilege of ceding their seats to the name partner. Fergy mooted the grand gestures by calling Powell's case first.

Figures. A trial judge with an eye on an open appellate bench would naturally cater to someone who had the ear of several U.S. Senators.

Team Powell surged forward, pulling Eva along in the wake. An opposing force of equal size and stature squared off against Powell's platoon. Lawyers and paralegals filled both tables and spilled into the jury box and front row.

All those mercenaries and only two speaking roles among them. A matching pair of silver-haired senior partners announced ready, on behalf of faceless corporations fighting over billions in a civil suit destined to drag on for a decade or more.

Cash quickly lost interest in the nitpicking over discovery and tuned out. He perked up only when Fergy called the morning break.

* * *

It took Cash two minutes to track down Paula in the hallway and two more for her to shake free from her client's general counsel. Paula and Cash found an empty bench at the far end of the floor.

"How do you think it's going for my side?" Paula sounded nervous.

"Not a clue. When the stiffs started arguing over the number of interrogatories, I put an end to my misery by puncturing my eardrums. One good thing about watching what the big firms do, it reminds me why I went into criminal law."

"Yes, a down and dirty trial by ambush suits your personality."

"You make that sound like a bad thing," he said.

"We don't have much time, so I'll get to the point." She took a deep breath and closed her eyes. "Eva is miserable."

Caught off guard, Cash tried to deflect the conversation. "Are you saying I ruined her for women?"

Paula snickered. "Quite the opposite. You set a very low bar for my gender. But you did ruin her for big firm practice."

"How so?" Not that Cash couldn't figure it out himself.

"Thanks to you, she sees a paralegal's role as interviewing witnesses, collaborating on trial strategy, sitting at the defense table at trial, and feeding questions to the litigators. That's not how real firms operate."

"Well, not your sweat shop anyway," Cash said. "You lock the poor paralegals inside windowless rooms, where they dig through boxes of dusty documents, or scroll though gigabytes of emails. All the while, billing out their time at three hundred dollars an hour. Cha-ching."

Paula's temples pulsed, but she didn't push back.

"That's not Eva," Cash said, "and it never will be."

She checked her watch and glanced over her shoulder. "Her unhappiness on the job is screwing up our relationship."

So that's why she's reaching out to me.

Cash had trouble mustering sympathy for Paula. Why should he be the only one to sacrifice for the greater good of protecting Eva?

"She may be unhappy," he said, "but she's safe. You have to sell her on sticking it out at your firm, at least for the short-term. I hope to bring her back when...if...."

Paula's eyes narrowed. "So your intent all along has been to park her with us until the heat's off."

He nodded.

"Would've been nice if you had let me know up front that we were only a way station. Even nicer if Eva had a clue."

"Trust me on this," he said. "Eva has a clue. And she rarely needs more than one."

Speak of the angel, Eva showed up. "Break's over." The chill in her voice dropped the temperature in the hallway. "But the next time you two get together to decide my fate, deal me in."

As Paula turned to leave, Cash grabbed her arm. "You and I," he said, "we're not finished. I need to know why you and your boss foisted Rhoden on Martin Biddle."

The color drained from Paula's face. It could've been due to Cash's question. More likely, it stemmed from Stewart Powell's sudden appearance at her side.

Speak of the devil.

Powell addressed Paula, his back to Cash. "The client is asking for you. Don't keep him waiting."

She rushed to the courtroom, leaving Powell and Cash alone in the lobby. Cash couldn't resist a jab at the rainmaker. "Surprised that a swell like you would slum with us working stiffs. Who gave you the directions to the courthouse?"

"I'm surprised, sport, that you still have a law license." Powell smiled. "In my role as president of the state bar, I'll have to look into that."

* * *

By the afternoon break, Fergy had flushed everyone from the courtroom, except Cash and his client. Even the government table—the one closer to the jury box—was empty.

After suffering through six sentencings, three re-arraignments, countless discovery disputes, and the swearing-in of a new lawyer, Cash had nearly fossilized into the bench. The break gave him a chance to stretch his legs on a stroll up and down the hallway, with Fine nipping at his heels.

"Man, oh man, I really screwed up." Fine had perfected the art of whining. "The judge couldn't stand Rhoden, but he fucking hates you even more."

Cash kept walking. "The good thing about Fergy is that he's an equal opportunity hater. He despises all living creatures, great and small. He just hates defense lawyers a tad more."

"That supposed to make me feel better?" Fine sounded as if he was about to lose his shit.

Cash stopped and faced his client. "Yeah, it should. There are judges in this building who are so hell-bent on helping the prosecution that they might as well sit at the government table. That ain't Fergy. Sure, he'll beat on me during trial, but he'll do the same to the prosecutor."

Cash checked the time. "We'd better head back."

After Cash and Fine had settled at the defense table, the door behind them creaked open. Cash swiveled around to see FBI Agent Stanley Bowers swagger into the courtroom, smirk in place.

Damn. Bowers must've bumped Maggie as the case agent.

Cash stifled any outward reaction to the bad break. No need to rattle the client any more than he already was.

Cash's spirits lifted at the sight of Maggie, five paces behind Bowers but gaining fast. Maybe he'd been too quick to count her out.

The courtroom door closed and remained shut for several seconds. It opened with a bang to reveal the new prosecutor.

Cash's jaw dropped. "Fuck. Me," he said under his breath, but loud enough for Fine to hear.

CHAPTER TWENTY

Regina Delgado—all five-feet-two and ninety-five pounds of her—blew into the courtroom, a minute after Judge Ferguson had taken the bench. "Sorry, Your Honor." She didn't sound near sorry enough. "American Airlines canceled my flight from D.C. last night and put me on the first flight this morning, which got delayed two hours."

Cash cringed. Fergy would never buy an excuse short of death.

The judge sat through Regina's apology, still as a statue. His natural scowl carved in stone. Gray eyes laser-focused on the supplicant. Wearing a black robe that could serve as a small tent.

Cash stayed loose and limber, ready to dodge thunderbolts from on high. Even if aimed at Regina, they would fly fast and furious and might hit innocent bystanders. Namely, him.

Instead, Cash witnessed a miracle. The corners of the judge's lips curled upward. Not a lot. Just a tick. No full-blown smile, but Fergy's closest simulation.

"No problem, Miss Delgado. Your assistant called to inform us of your travel issues." For someone without an ounce of compassion, Fergy sounded almost sympathetic.

What the hell just happened?

Cash's internal alarm went off. It dawned on him why Delgado had escaped with her skin. The sudden turn of fortune solved two mysteries: why Fine's case got called last on today's docket and why the Justice Department had sent Regina to take down the perv.

She had a history with Fergy. Almost twenty years ago to the day, she had moved to Dallas, fresh from Harvard Law School, to serve as his first law clerk. The clerkship had been rugged, more like a boot camp. A year of long days and short nights. Grueling schedules and impossible deadlines. Morsels of encouragement amid mountains of criticism.

A frontline federal prosecutor at the time, Cash had helped Regina through the trying year. Consoling her. Inviting her to happy hours. Introducing her to his colleagues. Now it was coming back to bite him.

Surviving the year had earned Regina two rare prizes: Fergy's blessing and a ticket to the United States Attorney's Office in Dallas, a plum post she had parlayed into a seventh-floor office at Main Justice in D.C.—shouting distance from the Attorney General.

Regina made the rounds in the room, receiving a hug from the longtime court reporter and a high five from the bailiff. Cash half-expected balloons to fall from the ceiling and ticker tape to rain down.

Finally, she made her way to the defense table. The bounce in her step testified to her home turf edge.

Cash stood to greet her. "What are you doing here, Gina? You traded in your trial spurs for a corner office on Pennsylvania Avenue."

Her smile faded. "Someone has to see that justice gets done down here. I go by Regina now."

"I'll try to remember that," he said, with no intent to do so. "But it won't be easy. I knew you when you were Gina and still had a sense of humor."

"I knew you when you had a sense of decency," she said, "before you went to the dark side to represent all manner of scum." She looked down on Fine, still seated. "Present company included."

Fine started to rise, but Cash stopped him with a hand on his shoulder.

"Are you going to let her talk to me like that?" Fine said to Cash.

"I'd push back," Cash said, "but unfortunately truth happens to be a defense to defamation."

Regina flashed a smile at Cash. The second miracle of the afternoon.

"I hate to interrupt this touching reunion"—sarcasm laced the judge's tone—"but we have the small matter of a trial to discuss. It's docketed for the twenty-seventh of this month. Will both sides be ready then?"

Cash and Regina pivoted toward the judge. Neither spoke, each waiting for the other to commit to a position.

During the awkward silence, the feds played a quick game of musical chairs. Three feds but only two chairs at the government table. Regina and Bowers claimed the open seats, banishing Maggie to the front row.

Tough break for Maggie, the odd woman out. For Cash as well. And most of all, for Fine.

Cash seldom suffered second thoughts over a defense strategy, but they swarmed him now. His game plan had been to request a short continuance of the trial date. That would be the sane, conventional approach for a new lawyer in a case with a terabyte of documents to pore over and a host of witnesses to interview.

Though loath to continue cases under any circumstances, Fergy would be hard-pressed to deny a delay of, say, sixty days for Cash to get up to speed. Perhaps ninety, if pushed.

An outright denial of more time to prepare would be grounds for reversal on appeal. The only thing the judge hated more than delay was a slap down by the Fifth Circuit Court of Appeals. Or as Fergy called the upper branch, the "Fifth Circus."

Regina's eleventh-hour appearance scrambled Cash's calculations. Better than even odds that she was equally unprepared, and the government had to mount its case first.

Advantage, Cash.

"I'm waiting," the judge said. "What says the government?"

Cash studied Regina's face, all clean lines and sharp angles. Pueblo ancestors had passed down dark eyes and a coppery complexion. He focused on her full lips. They parted. Closed. Parted again. A sign of indecision.

"Your Honor," she said, "while the government is prepared to proceed on the current trial date, we recognize that Mister Fine's previous counsel died recently and that Mister McCahill filed his notice of appearance only last week. Thus, to accommodate the defense, we will not object to a short continuance."

Riiiight. Like she's doing me a solid.

Cash whispered to Fine, "Do you trust me?"

Fine nodded tentatively. The fear in his eyes cast a dissent.

"I'm calling her bluff," Cash whispered to his client before addressing the court. "While we thank Miss Delgado for her kind offer, the defense will be ready to roll on the twenty-seventh. No delay necessary."

Silence gripped the room. Regina blanched. Bowers turned red. Maggie shot Cash a look like he'd lost his mind. Fine clenched his fists until the knuckles turned white.

Fergy recovered first. "Mister McCahill, I want to be sure you understand that this is your one and only opportunity to seek a continuance."

Cash doubled down. "Understood."

"You won't be able to wait until a week before trial and then beg for more time."

"I wouldn't dream of it," Cash said.

Regina found her voice. "The government moves the court to designate the case a complex one under the Speedy Trial Act."

Fergy looked perplexed. "To what end? Both sides have said they'll be ready for trial on the twenty-seventh, a date that clearly complies with the statutory deadlines. Why do we need to address this issue at all?"

"Strictly a fail-safe, Your Honor," Regina said. "If something unforeseen were to scramble the court's docket or if a critical government witness proved unable to travel on the scheduled date, it would be good to know in advance that the Speedy Trial Act won't preclude an emergency continuance."

"What's your position, Mister McCahill, on whether this case is complex and, thus, not subject to the deadlines in the act?" the judge said.

Cash saw through Regina's ploy. She was angling for an opportunity to lobby the court for more time later, if she got jammed during trial prep. Clever lass. Cash had boxed her in, but she was laying the groundwork to escape.

The good news, Cash could read her like a law book. Not that he'd bothered to crack open all that many law books, while in school or out.

The bad news, she could read him as well.

"Like most federal indictments," Cash said, "this one features a lot of fluff but not much substance. At the core, it's simple. So no, Your Honor, not complex."

Without further debate, the court slapped the c-word on the case, deeming it complex. Certain to be first of many rulings in Regina's favor.

After disposing of the last matter on the docket, the judge left the bench, and the courtroom went dark. Cash fully expected an ambush, as soon as he set foot in the lobby.

He guessed right about the ambush but wrong on who would waylay him.

CHAPTER TWENTY-ONE

Cash searched for Maggie outside the courtroom. No sighting of her.

No Regina either, though he was not so much looking for her as looking out for her. Little to gain from dredging up their past and plenty of downside.

Not a word had passed between Cash and Regina in over a decade. No contact between them since their short stint on a Justice Department strike force targeting public corruption on the border.

El Paso had offered a target rich environment. Charging corrupt officials had proven as quick and effortless as rounding up whores in a Juárez bar. Easy, sleazy. Couldn't throw a brick on either side of the border without hitting a crooked pol or a prostitute.

As if there was a difference.

Regina had led the task force and tapped Cash to be her top trial gun, but they had butted heads over strategy. Whatever chemistry had jelled in Dallas evaporated in the desert heat. One dead target had tanked the partnership for good.

The border gig had boosted her government career but aborted his. At the break-up, they'd left much unsaid. Fine with him.

The hall lights in the courthouse clanked off, row by row. The encroaching darkness chased Cash toward the exit. Batting zero for two in the ex-partner department, he decided to take off and leave the past to the past.

At the elevator bank, Cash ran into the absolute last person he wanted to see. FBI Agent Stanley Bowers' smirk invited a slap. Cash fought the urge.

"Delgado wants to see you." Bowers had a bad habit of making a simple request sound like a royal command.

"Tell her to make an appointment with...." Cash caught himself. He no longer had Eva to juggle his calendar and keep his life on track. Not that he had a lot on his plate these days. Nor much of a life.

"Now." Big mistake for Bowers to raise his voice. Made his double chin quiver.

Curious as Cash was to hear what Regina had to say, he had half a mind to brush past Bowers and hit the streets. Drive home the point that the agent's tough guy act needed work.

"Sorry, but I have a pressing appointment." Cash didn't try to sound sorry or sell the excuse.

"If you're looking for Maggie," Bowers said, "she doesn't want to see you."

"How do you...?" Cash clammed up. Better not to discuss Maggie with the Bureau's biggest backstabber. "She'll be the judge of that."

"She's already made her decision, and it's set in stone."

"What do you mean?" Cash said.

"Since that involves a personnel matter, it's for me to know and for you not to find out." Bowers pushed the button.

From the sixteenth floor, down was the only direction.

* * *

Cash followed Bowers to the corner office on the third floor of the courthouse, but he stopped at the doorway. "Hey, Gina, isn't this Webster's office?"

"It was." Delgado's stockinged feet rested on the desk, ankles crossed. "And I go by Regina now. That's twice you've been told."

Cash entered the office, wondering what would happen on the inevitable and imminent third strike. No need to guess what had befallen poor Webster.

The D.C. bigwig had rolled into town and displaced First Assistant U.S. Attorney Webster, who then bumped the Criminal Chief, who in turn booted the Civil Chief from her digs.

And so on and so forth. In the bloodless coup, only the high-and-mighty U.S. Attorney had held firm. Her minions had fallen like dominoes, surrendering their space in the bowl to the bigger fish.

Cash studied the familiar diplomas on the wall (Duke B.A., *summa cum laude*; Harvard J.D., *magna cum laude*), as well as the constellation of kiss-ass plaques from law enforcement agencies who owed Delgado big time.

"I see you've made yourself at home," he said.

"I'd be more than happy to pack up and leave." She swung her feet off the desk. "All you have to do is persuade your guilty-as-hell client to do the right thing."

"The right thing being...."

"Plead guilty and do a little stretch. He'll come out with plenty of time to line up a fresh crop of victims. Rinse and repeat."

"Define little," he said.

"Four."

"Months?"

She laughed. "Years. He cops to conspiracy, draws a nickel but does only four years behind bars. Maybe three if the judge has a soft heart."

It was Cash's turn to laugh. "Fergy and soft are not words found in the same sentence. Come to think of it, neither are Fergy and heart."

Bowers stood by the door, useless as an umbrella in a hurricane.

Cash nodded toward the agent. "What's doughboy doing here?"

Bowers clenched his fists but didn't make a move. Cash gave him a get real look.

"He's my case agent," she said.

"Thought by now you would've learned your lesson about saddling up the wrong horse." Cash pointed to the agent. "This nag will never cross the finish line."

Bowers took a step toward Cash, who stood his ground. Bluff called, Bowers backed away.

"Stan, let me talk to McCahill alone."

The agent started to protest but shook it off. He stormed from the office, slamming the door behind him.

"Now that you don't have to put on a tough girl act for the Bureau," Cash said, "care to make me a real offer?"

"I can do better than that. I'll make you a package deal."

"Define package."

"You deliver Fine to us," she said, "and we'll give you points for cooperation on your case, cut you an ex-friend and ex-family deal."

"My case?" Cash's knees buckled, but he recovered quickly. "A deal on what? A new car? A refi on my mortgage?"

"One that shaves a year or two off your sentence. Once we figure out your role in the murders of Mariposa Benanti and Rob Rhoden, you'll need a friend with a badge, and Agent Burns won't be around to bail you out this time."

The mention of Maggie rattled Cash, almost as much as the threat of a return to prison. He hoped his face didn't show it.

"This isn't El Paso," he said. "You actually need hard evidence to bring a case here."

"Both Benanti and Rhoden were killed shortly after you visited them. That makes you either part of a conspiracy or, like the media says, the Angel of Death. Not sure which is worse."

"If you had anything on me, you would've pitched Fine a deal to dime me out."

"Who says we haven't?" She smiled. "Between you and your client, let's see who flips first."

* * *

Maggie leaned against Cash's Porsche. Strike one. Her briefcase lay atop the roof. Strike two. Her flats adorned the hood like twin ornaments. Strike three.

The muted lighting in the underground garage played tricks on Cash's eyes. Made Maggie's blonde, white bread beauty look darker, more exotic.

"Scratch my wheels, young lady, and I'll have your ass." His voice echoed in the nearly empty garage.

"You've been there, done that." She managed a weak smile. "Practice makes perfect."

She pushed away from the car. "Practice? Is that what I am to you?" She sounded more sad than hurt. "Gutsy move back there in the courtroom, announcing ready for trial this month when you're nowhere close. Incredibly stupid and certainly suicidal, but gutsy as hell."

"At the end of a long, hard day, I knew I could count on you for some words of encouragement." He unlocked the car and tossed her briefcase into the backseat. "Care for a lift?"

"Sure." She opened the passenger door. "Take me to a fancy restaurant for a farewell dinner."

CHAPTER TWENTY-TWO

"Irst time since my arrest that I've set foot in the Ritz."
Cash recognized about half the diners in Fearing's,
mostly lawyers and those in need of their services.
"First time ever with you." He reached across the table and
took Maggie's hand.

Her hand was twitchy. No way would she pass a polygraph
in this condition. She pulled free of him. "Technically, it's the
second time, if you count the night we busted you here for jury
tampering."

"Let's not." He lifted his glass for a toast. "Here's to taking
our relationship to the next level."

She didn't reach for her glass. "What level would that be?"

"The one where you're willing to be seen in public with
me. In the past we've skulked around back streets and eaten at
holes-in-the-wall, like a couple of cheating spouses."

"Because I feel like one," she said.

He lifted his glass higher. "Here's to freedom from irratio-
nal feelings of guilt."

When she raised her glass, her hand shook. "In the gos-
pel according to Kris Kristofferson, freedom means you've got
nothing left to lose." She clinked glasses. "Here's to nothing
left to lose."

Cash savored the aroma of the Hall cabernet. "What was that nonsense about a farewell dinner?"

"I'm being transferred." Her tone turned bitter.

He killed the glass of wine. Didn't help. Not enough wine in the world to lift his spirits. Or deaden the pain.

"To a new division?" he said.

"New city."

"The bastards are sending you to the mother ship in D.C., aren't they?"

She shook her head. "Bismarck, so it's more like they're booking me on the *Titanic*."

"Bismarck!" Cash's raised voice drew glares from surrounding tables. A waiter hustled toward them. Cash waved him off.

He leaned in and whispered, "Is this some kind of sick joke?"

"Do you see me laughing?" Her eyes misted. "I thought that exiling fuckups to the frozen tundra went out with Hoover."

Cash's mind warped to defense lawyer mode, grasping for any loophole, delay, or backdoor deal that would keep her in Dallas. He had nothing.

He pounded the table hard enough to rattle dishes and diners nearby. A contagion of cleared throats and stern looks swept across the room. He could give a flying leap.

"You're not the fuckup here," he said.

"What would you call an agent who's sleeping with the lawyer voted most likely to be indicted? Make that, indicted again."

"I would call it the best thing that has happened to me in a long, long time."

A tear slalomed down her cheek. "Sorry, but it looks like you and me, well, it just wasn't meant to be."

Cash wasn't ready to give up. "Alternatively, this could turn out to be the best thing that has happened to us." He reached across the table. "Shake hands with your new partner."

She didn't take his hand. "What exactly are you proposing?"

The *proposing* part threw him for a loop.

She laughed. "You look a little green in the gills, Cash. Don't read too much into my poor word choice."

He breathed easier. "Quit the FBI and come work with me. I can use a crack investigator, especially one who knows where the Bureau has buried the bodies."

She laughed harder. "Me, working for you?"

"No, you working *with* me."

"You're not serious," she said.

"I'm dead serious."

"Dead being the operative word, because if we were thrown together twenty-four seven, I'd shoot you within a week."

"How do you know until we try?" he said.

The waiter filled their wine glasses, emptying the bottle. "May I bring another bottle of the Exzellenz?"

"Keep 'em coming," Cash said.

Maggie dabbed her eyes with a napkin. "I'm touched by your offer." Her smile faded fast. "But you're delusional if you think we could ever be on the same team."

"You believe that working with me would mean defecting to the dark side, but it's not like that. When the U.S. Attorney's Office tossed me out, I thought my world had ended. It took years to get over the blow to my ego. Hell, I never would've bounced back, if Goldy hadn't taken me in."

"You might want to share that with him someday," she said, "and make it soon."

Point taken.

"Sure," he said, "carrying a badge has its rewards. You work nine to five, try to do a little justice, go home feeling all warm and fuzzy inside, and sleep soundly. But the defense world has its own set of rewards, and I'm not talking about money."

"Though there is that." She made it sound like a bad thing.

"There's far more than that. People come to you at the lowest points in their lives, with no one else to turn to, desperate for a champion. The game is stacked against them, and they're the ultimate underdogs. You're their white knight in a land of dragons."

"Some might say more like a black knight," she said. "And correct me if I'm wrong, but didn't I hear this spiel about champions, underdogs, and dragons in your closing argument in the Campos trial?"

He smiled. "Good memory."

She stared into a bowl of tortilla soup, still untouched. "I can't leave the FBI."

He shook his head. Not in disbelief but in sadness. Hardly the first time he'd encountered A.S.S.—Abused Spouse Syndrome. Married to the Bureau for life, she'd take all the shit the agency could dish out and crawl back for more.

He made a last stand against the inevitable. "For someone who grew up in the Deep South, spent four years at Ole Miss, and scored plum postings in Miami, LA, and Dallas, every day in North Dakota will seem like a year in Siberia."

"You could travel north every month or so," she said, "to thaw me out."

"Yeah, maybe." He failed to muster an ounce of false hope. Reality hit him hard. She was already gone, and the asshole Bowers had been right. Maggie had made her choice, and it hadn't been close.

FBI, one. Cash, zero.

"I've lost my appetite," she said. "Can we get out of here?"

"Sure."

"But before we leave, hear me out." She paused until they locked eyes. "You're officially a person of interest in the murders of Mariposa Benanti and Rob Rhoden."

Cash nodded. Delgado had already dropped that anvil on him.

She went on. "You'll be offered all sorts of deals to cooperate. Get everything in writing. Don't trust Bowers and trust Delgado even less."

"Tell me something I don't know."

She leaned in and lowered her voice. "The FBI and DEA are waging a turf war over the *La Tigra* investigation."

"Same old, same old."

"No, this one's different. Bloodiest internal battle I've ever seen. It'll go up the ladder to the AG to sort out."

Bingo.

Maggie had come through with something he hadn't known. The agencies had brought guns to a knife fight. Possible that one or both would wind up wounded. Even better, she had offered something he could potentially exploit. Maybe an angle to keep her in Dallas. Or reel her back soon.

Before Cash could share his seed of a strategy with Maggie, his cell phone chirped. He made the rookie mistake of taking a collect call from the county jail.

A life-or-death one.

He stood and threw his napkin on the table. "Time to slay another dragon."

CHAPTER TWENTY-THREE

The collect call from the county jail came too late to spring Chris Campos before lights out. That would be a bummer for most prisoners but could be curtains for one whose survival turned on whether he got tossed into the clink as Chris or Tina.

DEA agent Duane Leroy Lee—the arresting officer—had given the trans prisoner a break by taking Campos home post-arrest and allowing her to shed the clingy dress, Cher wig, stiletto heels, and layers of makeup, before booking him as Chris.

Actually, Campos had caught a double break. Not only had Leroy done him a solid with the transformation from Tina to Chris, but the agent also had a history with Cash. Unlike most of his bros with badges, Leroy had a soft spot for the turncoat.

A dinosaur at the DEA, Leroy had roamed the streets of Big D since the days of dime bags and Dilaudid cocktails. In the distant past, he had worked a string of low-hanging dope cases with a green prosecutor who had a funny first name.

Cash. As in the stuff Leroy had too little of. Cash McCahill.

They had made a good team, with Cash not asking much of the agent, who had obliged by doing the bare minimum to secure convictions.

During his decade on the dark side, Cash had defended only a handful of druggies, never by choice but only on court appointments. Luckily, Leroy had not been the case agent on those court-appointed cases, so Cash had never crossed him on the stand.

Today, Cash made a flurry of calls to friends in low places, scrambling to locate Leroy. His feelers extended to smoky dives, dark bars, and rent-by-the-hour motels. He tracked down the agent at Spike—a bar in Deep Ellum that catered to teens with fake I.D.s and the pervs who preyed on them.

Slouching in a back booth, Cash watched Leroy chatting up an easy mark and noted how the sands of time had shifted. Back in the day, the agent had been broad-shouldered and narrow at the hips. Today, he was pear-shaped.

Susie Sorority's wide-eyed wonder made it clear that she was swallowing Leroy's bullshit. With both hunter and hunted perched on barstools, the seduction played out like a scene from *Beauty and the Beast*.

A more apt title would be *Beauty and the Bust*. The tragic tale of a clueless coed in the crosshairs of a grizzled grunt during the last gasps of the drug wars.

Cash's defense lawyer instincts kicked in. He walked to the bar and stuck out his hand. "Agent Lee, it's been years, but you haven't changed a hair."

True enough. Same patchy comb over and bad dye job.

Leroy didn't take Cash's hand. "Sorry, hot shot, but you've mistaken me for someone else." The *fuck off* was silent.

"Agent!" The prey had caught the keyword.

"Why, yes," Cash said to Muffy, or Buffy, or whatever. "Allow me to introduce you to a living legend in law enforcement. Special Agent Duane Leroy Lee has been with the Drug

Enforcement Administration for as long as runs the memory of man. What's it been now, Leroy? Twenty-five years?"

Long enough for the agent to recognize a cockblock when he hit one. He turned to the ashen-faced girl. "Twenty-two years, three months, and twelve days to be exact, and my next official act will be to arrest this asshole attorney for obstructing justice."

The teen took off, leaving behind an untouched Cosmopolitan but holding onto her fake I.D.

"Now that the minnow has wiggled off the hook," Cash said, "join me at the booth. I'll treat you to a beer."

"I'm on duty, so no booze."

Cash gave him a don't-shit-a-shitter look. The agent's claim of abstinence would've been more convincing, if he hadn't had a beer mustache and an empty mug in hand.

Leroy shrugged. "Okay, McCahill, one brewski before I bust you."

The tone told Cash that the agent wasn't serious about the bust. Nor about stopping after the next beer.

After they settled into the booth, Cash took the first shot. "Who'd you piss off to wind up on this shit detail? I mean, come on man, buy-busts of college kids? Can you go any lower on the food chain?"

The look on Leroy's leathery face straddled amusement and annoyance. "You want to take her room in the Graybar Hotel? Make my night, mouthpiece, and offer to buy a rock from me. Be sure to speak up, so I can get it all on tape."

"If the DEA is so hard up for stats that it's targeting trust fund babes," Cash said, "the agency needs to send in someone who doesn't remind the kids of their grandpa."

"A lot of these chicks dig older men."

Cash ordered a round of Coronas. "By older, Leroy, they mean thirty, not three hundred."

"What's your excuse for being here?" Leroy said. "You scrounging for a buck, a fuck, or both?"

The beers came. Leroy guzzled his. Cash nursed his drink but ordered another for the agent.

Leroy went on. "When you turned in your badge, you swore to steer clear of dopers. What a load of crap. Well, go ahead and spread your cards around the bar, then get the hell out of here. You're killing my business."

"I didn't come here looking for business," Cash said. "I came looking for you."

"Whatever favor you want from me, forget it." Leroy polished off the beer. "The statute of limitations has long since run on anything you did for me back in the day."

"Get this through your thick skull. I'm not looking for a favor." Not close to being true. "I'm trying to do you a solid." Closer to true but not 100 percent there.

"I know I'll regret asking this," Leroy said, "but what favor are you dying to do for me?"

"I hear that your broke ass agency is at war with the big, bad FBI over who runs point on the *La Tigra* investigation."

Leroy perked up. "So?"

"So the enemy of my enemy is my friend."

Leroy laughed. "You, a friend of ours. No fucking way."

"With Rob Rhoden out of the picture, I'm *La Tigra's* go-to guy north of the border."

"Your mother must be so proud. Still doesn't explain why you'd give a rat's ass over which agency comes out on top."

"The Bureau is fucking over my girlfriend. The brass took issue with our relationship and plan to bury her in Bismarck.

Nothing would please me more than screwing those self-righteous pricks."

"Revenge is a dish best served cold," Leroy said, "much like beer." He banged his mug on the table. The bartender returned with a full pitcher.

It wasn't full long.

"I'm still not buying what you're selling," Leroy said.

"I prefer dealing with people I trust. Say the word, and I go through you and you alone in my negotiations for *La Tigra*."

Leroy did a double take. "What's in it for me? You know what the old-timers say. Little cases mean little problems. Big cases, big problems. You show up out of nowhere, offering me the mother of all monster cases, and expect me to jump on this live grenade?"

Cash had anticipated pushback. The agent's initial reaction would be suspicion, followed by heightened suspicion.

Cash sweetened the pot. "It'd be a helluva capstone to a career with lots of ups and downs." He didn't point out that recently there'd been far more downs than ups. "Plus, taking the lead in catching *La Tigra* would spring you from this shitty detail."

The agent scratched his salt-and-pepper stubble. Far more salt than pepper. Didn't take a mind reader to know the hook had been planted. "What's in it for you?"

"I need a get-out-of-jail-free card for a trans prisoner you arrested earlier tonight." Cash wrote her name, date of birth, and social security number on a napkin and slid it toward Leroy. He figured the agent was a few beers past remembering those details.

"What's the tranny to you? Is she your client, or are you hers?" Leroy waved off an answer. "On second thought, I don't want to know." He grabbed the napkin. "I suppose you expect me to arrange for a limo to pick her up at the jail." Said with sarcasm to spare.

"That won't be necessary," Cash said, "but deep-six her case."

Leroy grunted. "I'll see what I can do, soon as I finish my beer."

Cash left the bar, confident that Leroy would step up. Cash had a favorite quote from Churchill. How he could always count on the United States to do the right thing, but only after it had exhausted the alternatives.

The saying applied in spades to Leroy, who would get around to doing the right thing. The only question was whether it would be in time to save Campos.

CHAPTER TWENTY-FOUR

A knock on the office door interrupted Cash's text to Maggie. The odds of the message being finished and sent were roughly the same as those of her remaining in Dallas.

Less than zero.

He checked the time. 1:17. Toby Fine must've jumped the gun on his two o'clock appointment. Cash deleted the draft and yelled for the client to come in.

The door opened to reveal not a current client, but a past and future one. For someone who had left the county jail only hours earlier as Chris Campos, the reincarnation as Tina came off as stunning.

Crossing the office to take a chair, Tina exaggerated her sway. In her case, the hips might lie.

"Where's Eva?" she said.

"She's gone."

"What do you mean gone?" Her voice was high-pitched but husky enough to keep the customers guessing.

"I ran her off."

"That was a dumb shit move." She placed her Kate Spade purse on the desk and smoothed her dress.

"Seems to be the consensus."

"If you have a brain cell left in that thick skull of yours," Tina said, "you'll beg her to come back."

"Too late for that. She landed a better job."

"Yeah, well, low bar."

Cash changed the subject. "Hate to interrupt your fun at my expense, but while we're on the subject of expenses, any chance you're here to settle your legal bill?"

"I don't have the cash on me now." She paused. "But I should have it for you by...let's say midnight."

"To borrow a line from Clarence Darrow, I cannot accept as payment of my fee the proceeds of a crime." He paused for effect. "Committed so recently."

Her laugh tipped the scales to the feminine side. "Then perhaps we can agree on an alternative payment plan."

"If you came here all dolled up to seduce me, sorry but I don't date chicks with dicks."

"Certainly not those of us with bigger dicks anyway."

"If you've got something to say beyond simply busting my balls, make it quick. A client will be here any minute. A *paying* client."

Tina looked crestfallen. "I came to thank you for saving my life last night. Your DEA buddy pulled me out of the holding cell, before I got thrown into gen pop."

"All in a night's work."

She started to speak but held back. Rose and walked slowly to the door, looking like she'd lost her last friend.

It hit Cash that she might be down to a single soul in her corner. Him. He extended a lifeline. "Hey, wait a minute. Maybe you can help me with this case."

She hurried back, heels clicking on the hardwood floor, and perched on the edge of the chair. "I'm all yours."

"Do you advertise in the *Backdoor?*"

"Of course."

"Why?"

Tina smiled, as if the answer was obvious. Straight out of Hooking 101. "For starters, all the girls are on the site, and most with more than one ad. I have six up and running, each geared to a specialty. Vanilla, couples, dominance, submission, bondage, and switch."

She went on. "From time to time, I tweak the wording in my ads to keep them fresh. Everybody wants the new girl in town, which is challenging when you've been on the site forever. Like me."

"How long exactly?"

Tina ticked off the years finger by finger, until she ran out of digits. "Almost twelve years."

Cash did the math in his head. "How old are you?"

"That's not a question to—"

He cut her off. "I wouldn't ask if I didn't need to know."

"Twenty-five."

Which made her fifty in street years.

"Are you telling me that you placed your first ad in the *Backdoor* when you were thirteen?"

"That's not exactly how it went down. My first ad was placed for me on another website by the man I was living with at the time."

Cash shook his head. How the hell had she survived in the life for more than a decade? He hoped her gateway pimp hadn't been so lucky.

"The scumbag who broke you into the business," Cash said, "is he still in the picture?"

"Yes and no." She blushed. "Rocky has a stable, but I'm no longer in it. He likes them young, so he turned me out when I hit eighteen. I know he's still active, because I can spot his ads."

"How do you know which ads are his?"

"By his code words. Babysitter. Barely legal. Lolita. First time. Words that mean something in the trade."

Cash didn't need a primer on their meaning. "How did you meet him in the first place?"

"He bought me." She wouldn't say from whom.

* * *

Toby Fine filled the chair left warm by Tina. More like flowed over the seat, his ass hanging low like saddlebags.

The royal blue jogging suit didn't flatter his roly-poly body, and the matching headband was purely decorative, since he never moved fast or far enough to work up a sweat. He looked pale, soft, and lumpy. Reminded Cash of the Pillsbury Doughboy.

Cash had a rule of thumb for newbie clients. If they came to the first meeting in a suit, the attorney-client relationship would be smooth sailing. If they wore business casual, choppy waters ahead. And if they sported sweats, batten down the hatches.

"For what it's worth," Fine said, "you were my first choice of counsel. She made me go to Rhoden."

It wasn't worth spit to Cash. "No problem."

Long as you don't have a third option in the wings, making me as expendable as Rhoden was.

"What's your plan for getting my indictment tossed?"

There it was. Cut to the quick. The question that had triggered Rhoden's execution. Fine never planned to win at trial. His sights were set on a dismissal of the indictment pretrial.

"And how soon can you get it done?" the client said.

Cash's mind reeled. With Fine's expectations pegged way too high, a simple home run wouldn't do. The ingrate demanded a grand slam, along with an apology from the opposing team for showing up.

Cash had to level the playing field. Lower the client's expectations. Regain the high ground. He should be throwing out the questions. High, hard ones, aimed at Fine's head.

"Do you have any idea what the odds are of having an indictment dropped at this stage?" Cash said. "What you're asking is next to impossible."

"I'm not asking," Fine said. "I'm telling. And what it takes is one phone call."

"And who's on the other end of this magical call?"

Fine shrugged. "The judge, U.S. Attorney, Attorney General. I don't give a shit who pulls the plug on my case. Just get it done."

"That's not how I practice law."

"Then stop practicing law and start playing politics."

"When I entered law school, my plan was to go into politics," Cash said, "but unfortunately, I passed my ethics exam."

The line failed to draw a laugh from Fine, or even a smile. Cash tried a different tack. "If I'm going to spring you, I need to know more about your background and business model."

"Fire away," Fine said. "I'm an open book."

"How many underage girls and boys advertise in the *Backdoor*?"

"None."

"Guess again. Another client of mine has placed scores of ads on your site since her early teens."

"Who?"

Cash shook his head. "That's privileged. Attorney-client."

"But I'm the client." Fine's voice rose an octave.

"So is she. I can't reveal her confidences to you or *vice versa*."

"What if she has info that can help me?"

"If she took the stand, her testimony would bury you." It took several seconds for Cash to process the import of his words. A door had opened for him. Just a crack, but he saw a way out.

Over the years, conflicts between clients had proven to be professional hazards, ethical traps, and hell on the bottom line. This one, however, might be his salvation.

He'd hit on a strategy to scratch his name from the lineup and watch from the cheap seats as Fine went down swinging.

"Fix me a drink," Fine said, "and make it a double."

You're going to need more than one.

CHAPTER TWENTY-FIVE

F ace to face with Goldberg for the first time since the firm imploded, Cash couldn't tell whether the breakup had affected the old man at all.

On the one hand, Goldy looked rested, rambling around his downtown apartment in silk pajamas. His slippers slapped the floor in a steady beat, and his limp had all but disappeared.

On the other, a warhorse like him lived for courtroom battles, where tyrants in black robes wielded gavels and lawyers fired off objections. Whenever peace broke out on the legal front, he suffered from withdrawal.

Cash followed Goldy to the kitchen. His eyes swept the room, which would be the only thing to sweep it in weeks. Crumbs littered the floor. Towers of greasy dishes filled the sink. Trash bags barricaded the pantry door, the last line of defense against an army of ants laying siege to the dwindling provisions.

Cash promised himself not to ask about Eva, or at the very least, not to lead off with her. Show no concern.

As soon as he sat at the table, he caved. "How's Eva doing?"

Goldberg planted his elbows on the table, fingers laced around a coffee cup bearing the inscription: WAIT UNTIL YOU SEE MY BRIEFS.

"Give her a call and hear for yourself," Goldy said.

"She won't take my calls or return my messages."

"Should've thought of that before you fired her." Goldy shuffled to the counter and poured himself a fresh cup of coffee. He didn't offer one to Cash before returning to the table. "What's the first thing I taught you?"

"Get the fee up front," Cash said.

"Okay, what's the second?"

"Never fly solo."

Goldy nodded. "Any lawyer who claims to have won a case all by himself is either a fool or a liar. You need a skilled copilot and a solid crew to bring the passengers home safely. And it takes a damn jackass to bust up the A-team."

"That's a hard lecture to stomach coming from you," Cash said. "I lost count of the secretaries, paralegals, bean counters, and baby lawyers your zipper problem drove off."

"To quote our fellow Dallasite, president number forty-three, 'When I was young and foolish, I was young and foolish.'"

Cash gave him a get real look. "The last time was three years ago, old man. But I didn't come here to dredge up the past."

"Then why are you here?"

"I've hit on a way to put the firm back together," Cash said.

"To quote another Dallasite, who also ran for president, 'I'm all ears.'"

Cash took a deep breath. "You remember Chris Campos, a.k.a. 'Tina'?"

"Sure, the hotheaded tranny you got off."

"Depends on what you mean by 'got off,' but she was acquitted. By the way, they prefer the term transgender these days. Try to keep up with the times."

"Yeah, right." Goldy's tone conveyed no intention of doing so. "I remember him, her, them, whatever."

"Turns out that Campos has been advertising on the *Backdoor* since her early teens."

"What's the *Backdoor*?" Goldy asked.

Cash shook his head. The old man really hadn't kept up.

"It's a website owned by Toby Fine—at least on paper— where all manner of prostitutes advertise." Cash's tone took a sharp turn. "Did you even bother to read the indictment against Fine before he came to our office?"

"Of course not," Goldy said. "I wouldn't do a damn fool thing like that until his check cleared. Remember the prime directive: cash in or client out."

"Back to my plan to reunite the band," Cash said. "Tina has been featured on the site for more than a decade."

"So?"

"That could make her a witness for the government against Fine. Because I've represented Tina in the past and will likely do so in the future, I can't both defend Fine and impeach her on the stand."

Goldy looked skeptical. "What's the endgame here?"

"I flag the conflict of interest between Tina and Fine, which results in the government bumping me off the latter's defense. Even better, since the feds force the issue, no one can blame me for exiting the case. Not Fine. Nor, more importantly, *La Tigra*."

"That's the means to an end. What's your ultimate goal?"

"To rebuild the firm," Cash said. "You, Eva, me, and an associate to be named later."

Goldy shook his head. "Maybe not the worst plan you've ever cooked up, but definitely ranks in the bottom five."

"What's wrong with it?" Asked as if Cash already knew the answer.

"For starters, of the hundreds, maybe thousands of victims available to testify against Fine, what makes you think the feds will call on Campos to make their case?"

"A little birdie could whisper in Delgado's ear that Tina would be a dynamite witness for her."

"And what happens if Delgado blows off the tip and decides not to put Campos on the government's witness list? After all, any prosecutor worth her salt would be wary of a gift from you."

"Gina would never pass up the chance to throw me off the case," Cash said. "She wants no part of me."

Goldy took a swig of coffee. "That leads to the final, fatal flaw in your plan. You said there was nothing *you* could do about the conflict between Fine and Campos, and that may be true. However, there is definitely something *La Tigra* could do about it."

Here it comes. The insurmountable hurdle that had driven Cash to seek Goldy's counsel.

"She could have Campos killed," Goldy said. "Conflict resolved."

"Well, when you put it like that...." Cash's voice trailed off.

With Cash on the ropes, Goldy pounded away. "I see what's in this scheme for you, but what's in it for Campos?"

Cash couldn't look Goldy in the eye. "She'd earn major brownie points from the feds, which might come in handy, given her occupation."

"Only if she lives long enough to call in the marker," Goldy said. "Your ploy involves taking a lot of heat off you and a little heat off Eva and me by shifting all the heat to Campos. You would be signing his...her death warrant. Can you live with that?"

"Can't live with it," Cash said, "probably can't live without it."

"To paraphrase the greatest president of the twentieth century," Goldy said, "if you can't stand the heat, stay out of the courtroom."

* * *

Outside Goldberg's apartment complex, Cash spotted a black limo with tinted windows parked across the street. He picked up his pace to the lot, where his Porsche waited.

The limo pulled away from the curb and rolled slowly toward the lot. A black Tahoe swung into view from around the corner and trailed the Lincoln by a half-block.

The tail had picked up a tail, both keeping their distance from each other and from Cash. Like race cars under a caution flag.

Cash memorized the license plates of both vehicles. His only question was, which one belonged to the feds and which to *La Tigra*?

CHAPTER TWENTY-SIX

The black Tahoe zipped around the limo and screeched to a
stop between Cash and his Porsche.

Faced with a choice of fight or flight, Cash hit upon
a third option: freeze. He stood his ground. His heart pumped
like mad. Sweat glands gushed. Miraculously he managed not
to piss his pants.

Beaten to the prey, the limo sped away, leaving fewer witnesses to Cash's fate. Whatever that might be. He still had no
clue as to who loomed behind the dark windows of the SUV:
the feds or a cartel.

Both had a nasty habit of snatching folks off the street.
Both bought Tahoes by the fleet and stole them by the score.
The cartels had branched out into carjacking. The feds had a
euphemism for their brand of theft. Called it "asset forfeiture."

A ruse by any other name....

Two goons bailed from the vehicle. A squat Latino and a
pale beanpole.

Cheech and Long.

They pulled the old coat-flip trick, revealing the pistols
on their hips and flashing gold badges too quickly for Cash to
catch the fine print.

"Can I see those badges again?" he said.

Cheech shook his head. Long lifted Cash's watch, wallet, and phone.

"Am I under arrest?"

"Not yet," Cheech said.

They shoved Cash into the back of the Tahoe and blindfolded him. The loose blindfold left a partial view of the driver's face but no line of sight to the front seat passenger.

"Is this really necessary?" He started to point out that he'd already seen their faces but caught himself. It wasn't good for his health to remind the captors of that.

"Keep it on." Cheech had a heavy Hispanic accent. "Or we'll cuff you."

Cash nodded. They say the loss of one sense, like sight, sharpens the others. It sure as hell spiked Cash's sense of foreboding.

He tried to keep it together by assuring himself that the street pickup was more mind game than endgame. The badges could be counterfeit, but the cheap suits suggested they were feds, not cartel.

Into the frying pan but not the fire.

His panic level flared again. How hard would it be for *La Tigra*'s soldiers to play dress up? Or in this case, dress down?

During the short ride, no one spoke. Other than Cash, of course. He rattled off questions, all unanswered. The one most often repeated: "Where are you taking me?"

The Tahoe stopped, and the goons pulled Cash—still blindfolded—from the SUV. The hot breath of a revving plane swept over him. Rough hands dragged him onto the plane and strapped him into a leather seat.

"Let me go now, and we'll forget all about this." Cash tried to sound more put out than freaked out. Didn't work.

An elbow drilled his gut, and he doubled over, far as the seatbelt allowed. As soon as the plane went airborne, he got yanked to his feet and dragged to the back.

A heavy door closed behind him. All was black and still. No sound other than the pounding of his heart.

The blindfold came off. He stood in an enclosed space the size of a storage shed. It had the personality of one too. Reinforced steel for security. Spongy padding on the walls for soundproofing. No windows. No pictures or paintings.

Recessed lighting bleached out the complexions of the two feds seated at a round table for eight, each station with its own keyboard and phone. Cash recognized Attorney General Karen Washington and FBI Director T. Baker Danfield from media overexposure.

Washington wore a black ball gown. The FBI director, a tux. The bigwigs were either coming from or going to a formal event.

The two agents who had snatched Cash off the street stood by the door. Their presence gave the Bureau an edge in raw numbers. Made the tally: FBI, three; Main Justice, one; defense bar, one.

Cash took note of who wasn't at the table. No DEA. Also no rep from the U.S. Attorney's Office in Dallas. No local color.

"Where are you taking me and why?" Cash said.

"Welcome to our flying SCIF," said Washington.

"What's a skiff?"

"A sensitive compartmented information facility," Danfield said. "Basically, a room protected from breach by outside eyes and ears."

"Oh, like the cone of silence on *Get Smart*," Cash said, "only more expensive and less effective."

No one laughed or even smiled. Either not catching the pop culture reference or not finding it funny. Cash couldn't decide which was more unforgivable.

"Seriously, where are we going?" Cash said.

Danfield cleared his throat. "That's strictly need to know."

"Well, I need to know, so I can figure out where venue lies for the kidnapping charge I'm bringing against the lot of you."

That brought a collective smile to the room, except for Danfield. He could hold a glare for hours. A grudge, forever.

"Before you run your mouth," Danfield said, "better check the fine print of the Patriot Act."

"Read the United States Constitution before you grab a law-abiding citizen off the street, force him onto a plane, and hotbox him in the air." Cash's voice reached a closing argument crescendo. "I suggest you start with Article Four of the Bill of Rights."

Washington couldn't have looked less concerned. Her hair had been styled by a pro. Dark brown with blonde highlights. Layered and lush. The cut, like the evening dress, definitely not for Cash's benefit.

"The sooner you hear us out," she said, "the sooner we can go our separate ways."

Cash took a seat and picked up the phone at his station. The line was dead.

"I'm listening," he said. "By the way, which agency do I bill for my lost time at the office?"

"We can't offer money as compensation for your time," the A.G. said, "but you of all people should appreciate the value of pocketing a favor from us."

"I'd want any IOU in writing," Cash said.

"Why? You don't trust us?" When Danfield got angry, the southern drawl made a comeback.

"Exactly as much as you trust me." Cash had a surefire way of getting under Danfield's skin. "Like your boss said, let's get this meeting over with." He played on the common knowledge that nothing rankled the FBI director more than the suggestion that he had a boss. On earth or in heaven.

With the meeting heading south fast, Washington picked up a ballpoint pen and clicked it while speaking. "What we're about to share with you cannot leave this room and definitely cannot be put in writing." She paused until Cash nodded. "You represent someone who faces the very real prospect of dying behind bars."

"Look, if you want to conduct plea bargaining," Cash said, "you don't need to impress me with a ride on the agency jet. Just make an offer. I'll talk it over with my client and get back to you. Save the fuel."

The A.G.'s pen hit hyper-click. "This isn't your typical plea bargain situation," she said. "The highest levels of government on both sides of the border are silent partners to our negotiations. Whatever we work out has to be approved by Justice, State, Homeland Security, the NSC, and a half-dozen other agencies before word of it reaches the Oval Office."

Danfield jumped in. "Even if POTUS were to green light an agreement, that wouldn't change the official line that he played no role in the negotiations and knew nothing about the deal beyond what was public."

More rewriting of history in the works.

"I get that you folks brought me here to conduct double secret negotiations," Cash said. "What I don't understand is why you consider Toby Fine such a big fish."

The pen fell silent.

Danfield came out of his seat. "Fine! Who gives a shit about that dirtbag? We're talking about a deal for *La Tigra*."

CHAPTER TWENTY-SEVEN

"Y ou might as well throw me off the plane now," Cash said. "I've got a better chance of surviving a fall of thirty thousand feet than of keeping my scalp, if I take your offer to *La Tigra*."

The jet hit a rough patch and nearly bucked Cash from his seat at the table. Attorney General Washington picked up the phone at her station and talked to the pilot. The plane banked left and slowly descended.

She hung up the phone and turned to Cash. "You'd be bringing *La Tigra* her one and only shot at survival. She's bleeding support, in and out of Mexico."

"Let me make sure I've got the terms down," Cash said. "*La Tigra* forfeits a compound with a forty-thousand-square-foot mansion, an eighteen-hole golf course, the sixth largest zoo in the world—"

FBI Director Danfield cut in, "She can keep her precious white tiger. I'd be happy to arrange for her to share a cage with it."

Cash went on. "She also throws in an indoor pool that flows into an outdoor infinity pool, a massive wine cellar, a the-atre that seats three hundred, three master chefs, and a private masseuse." He considered bringing up the fleet of SUVs, jets, and helicopters, but he'd made his point.

"In return for surrendering everything," Cash said, "she gets a lifetime lease on a ten-by-twelve-foot cell. No extra charge for the rats and roaches. Of course, what your sales pitch failed to disclose is that in order to have any hope of staying alive, she'd have to rot away in solitary. That means twenty-three hours a day in a box half the size of this room on an express train to crazy town."

"Whether *La Tigra* takes our deal or not," said Danfield, "she's already lost the compound, along with all the bells and whistles you ticked off. She just doesn't know it yet."

"So says the United States government," Cash said, "which doesn't have the best track record of honest dealing."

Danfield's face turned red. "So says the Mexican government too."

The plane leveled off, settling into a smoother ride.

"You must be talking to the one or two *federales* not in *La Tigra's* pocket." Cash sounded more confident than he felt, aware that the Mexican police had a bad habit of switching sides on a dime.

Like their counterparts to the north.

Washington resumed her annoying tic with the ballpoint pen. "For every government official on *La Tigra's* payroll, *Los Lobos* own two."

Instinct kicked in, and Cash jumped to *La Tigra's* defense. Occupational hazard of a criminal lawyer to suffer under the delusion that even the damned deserved a champion.

"A woman doesn't rise to the top of the most powerful cartel in Mexico and hold onto power for two decades by allowing herself to be outflanked by a ragtag band of butchers."

Danfield snorted. "To call *Los Lobos* a ragtag band is like calling ISIS a chess club. They're the most lethal cartel in the world, and they control half of Mexico. Their sights are set on Sinaloa, and they won't stop the slaughter until they have it."

"To make matters worse for *La Tigra*," Washington said, "the Mexican government can't afford another bloodbath between cartels. Not while Mexico is negotiating a new trade deal with us and bidding for the 2032 Olympics. The *federales* have picked a winner, and unfortunately it's not your client."

Cash shook his head. "That makes no sense. Why would the Mexican government go with *Los Lobos* over *La Tigra*? Better the devil you know...."

"The Mexican government isn't leading the victory parade for *Los Lobos*, only trying to get in front of it."

"Even if all that were true," Cash said, "what makes you think that *La Tigra* will be the first cartel chief in history to give up her empire without a fight to the death?"

The A.G. leaned in. "For one thing, your client belongs to the smarter sex. For another, we have you to sell the deal to her. No one understands better than a lawyer who's done time himself that not all confinements are created equal."

She eased back. "We might be able to make some concessions to your client, while she's under our tender, loving care. Give her something to look forward to every month."

Cash caught the drift. "Not sure monthly stud service will do the trick."

"How about weekly?" Washington said.

"While the way to a man's heart goes through his pecker," Cash said, "according to you, women are smarter than that."

"Smart or not," Washington said, "no one wants to believe that her sex life is over." The clicking stopped. "We can work out the details of her living conditions later. Prison can be very hard, especially on a woman. Or not. As the poet wrote, stone walls do not a prison make; nor iron bars, a cage."

"Yeah," Cash said, "but they're a pretty good start." He shook his head. "Color me underwhelmed by your offer. And if I'm not sold, she won't be either."

"Your client has a daughter at NYU." The A.G. didn't say more. Didn't have to.

"The kid has a private security detail to rival the president's," Cash said. "Besides, she has nothing to do with the business."

"Neither of which will save her," Danfield said. "Only we can do that." He stood and stretched to his full six-four frame. Lanky, lean, and lethal. "I'm tired of dancing around. *La Tigra* has thirty-six hours to grab the lifeline. After that, *Los Lobos* and the *federales* will join forces to hunt down and kill her and her daughter."

"Thirty-six hours!" Cash stood and locked eyes with Danfield. "That's impossible. I have to set up the meeting with *La Tigra*, kill a day in transit to the compound, go over the deal with her, give her time to consider it, and then travel back to the States. I'll need at least a week."

"You've got thirty-six hours," Danfield said, "minus the minutes you just wasted whining."

Washington tugged on Danfield's sleeve until he sat. "Your transportation has been arranged," she said. "We're getting off in Houston. Then our plane will take you to Sinaloa and land on a private strip near *La Tigra*'s compound. That gives you about thirty-three hours to sell the deal to her, after which the plane will return to Dallas, with or without you."

In all the talk about *La Tigra*, Cash had almost forgotten about his other client. The one facing trial this month. "What about Toby Fine? Where does this leave him?"

"In limbo for now," the A.G. said.

Cash didn't have to ask where he stood. Stuck in the middle, of course.

Guilt by association with clients made it old hat for the feds to target him for tax evasion, money laundering, and the like. He lived in the crosshairs. But being squeezed between two governments and two cartels pushed the risk level off the charts.

La Tigra wasn't alone in needing a lifeline.

"Fine is the least of your worries," Danfield said, "and that weasel is four steps ahead of you and *La Tigra*. He's already reaching out to *Los Lobos*, and he'll offer up your scalps to save his own."

It was news to Cash that Fine had made overtures to *Los Lobos*. No surprise, however, that he'd sacrifice his mother to save his own skin.

Cash had two final questions. "Do you have a sealed indictment against *La Tigra*?"

He expected no answer and got none, so he didn't waste his breath asking the follow-up.

Do you have a sealed indictment on me?

CHAPTER TWENTY-EIGHT

As soon as the FBI's G-jet taxied to a stop, a SWAT team stormed the landing strip and boarded the plane. Cash tried to tally up the troops on the takedown crew. Twice he made it to thirteen before losing count. Too many moving targets in identical uniforms.

The soldiers wore black from their boots to riot helmets. Tinted face shields were down, and weapons drawn. FN Five-SeveNs in one hand and steel-capped batons in the other. They looked like the bad guys in a *Star Wars* flick.

Dragged from the plane, Cash and the pilot wilted in the triple-digit heat of dusk. The night had yet to offer any balm from the sun's toll.

A Boeing 747-430 on the runway overshadowed the G-jet. *La Tigra's* plane was painted orange with black stripes, with the name emblazoned along the body: *The Flying Tigress*.

The troops split up. The pilot forced one way. Cash, the other.

Cash gave the pilot a parting look that said, *don't dare leave without me*. The pilot's blank expression made no promises.

A ten-minute hike brought Cash to the theatre in *La Tigra's* mansion. Took his eyes a minute or so to adjust to the dark, but only a few lines of dialogue to nail the neo-noir classic on the screen:

> *Matty (to Ned): You're not too smart, are you? I like that in a man.*
> *Ned: What else do you like? Lazy, ugly, horny. I got 'em all.*
> *Matty: You don't look lazy.*

Two goons ushered Cash to the seat next to *La Tigra* and left. A sea of empty seats surrounded the couple.

"So you're a fan of *Body Heat*," Cash said. "That gives us something in common."

Her eyes stayed on the screen as she spoke. "You seem surprised by my taste in films." A hawk nose and high cheekbones dominated her profile. No need for *ancestry.com* to figure out her roots.

"I thought you might try to intimidate me with a private showing of *Scarface*."

"I suspect that a film about a woman outsmarting the men around her terrifies you far more than Tony Montana and his little friend."

Copy that.

"Speaking of little friends," she said, "I have warehouses of weapons, including missiles that could have downed your plane from two thousand kilometers away."

Cash resisted asking why she hadn't. Figured she was about to tell him anyway.

"I received word from your government, by way of my government, that you had an important message for me."

"Right." Cash found himself sweating more than the characters on screen. "Before we get down to business, have you heard the expression: don't shoot the messenger?"

"Of course."

"Good," he said. "Because I have a very limited role here. I'm only a delivery boy."

"I am all ears." She smiled. "Is that not also one of your expressions?"

He took a deep breath and dived in. "The United States government is willing to throw you a lifeline."

He caught her reaction, slight as it was. The faintest of lines bracketed her eyes and the corners of her mouth.

She recovered quickly. "Not what I expected to hear from you. I thought you had come to report on Mister Fine's case."

"The feds don't care about him," Cash said. "It's you they want to save."

"That assumes I need saving."

"According to the FBI, *Los Lobos* and the Mexican government are teaming up to take you out."

If that was news to her, she didn't let on. An arson on screen lit up her face, illuminating the worry lines.

"Do you believe everything the FBI tells you?" Asked as if she already knew the answer.

"The better question is whether I believe *anything* the FBI tells me."

She turned to face him. "Then why would you believe this?"

"Way above my pay grade to know whether the Bureau is shooting straight here. Even if the intel turns out to be true, I'll be damned if I know why they'd lift a finger to rescue you. All I can say is that the message comes straight from the FBI director and the Attorney General. So if we're being lied to, at least it's by liars in high places."

"Your government leaders have a history of deception."

"I wouldn't limit that charge to my government."

She nodded. "What exactly is the offer?"

Cash laid out the details, opening and closing with the feds' claim that the deal was her best and only shot at survival.

Her eyes returned to the screen. She clicked a remote, freezing the film on a close-up of Matty, right after she had informed Ned that her temperature ran a couple of degrees high.

"That is my favorite line in the movie," she said, "because mine does as well."

"I'd wager that your blood pressure is running a little high also," he said.

"If the choice is between living in a box for the rest of my life or waging war on *Los Lobos*, what makes you think I would choose the former?"

"The feds believe you will do anything to protect your daughter."

Her eyes flashed, and her fingernails dug into the armrests. "Are you threatening my daughter now?"

Cash sweat bullets. Bringing up the kid had tripped a land mine. He had to defuse it or die trying. "Remember, I'm just the messenger here."

The one you shouldn't kill.

She loosened her death grip on the armrests. "Tell your friends in the government that *mijita* is protected by the best security money can buy."

"They aren't my friends, but they're willing to do whatever it takes to protect you and your daughter."

"Do you trust them?" It came off as accusatory.

An inner voice warned Cash to wrap it up. His job was done. The lines delivered in the farce, or tragedy, or whatever it was.

He blew past his better judgment. "It's one thing to go to war against a rival cartel. Something entirely different to take up arms against your own government. The former is self-defense. The latter, treason."

"Governments come," she said, "and governments go. Even yours."

"Amen to that." Another silent warning urged him to stop now, so of course he continued. "But cartels come and go too. Perhaps the time has come for you to retire. You've had a long run on top and amassed more wealth than a person could spend in a hundred lifetimes."

She fast-forwarded the film to the final shot of Matty basking in the sun on a tropical beach. To reach the end frame, she had to scroll past a scene of Ned the lawyer behind bars. Took Cash back to his two years at Club Fed.

"As a little girl, I loved the beach. Not so much for the water. I was never a strong swimmer. For me, it was all about the sand. The grit and warmth of it."

"Living like a prisoner inside a compound in the mountains," he said, "isn't exactly a day at the beach."

"Neither is serving a life sentence in Supermax."

"Who said anything about Supermax?"

She had obviously done homework on the federal prison system. Cash took that as a good sign.

"Even if the Bureau wanted to send you there," he said, "we'd never jump at the first offer. I've been on both sides of the bargaining table, and I can promise you one thing. When the stakes get high enough, everything is negotiable."

"Can you find me a place in the sun?"

"I think so. Two governments want you out of business, and they want it badly enough to deal through me. A person with your firepower can hang up her spurs the hard way or the easy way."

"But can you guarantee that I will not end up in prison and that my daughter will be safe?"

"There are no guarantees in my business," he said.

"There are in mine."

Cash let the threat slide. Not the first time he'd heard that line from a client who could carry through on it. "Have I ever let you down?"

"The jury is still out on that," she said. "But what happens if the FBI will not offer something my daughter and I can live with?"

"We bring in a new bidder."

As the film credits scrolled, Cash rose to leave. She grabbed his arm. "I have a message for you to take back. Only two words."

CHAPTER TWENTY-NINE

ash returned to the States with two messages from *La Tigra*, each of two words. The first was to the Justice Department: keep talking.

The second, to Toby Fine: stop talking.

A flock of feds boarded the G-Jet at Love Field Airport in Dallas. Eight stiffs from the Bureau flanked FBI Director Danfield and General Washington and whisked Cash into the SCIF at the back of the plane.

Danfield wasted no time on small talk. "Did she take the deal?"

"*La Tigra* didn't get where she is by accepting first offers," Cash said.

Danfield turned to the A.G. "I told you we were wasting our time with this slimeball."

Cash stood. "That's Mister Slimeball to you." He walked toward the exit. Two agents blocked his path. Even if he could manage to slip through them, reinforcements waited outside the door.

Cash turned to Washington. "Look, you asked me to deliver a message, and I did. Shuttle diplomacy is not my thing, so find yourself another gofer. I have a trial to prepare for."

Washington motioned for Cash to return to the table. Against his better judgment, he did.

"Did you explain to your client that time is running out for her?" Washington looked beat. Her coiffed hair, expertly layered on their last visit, had collapsed into limp strands.

According to media reports, time wasn't on her side either. With the president's poll numbers tanking, he had made noises about purging the cabinet, starting with Washington.

"*La Tigra* knows the score," Cash said, "and she's not suicidal. We'll stay at the bargaining table, at least long enough to see if you come up with an arrangement she can live with. If you don't, she has the firepower to fuck up business on both sides of the border for years to come."

"Did she tell you what she would accept?" Washington said.

Cash rubbed his chin. "*La Tigra* loves long walks on the beach, and her favorite color is white, as in sparkling white sand."

Danfield rocketed to his feet. "I don't give a flying fuck what her favorite color is." His southern accent flared, along with his temper. "It had damn well better be orange, because that's what she'll wear for the rest of her life."

The A.G. tugged on Danfield's sleeve until he sat. She turned to Cash. "What do you suggest our next step should be?"

"Offer her one of our states with beaches, preferably one we could lose without hurting the bottom line. How about South Carolina?" No accident that Cash picked Danfield's home state.

Danfield's face went red. He started to speak, but Washington stared him down.

"Do you have a suggestion that wouldn't cost my party nine electoral votes?" she said.

"Think tropical," Cash said.

"And you, asshole." The FBI director couldn't hold his tongue any longer. "What do you hope to gain out of this?"

For a nanosecond, Cash considered giving a straight answer. Truth be told, he'd settle for resuming his old life. No drug work. No cartel cases. No death threats. Eva and Goldy back in the fold.

The nanosecond passed.

"If I pull this off without a shot being fired," Cash said, "I deserve nothing less than the Nobel Peace Prize."

* * *

For a packed restaurant at noon, Tei-An was eerily quiet. Patrons spoke softly or not at all.

Cash honored the ambience. "She knows." His hushed tone amplified the threat.

Toby Fine froze, sushi suspended inches from his mouth. He put down the chopsticks and proceeded to do what he did best. Lie. "I don't know what you're talking about."

"*La Tigra* knows you're playing footsy with *Los Lobos*."

"I would never—"

Cash cut him off. "Oh, I know. You would never betray her. At least not until someone offered a sweeter deal."

The client feigned silent outrage. His act needed work.

"Personally, I don't give a shit whether you remain on *La Tigra*'s team or defect to the bad guys. Make that, the badder guys. Hell, I wouldn't care whether you survive the day, but for the effect it has on my schedule."

Cash took a piece of sashimi from Fine's bento box and nibbled around the edges. He winced. "Never developed a taste for the raw stuff."

"You're my lawyer, and you owe me—"

Cash cut him off again. "I owe you my duty of loyalty for as long as you're alive, which in your case might be a matter of minutes."

Cash washed the taste from his mouth with sake. "Ordinarily you'd owe me a hefty fee in return. However, since you're a freebie, I'm in that rarest of situations where losing you as a client would actually boost my bottom line."

"It can't be good for business," Fine said, "to lose a case or a client."

"Except that here if the client were to go first, I no longer have to worry about losing the case."

Fine leaned in to whisper. "You've got me all wrong."

"How's that?"

"I'm not talking to *Los Lobos*," Fine said. "They're talking to me."

Cash's spine stiffened. "And what are they saying?"

"The same question they have for everyone. Which do you want: gold or lead?"

Cash remained silent.

Fine went on. "Translation, get rich with them or sleep with the worms."

"Yeah," Cash said, "I got it the first time." Another sip of sake. "You may have a third option."

"I'm not working with the feds." His voice rose above a whisper.

"Not asking you to," Cash said. "The feds could care less about you."

"Is that supposed to cheer me up?"

"It should, because if I can negotiate the terms of *La Tigra*'s retirement, the prosecutors might let you drift away in her wake."

Fine uncorked a one-note laugh. "There's no way *Los Lobos* will let her live. Or me either, unless I play ball with them."

Cash shook his head. "I came here to deliver a message from *La Tigra*. Stop talking. To *Los Lobos*. To the feds. To anyone."

"Funny, because I came here to deliver a message from *Los Lobos* to you. Gold or lead?"

CHAPTER THIRTY

C ash talked his way into the apartment Maggie had vacated by feigning an interest in renting it. He suffered a tinge of regret over lying to gain entry and a ton of regret over viewing the space.

"Great choice." The henna-haired landlady made a nonstop sales pitch during the tour. "Best unit in the whole complex."

He nodded to everything she said, devastated by the reality that Maggie had gone for good. The Bureau had lifted a page from Hoover's playbook and exiled her to North Dakota, the Siberia of the States.

Goodbye frozen margaritas. Hello frozen tundra.

She hadn't blamed Cash for her exile, at least not expressly. Then again, she didn't have to. He lost the blame game by default.

He should've seen the transfer coming from months away. If life had taught him anything, it was that women didn't stay.

Not even mothers.

He second-guessed the decision to visit Maggie's old haunt. Nothing in the world is more depressing than an empty apartment.

Well, almost nothing. He thought of the cell he'd shared with Big Black and Martin Biddle, reminding him that things had been worse. It also reminded him of unfinished business at Seagoville.

There was unfinished business here as well. He hadn't needed a site visit to accept the loss, but he clung to a hope that Maggie had left behind a memento. A poster on the wall, a knickknack in a closet, a book on a shelf. Anything to remind him of her.

Of them.

The smell of chili permeated the place, stirring memories of Maggie's one-two punch in the kitchen. Enchiladas for dinner and migas in the morning. She followed the cardinal rule of cooking: Hatch chile improves everything.

The aroma dogged him from room to room on the treasure hunt. The landlady rattled on about the apartment. Her litany of half-truths negotiated a narrow path, falling north of puffery but south of fraud.

He found no sign. No hidden keepsake. Maggie had vanished without a goodbye note.

Just like his mother.

* * *

Fine and Cash sat across from each other at a round table in a conference room at the law firm. Three stacks of paper loomed between them.

Fine looked up from the page in his hands. "Is there a woman in the courthouse you haven't fucked?"

Cash did a double take. The question had come out of nowhere. He smelled a stall. "Keep reading."

"This is boring me to tears," Fine said.

"Read through your tears."

"Lawyers have to sift through shit like this," Fine said, "but not real people with real lives."

Granted, there was a lot of dreck to wade through. Cash had printed the client's email exchanges. Not all of them, of course. That would take a lifetime to review.

By using search terms, the date range set out in the indictment, and a list of key players, Cash had whittled the universe of documents down to the subset most likely to contain relevant exchanges between Fine and his unindicted co-conspirators.

Even the subset, however, had produced a paper tower half as tall as Cash. By day three of the document review, he and Fine had subdivided the tower into three stacks: a tall one of pages yet to be read, a shorter stack of those reviewed and discarded as irrelevant, and a small collection of hot documents.

Hot docs were either very good or very bad for their case. At the outset of the review, Cash had laid down for Fine the prime directive: show me the good ones at any time but the baddies immediately.

Fine rose and headed toward the door. Cash called his bluff. "You walk away from the table, and so do I."

"You can't do that. You have to stay here and prepare my defense."

"Here's the great thing about being the lawyer and not the client. If the jury hands down a guilty verdict, you're shipped off to prison on the spot, while I go home and pour myself a stiff drink."

"Do you make all your clients suffer through shit work like this?" Fine took whining to a new level.

"Only the cut-rate ones. As a no pay client, you owe me a ton of sweat equity."

Fine trudged back to the table. "You never answered my question."

"Which one?" Asked as if Cash had forgotten.

"Is there a woman in the courthouse you haven't screwed?"

Cash stroked his chin, as if pondering. He meant the gesture as a joke. Wasn't sure it came off as one.

"What about the spitfire from D.C.? You tap that?"

Cash recoiled. "What would give you that idea?"

"Sparks flew between you two in court last week. Makes me think there's a backstory I need to hear."

"Gina and I have a past," Cash said, "but it's got nothing to do with sex."

Cash tried to drop the subject, but Fine wouldn't let go. "Fess up, McCahill."

Cash sighed. "Well, I guess you deserve to know who you're up against."

"Let me guess." Fine sounded glum. "You're about to deliver the bad news that she's never lost a case."

"I can't say that, but she has won several that should've gone the other way." Cash owed the client the whole truth, or at least more of it. He went on. "Gina will lie, cheat, and steal to win a case. I'm telling you that, and I'm her friend."

"And that makes her different from other prosecutors how?"

"Fact is, most prosecutors are pretty decent folks," Cash said. "Remember the old saying that in our system, it's better for ninety-nine guilty people to go free than for one innocent person to be convicted?"

Fine nodded.

"Gina flips that on its head. In her world it's better for ninety-nine innocent people to be convicted than for one guilty person to walk."

"Is this something you've heard about her," Fine said, "or something you've seen?"

"Oh, I know it firsthand. Back in my days at DOJ, the Deputy A.G. sent Gina and me to El Paso on a task force to take down a crooked county judge. At the outset, the sledding was tough because our target had the witnesses by the short hairs. We couldn't get anyone to roll on him."

"Win some," Fine said, "lose some."

"That wasn't good enough for Gina. She cooked up a bull-shit bank fraud charge against the judge's wife and threatened to indict her, unless hubby copped to bribery."

"So what happened? Did the judge fall on his sword?"

"He didn't have to," Cash said. "The wife hung herself the day before she was to be indicted."

"So the bitch's plan didn't work," Fine said.

"Plan A didn't, but Plan B worked like a charm. After the judge's wife killed herself, Gina turned her guns on the daughter, and the judge folded like a cheap tent."

Fine's shoulders slumped, and his chest caved. Beaten before the first punch.

"Cheer up," Cash said. "On the plus side, you don't have a wife or daughter for Gina to threaten."

He didn't bring up the downside. A little pressure from Gina, and Fine would snap like a twig.

CHAPTER THIRTY-ONE

ash resorted to the time-honored strategy called shake-the-tree-and-see-what-falls-out. For good measure, he'd shake two.

Ladies first.

Cash sat across the desk from Regina Delgado in the office she had made her own, to the point of replacing the First Assistant's battle-scarred desk with a larger one. Worked for Cash. More space between them.

"You know what they say about karma," he said.

"That it's a bitch?"

He nodded. "Thought you should know what the high muck-a-mucks from D.C. are up to." He paused to build tension. "They're playing games with our case."

"What kind of games?"

"Your boss had me swept off the streets and put on her private jet, where the subject of Fine's case came up. I looked around the plane and noticed you weren't on board."

Her eyes narrowed. "Who was?"

"For your side, only the A.G. and the FBI director. First time I've been hustled by Mister and Missus Big."

"What exactly did they offer you?"

"The moon." More stalling to stoke her paranoia. "Plus the sun and stars."

"Were you offered anything on this planet?" Her voice had an edge.

"A walk for Fine, if I delivered *La Tigra*."

She stiffened in her seat. "In the unlikely event that this turns out to be true, why would you tell me?"

"Figured I'd save you the time and trouble of prepping for a trial that will never happen."

"I still fail to see why it's in your interest to enlighten me," she said.

"I do you a solid. In return, you do one for me. Karma."

She looked askance at him. "What are you fishing for?"

"I need intel on a closed case this office brought against Martin Biddle."

"Who's he?"

"A nobody who got popped for bank fraud and money laundering. He died in the pen."

"What is it you want to know?" she said.

"Why this office went after only Biddle? Why weren't others indicted with him?"

"If it's a closed case and the defendant is dead, what's the point?"

Cash had been asking himself the same question for weeks. He had a ready answer. "The widow deserves to know whether Biddle took his own life or was murdered. If the latter, who had a motive to shut him up permanently? Numbers one through one hundred on my suspect list are the co-conspirators who dodged indictment."

"That explains why Missus Biddle cares and maybe why you do as well," she said, "but why should I?"

"It's no secret you're after the top job at Justice, and so is Jenna Powell. Ambitious U.S. Attorneys like her are always angling for the mother ship in D.C., and Daddy Warbucks has a senator or two in his pocket to grease the skids. The intel I'm seeking could knock your rival right out of the running."

* * *

Duane Leroy Lee slouched on the barstool at Spike. While the teens packing the Deep Ellum bar tried to pass for older, Leroy struggled in vain to play younger.

The undercover agent's glazed look and boozy breath signaled the lowering of his guard. Time for Cash to make his pitch. He took the stool next to Leroy and ordered two Tecates.

Leroy nodded in silent thanks for the drink. "I don't hear from Mister Big Shot Shyster for years and then two visits in two weeks. What do you want now?"

"Are you playing hard to get," Cash said, "or are you just too damn lazy to pick up the career case that landed in your lap?"

"Career case, my ass. More like career killer." Leroy went from pissed to piteous in two syllables flat. "I told the SAC about your lead, and he split a gut laughing at the mention of your name. Said if I was fool enough to fall for your bullshit, he had a bridge to sell me."

"Let me talk to your boss," Cash said. "I'll turn him around."

"I'm not near drunk enough to go along with your suicide pact."

"Then we'd best get to work on your alcohol intake." Cash lifted his mug. "Bartender, another round for my friend and me."

"It's against my religion to turn down a Tecate." Leroy slid his empty mug to the bartender. "But if anyone asks, we're not friends."

*　*　*

A stone's throw separated DEA's glass-and-steel complex in northwest Dallas and FBI's taller, more imposing headquarters. Leave it to the Bureau to one-up the competition.

The idea behind building the structures side by side had been to break down barriers between the notoriously territorial bureaucracies. Encourage cooperation. Foster teamwork. It must've seemed like a good idea at the time.

Today, not so much. Not to Cash anyway. In light of his plan to play off one agency against the other, it gave him the willies to know that the FBI could watch him enter and leave DEA's den.

Cash surrendered his phone and passed through two levels of security at DEA headquarters: a metal detector followed by a rougher than necessary pat-down. Leroy took him to a windowless conference room on the top floor.

The two waited in silence ten minutes before Special Agent in Charge Victor Valdez entered the room. Even with lifts and a pompadour, the SAC struggled to hit five-eight. He had the build and black hair of a twenty-five-year-old. The body was solid, but salt-and-pepper stubble copped to a dye job.

With twelve seats at the table, Cash had expected an entourage to accompany the chief, but he came alone. The SAC squeezed a grip exerciser ten pumps with the right hand, then with the left. Ten right, ten left. Over and over.

Cash rose from the table and held out his hand for what seemed an eternity. Valdez gave him a bone-crunching shake.

"McCahill, you've got five minutes." The SAC sounded distracted and disinterested.

Leroy looked as if he was about to lose his lunch. Could be a hangover from last night's drinks. Or a sense of dread over the prospect of an imminent reaming from the boss.

Five minutes, no problem. Judges had given Cash less time to close. If only he knew where to begin. After burning the first minute in false starts, he opened in the middle. "I represent a defendant named Toby Fine, who—"

Valdez cut him off. "Not our case, not our problem." He squeezed the exerciser faster and harder.

"Not your problem," Cash said, "but could be your passport to D.C."

The SAC's fake yawn didn't fool Cash. Valdez was nibbling on the baited hook. Twice passed over for the Deputy Administrator's job, he had one last bite at the big time.

"If you want to plead your guy," Valdez said, "deal with the prosecutor. I don't poach cases, and I don't have time for your games." He pushed back from the table.

Cash spooled the story back to the beginning. "Fine works for *La Tigra*."

Valdez froze in a crouch, halfway between sitting and standing.

"He reports directly to her," Cash said, "and I would hardly call it poaching on your part, when the Bureau has cut you boys out of the biggest cartel case in a generation."

The SAC eased back into the chair. "Two minutes left on the clock."

"I never would've represented a lowlife like Fine, except *La Tigra* called in a chit. She's not someone you turn down."

"If you want absolution for representing scum," Valdez said, "try a priest."

"Absolution is off the table. I'd settle for discharging my ethical duties to Fine and *La Tigra* and getting the hell out of the drug world." Cash nodded toward the field agent. "Leroy here can vouch that I draw the line at representing druggies and pimps."

Leroy snickered. "Yeah, he's much more comfortable with con men and whores."

Cash couldn't argue with that.

"So you're saddled with a client who should burn in hell," Valdez said. "I still don't see why I should give a damn about you or your client."

"All roads lead to *La Tigra*," Cash said, "but Fine is the expressway to her."

With his free hand, Valdez stroked his chin. "What makes you think he would turn on her?"

"The question," Cash said, "is whether he would turn *with* her."

"You lost me," the SAC said.

"I'm offering you a two-for-the-price-of-one special. A package deal for *La Tigra* and Fine. Be a helluva bargain for you guys."

Valdez uncorked a full-throated laugh. "A deal for *La Tigra*! The only deal I'd offer that bitch is to let her choose the method of her execution."

Cash stood. "Then I'm sorry to have wasted your time. FYI, the Bureau beat your offer."

The SAC stopped pumping the grip.

Now it was Cash's turn to squeeze.

CHAPTER THIRTY-TWO

DEA chief Victor Valdez whisked Cash to the El Paso Intelligence Center, EPIC for short, proving two things in the process. The Bureau wasn't the only agency with a jet, and Valdez shared Cash's paranoia about meeting next door to FBI headquarters.

Cash went along for the ride, hoping to find a maverick with the balls to bid against the Bureau. EPIC seemed as good a place to start as any. He entered a packed conference room, where the suits outnumbered street agents four to one.

Not a good sign.

With fifteen agents in the room and only twelve chairs at the table, a mad game of musical chairs broke out. The lone female in the room, an exotic beauty, captured Cash's attention and the first seat at the table. The others went fast, with the losers banished to chairs against a wall.

In jeans, a Dallas Mavericks t-shirt, and scuffed boots, Duane Leroy Lee drifted to the chair nearest the door and faded into the woodwork. Nearly out of sight. Definitely out of the loop. As far from Cash as possible.

Cash couldn't allow such injustice to stand. "Lady and gentlemen, our first order of business is to make room at the table for the lead agent in the biggest cartel case of your careers. For those who haven't had the privilege of meeting the man of the moment, allow me to introduce Duane Leroy Lee. Close friends like me call him Leroy. You may address him as *Special Agent Lee*."

Lee's face flushed red. Sweat beaded his temples. "I'm fine right here." He didn't sound fine, his voice more gravelly than normal. "And to set the record straight, McCahill and I are not friends."

"Nonsense," Cash said. "I need my right-hand man at my right hand."

Cash elbowed his neighbor, a suit with a unibrow. The nudge jolted him to his feet.

Unibrow looked to an African-American with the wingspan of an NBA power forward and a graying goatee. The silent appeal for help told Cash who swung the biggest dick in the room.

Goatee shrugged, and Unibrow ceded his place at the table. Leroy trudged over, as if he were walking the last mile. After taking the hot seat, he whispered to Cash, "Thanks for nothing."

"*De nada,*" Cash whispered before addressing the group. "Since this is my first dance with DEA brass in a decade, what say we start with a round of introductions?"

"What say we don't," Goatee said, confirming Cash's read of the pecking order in the room. "All you need to know is that I'm John Price, and I'm in charge here." His rolling thunder voice kept the clash of egos in check.

"And you are?" Cash said.

"The person in charge here." Price's tone went from no nonsense to kickass. "You may be accustomed to running roughshod in the courtroom, McCahill, but that don't cut ice with me."

"I don't take over all courtrooms. Just those where the judges let me get away with it." Caveat aside, Cash gave the agency a gold star for doing its homework on him.

"Let's get this straight," Price said. "*If* we decide to open a file based on your intel, Lee will not be the lead agent. Instead, *Supervisory* Special Agent Tanaka will run point."

"Who's he?" Cash said.

"He is a *she*." The voice came from the lone female, who sat to Price's left. "I'm Dani Tanaka, and I drew the short straw. I'll be your minder."

Since Cash had entered the room, his eyes had rarely strayed far or long from Tanaka. The agency really had dug into his background. Playing on his weakness for women in general and Asian-Americans in particular. She would be lucky to reach five-two and a hundred pounds, but she still packed a punch. Hitting him below the belt.

Though Cash had been set to take a my-way-or-the-FBI-way stand on the Leroy-for-leader ticket, the brief exchange with Tanaka gave him pause. He came up with a compromise. "Price, you may be accustomed to intimidating your underlings, but I don't take orders from anyone not wearing a black robe. Hell, half the time I don't listen to judges." He let the lesson sink in. "Tanaka's on the team, but only if we're clear that Leroy is my point person."

Leroy cursed under his breath. "Thanks for digging me a deeper hole," he whispered.

"Anything for a friend," Cash whispered back.

"Lee can hang on," Price said. The *for now* was silent.

Because Price caved on Leroy so quickly, Cash second-guessed himself over whether he could've driven a harder bargain. Then again, adding Tanaka to the lineup had its advantages. And not just the skin-deep ones.

She had the vibe of a woman who got shit done. If Cash could sell her on a deal for *La Tigra*, then....

Price punctured his balloon. "Don't get too far down the road with talk of a team, until I hear what you bring to the table."

"I can convince *La Tigra* that it's time to retire." Cash paused for pushback. None came, so he went on. "The question for you is whether she steps aside peacefully or goes out guns blazing, leaving hundreds, maybe thousands of bodies piled up on both sides of the border."

"This is total bullshit," Price said. "*La Tigra's* no fool. No one retires peacefully in her business, and she knows it."

"Your sister agency begs to differ," Cash said.

Price looked puzzled. "Sister agency?"

"The FBI," Cash said, "though perhaps it's more accurate to call it your big brother."

"The Bureau doesn't know shit about Mexican cartels." Price practically spat out the words.

"They know enough to back the winner in a cartel war that's about to go to DEFCON One," Cash said.

Price snorted. "There are no winners in a cartel war. Only those who lose today and the rest who'll lose tomorrow."

"Once again," Cash said, "the FBI director and the Attorney General beg to differ. The rising body count of the cartel war threatens the ruling parties there and here. The bloodbath has to end, which means a clear victor and an out-of-business loser. *La Tigra* gone. *Los Lobos* rule."

Price looked like his head was about to explode. "That's insane. *Los Lobos* are animals."

Cash shrugged. "To the powers that be, all cartels look gray in the night."

"All cartels are bad," Price said, "but not all are equally bad."

"The same could be said for your options." Cash poured himself a glass of water and drank. "All bad but not equally so. You can sit back and let the FBI have its way with *La Tigra*. Or you can compete for her affection."

Price pounded the table. "Your client's the one with shitty options. She can stay put until *Los Lobos* carve her into tiny pieces. Or surrender to us and spend the rest of her life behind bars."

"I was thinking more along the lines of her kicking back on a tropical island. Wasting away in Margaritaville. Out of sight. Out of the drug trade. And out of your hair."

"And what would we get in return for sending a mass murderer on a permanent vacation in paradise?" Price said.

"The thanks of two grateful nations for saving countless lives," Cash said.

Price grunted.

Cash upped the ante. "Plus all the intel in *La Tigra's* pretty little head."

Price stroked his goatee. "I'm listening."

"Including a depressingly long list of politicians and law enforcement officials in both countries on her payroll."

Dani wrote a note and slid it to Price. He read the note and looked at Cash. "What about *La Tigra's* daughter? What do you propose we do with her?"

Bringing up the daughter proved the agency hadn't come to the meeting cold, at least Tanaka hadn't. Cash figured her to be a step ahead of everyone in the room, including him.

"You keep her safe," Cash said, "and with the mother."

"What if Marisol doesn't want to go with her mother?" Tanaka asked as if she already knew the answer.

"Knowing *La Tigra* as I do," Cash said, "I doubt the daughter has a choice."

Price stood, signaling a wrap to the meeting. "Yeah, we wouldn't want a mother to vanish without the child having a clue as to her whereabouts...without the kid knowing what happened to her." His tone carried not an ounce of concern for the mother or the child.

Damn, the assholes really had done their homework on Cash.

CHAPTER THIRTY-THREE

John Price led his entourage from the EPIC conference room, leaving behind only Supervisory Special Agent Dani Tanaka, Special Agent Duane Leroy Lee, and Cash.

Tanaka stood at one end of the table, a remote control console in one hand and a laser pointer in the other. Leroy and Cash sat across the table from her.

"Agent Lee," Tanaka said, "dim the lights."

Leroy jumped on command. "Hey, if you two would like to be alone...."

"Excellent idea," Cash said. "Cue the soft music on your way out."

She ignored Cash and spoke to Leroy. "You wanted to be on the team, so you stay and suffer with me."

Leroy lowered the lights and his voice. "Never said I wanted to be on the team."

"Well then," she said, "you can thank your buddy for signing you onto this suicide mission."

Cash hoped she was talking about *career* suicide. Hard to tell from her end-of-days tone.

Leroy returned to the table and sat two seats away from Cash. "Again, he's not my buddy."

Tanaka pressed the console, and a projection screen descended behind her. Another button brought down blinds over the windows. The dark room turned darker.

She passed across the screen, like a shadow. "McCahill, they say you're a quick study."

"I'll cop to that."

"You'd better be," she said, "because you've blundered into cartel hell, without a clue as to who or what you're dealing with. So get ready for a crash course on the drug world. Everything you need to know to have any chance of getting out of this alive. Welcome to *Los Lobos* 101."

"Will there be a test at the end of class?" A long silence warned Cash that his crack hadn't broken any ice. No surprise there. A fella could freeze a margarita next to Tanaka's heart.

He tried a different tack. "Look, though I don't represent dopers as a matter of principle, I follow the news. I don't need a lecture to know *Los Lobos* are badasses."

"It's one thing to know up here." Her forefinger tapped her temple. "Another to know where it counts." She patted her heart. "We have a three-week saturation course for new agents that barely scratches the surface."

"We don't have three weeks," Cash said.

"Understood. We also have a three-day compressed course for desk jockeys."

"I doubt we have three days."

"Last and least," she said, "there's a three-hour executive summary, but then you're not an executive."

"Can we cut the shit and get down to the business of negotiating the fine points of *La Tigra*'s future plans?" Cash feigned impatience. "I need to know whether my client should stock up on Stinger missiles or sunscreen."

"I know you can be glib," she said. "What I don't know is whether you can be serious."

He took a sober tone. "If you need me to sign some C.Y.A. form to protect the agency from liability, in case I get hurt or killed, I'll do it. Anything to escape the dreaded death by PowerPoint."

"If we're going to work together," she said, "you have to do less talking and more listening. For a change try not to act like an asshole attorney."

"Asshole attorney is redundant," Leroy said.

She smiled for the first time in Cash's presence. Maybe for the first time ever.

"The flaw in all our courses," she said, "is that to make it through any of them, you have to numb yourself to the violence. The longer the presentation, the more you have to shut down inside. In the end, that defeats the whole purpose."

"Does that mean I'm getting a pass on the coursework?" Cash said.

"Not a complete pass." She pressed the console, and a grainy image appeared on the screen. A frozen shot of a young girl on her knees, gagged and stripped to her panties. Whip marks crisscrossed her breasts, belly, and thighs. With her hands bound behind her back and her ankles lashed together, she would've fallen on her face, but for the noose running from her neck to a ceiling beam.

Another click of the console brought the torture scene to life. The girl's muffled screams and guttural sounds were piercing. Her tears proved contagious.

The action took place in a nondescript living room. The girl knelt on a plastic sheet that protected a beige carpet from her tears, sweat, and blood. A *telenovela* played on a big-screen TV behind her, the sound turned low but not off.

Tanaka froze the film and aimed the laser at the TV. "That particular episode of *La Reina del Sur* aired about six weeks ago. Helped us pin down the date Sofia got snatched on her way to school."

She hit the play button. Smack talk in Spanish gave evidence of three or four males in the room, all off-screen. Cash picked up enough of the trash talk to realize they were playing cards and high on something. The banter drowned out the *telenovela* but not the girl's stifled pleas.

Nothing would drown that out. Ever.

The camera zoomed in on the teen's tear-streaked face. Her eyes were wild with terror. Drool stringed from the corners of her mouth. Snot flowed from her flaring nostrils.

The camera slid down her quaking body from head to toe. A sheen of sweat on her skin made the whip marks stand out.

Tanaka stopped the action again. Cash prayed it was for the last time. He had seen enough to know how it would end.

"How old do you think she is?" Tanaka said.

Neither man rushed to respond. Cash took a stab. "Sixteen."

"She's fifteen," she said. "*Was* fifteen."

"Who is she?" Cash started to correct the tense but didn't.

"The daughter of the Veracruz police chief, Hector Flores. A cop's cop who couldn't be bought." She spoke softly.

"Let's hope Hector gets revenge on the animals who did this to his daughter."

"It won't be in this life," she said. "Hector witnessed this in real time. *Los Lobos* forced him to watch the rape, torture, and death of his daughter. The butchers then did the same to his wife, before killing him slowly. It took three days to erase the family, all save one."

"How do you know the video is real and not a fake snuff film? How did you get it?"

"The easy way," she said. "*Los Lobos* posted it online, as a message to law enforcement on both sides of the border."

Cash stood on shaky legs. He felt the need to say something bold, but no words came out.

"Sit down," she said. "The show's not over."

Cash lowered to the chair, still at a loss for words.

She pressed play. A beanpole moved behind the girl. He wasn't much larger than she was. Couldn't weigh more than a buck thirty. His face stayed outside the shot.

An off-screen companion handed beanpole a machete. He gripped the weapon with both hands, like a baseball bat, and took several practice swings before stepping up to the prisoner.

Her pleas hit a new pitch. She jerked and twisted, as far as the ropes allowed. It wasn't far enough.

Cash turned away from the screen and closed his eyes. Tried but failed to shut his ears to the sickening swoosh, followed by a thud.

No screams now. Just laughter and more smack talk from the players. The card game resumed.

"It's over, "Tanaka said. "You can look now."

Cash forced himself to turn back to the screen, frozen on the blood-splattered face of a grinning kid, licking the blade of a bloody machete.

The close-up of the executioner gave Cash another shock. He had conjured an image of a hardened, scar-faced thug. Not a skinny punk with acne and an Adam's apple the size of a golf ball.

"How old do you think he is?" she said.

Cash would've guessed fifteen, but his vocal cords locked down. Leroy too remained silent.

"Fourteen," she said. "His name is Julio, and he's Sofia's younger brother, Hector's only son. Meet the new face of *Los Lobos*."

CHAPTER THIRTY-FOUR

F amine or feast, Cash's world turned on a dime. As in, brother, can you spare one?

His rollercoaster career whipsawed between highs and lows, with far more dips lately. This week sank to an all-time nadir, and the prospects worsened by the hour. A single appointment kept Friday from being a lost day.

The meeting scheduled for ten would give Toby Fine and Cash a start at crafting a defense. Crafting a defense was how Cash put it. The government would call it concocting one.

Before Fine showed, three women visited Cash, not together but separately. A rule of nature dictated that trouble came in threes, like the Fates. Or the witches in *Macbeth*.

The trio of visitors sparked Cash's full gamut of emotions, from desire to despair. Like contestants in a game of fuck, marry, and kill. The women didn't necessarily come in that order. Nor necessarily out of that order.

At nine sharp, Tina Campos ambushed Cash in the lobby. She carried a cardboard tray, with coffees wedged into the four corners and a pyramid of scones in the center.

"What's the occasion?" The unscheduled visit took Cash by surprise, as did Tina's wardrobe. She favored obscenely short dresses that barely cleared her hips, even for business meetings.

Given her profession, especially for business meetings.

Today, however, she wore a conservative black dress that brushed her knees. Her heels were high but not to fuck-me extremes. A light touch on the makeup shaved years from her face.

"Can't I bring breakfast to my favorite lawyer?" she said.

"You mean your only lawyer. Don't tell me you got busted again." His tone suggested that was exactly what he expected to hear.

"Thanks for the vote of confidence, counselor." She sounded hurt, but then she was an actor, of sorts. "This time I'm here to bail you out, and I came bearing gifts." She handed the tray to him. "From the look of you, I arrived in the nick of time. You're losing weight."

Good eye. Lately he hadn't been eating all that well, and the same went for sleeping. He was below one-sixty and still dropping. Living in the crosshairs of one, maybe two cartels plus one, maybe two governments had that effect on him.

He placed the tray on a table and took a scone and a latte. "I'll be sure to deduct this from your legal bill." He immediately regretted bringing up her debt, but in his defense, handling the Fine case *pro bono* had wrecked the bottom line.

No payments for the month but lots of expenses had left his accounts drier than Dallas in August. Tough to fend off one, maybe two cartels plus one, maybe two governments on maxed out credit cards.

Tina followed him into his private office and sat. "About my outstanding bill, I have a proposal for you."

He flashed a not again look. Not that he wasn't tempted. While he kept an active roster of prostitutes as clients, he was client to none. That was one line he hadn't crossed, not know-ingly anyway.

She countered with an eye roll. "Get your dirty little mind out of the gutter." She looked around the room. Her frown signaled that it had failed inspection. "Without Eva to run things, you're floundering."

"I wouldn't say floundering." Granted, it was true. He just wouldn't *say* it.

"How about I work off my debt by being your new girl Friday?"

He was at a loss for words and not simply because he had never considered the possibility that Tina would give up the streets for an office job. Even more jarring, he had never faced the hard reality that Eva might be gone for good.

Much as he needed help, he hadn't steeled himself to hire Eva's replacement. That would make the separation feel more like a divorce.

Or a death.

"No one will ever take Eva's place," she said. "I realize that. But I can type, handle calls, juggle your calendar, and try to keep the business afloat until she comes back."

"I can't ask you to do that."

"You didn't ask," she said. "I volunteered."

He stalled by scarfing down a scone and chasing it with a latte. His mind erected a hundred hurdles, starting and ending with the most obvious. "If you knew how cash-strapped I was."

"That's the beauty of hiring me," she said. "My debt will take an eternity to work off."

He gave in, unsure whether he'd been convinced by her logic, worn down by her doggedness, doomed by his despera-tion, or all of the above. "I won't let you work for free. I'll pay you what I can, and you reduce the debt as you're able. So when can you start?"

She snapped off a crisp salute. "Private First Class Tina Campos, reporting for duty, sir."

Minutes later, she buzzed Cash to announce the second surprise visitor of the morning, Paula Marshall. Though pressed for time, he took the meeting, because he had a score to settle with her. Saddling Martin Biddle with a snake like Rhoden was inexplicable and unforgivable, and he had to know her motive for doing so.

Tina ushered Paula into the office and left her alone with Cash. Slumped in a chair, she looked haggard, as if the tens of thousands of billable hours had finally taken a toll. She wore jeans, a t-shirt, flip-flops, and no makeup.

It was as if Paula and Tina had swapped wardrobes. Another touch of weirdness in a day off to a strange start.

"Are you okay?" he said.

No response from her, other than a shrug.

"Is something wrong?"

Silence. This must be serious. He'd never known Paula to be short on smack talk.

"Is Eva all right?"

"She's gone, and I can't find her." The floodgates opened, and she broke down.

Cash's mind reeled. If Eva was missing, he had a prime suspect in mind and a new number one priority.

Paula pulled herself together, more or less. "I've been trying to get hold of her for two days. She hasn't returned my calls or texts." Her voice was raw, as if she'd had a rough night. Probably a string of them.

No mystery now why she had come. In the wake of Eva's disappearance, the iron lady of the law had shattered like glass.

Cash didn't confront Paula about Biddle. Not the time for it. Not while Eva was AWOL.

"I'm sure she's fine. Probably off licking her wounds from your latest lovers' spat." His voice, more confident than his gut. "At the courthouse, you said Eva was on the verge of leaving your firm. I take it she did."

"When I told you that, I didn't realize she'd also leave me." She broke down again.

Though Cash had a client on the way, he let her cry in peace. Get it out of her system, for now.

"I thought she might come here." More waterworks drowned out her next words. "Or at least reach out to you."

"I wish," he said.

"We have to find her."

Wow. Had to be hard for Paula to draft him for the hunt. He weighed how much of the truth he could afford to share with her. Not much, he decided. "I'm on it. Now go back to your place and wait. Odds are she'll come back to you soon."

"If she doesn't," Paula said, "I'm counting on you to find her." She rose shakily. "You and I have never been close. We're not even friends really, but here's some free advice. The no-friends-and-no-family plan is a shitty way to go through life."

She had him there.

No sooner had Paula left than Regina Delgado strode into the office and looked around, acting like she owned the place. Given the federal forfeiture statutes, that outcome wasn't farfetched.

She came dressed for war, peace, and everything in between. Royal blue suit, cream-colored blouse, blood red scarf, and black heels. She had gone heavy on the makeup. Maroon lipstick. Eyebrows freshly plucked. Bold blush. She looked more like an actor playing a lawyer than the real thing.

Cash didn't delude himself into thinking her extra touches were for his benefit. Dollars to donuts, she had a date with the TV cameras later.

He made a point of greeting her as Gina. "To what do I owe the honor of a rare visit by a high-ranking DOJ official? You feds usually makes me schlep to your office, under the mistaken belief it gives you a tactical advantage."

Her smile looked forced. "I can glean a lot from a lawyer's office." She looked around again. "For example, yours screams S-O-S."

"And here I was going for V-I-P."

She laughed. "Only if that stands for Vain and Insane Prick."

"Can I get that on tape?" he said. "I might need an insanity defense someday."

"Maybe sooner than you think." She helped herself to a scone and sat. "Last week the Attorney General threw lifelines to *La Tigra*, Fine, and last and definitely least, you. Why haven't we heard back?"

"I need more time. Fact is, I'm meeting with Fine this morning. He should arrive any minute now, and I'd rather he not see you here. Might give him the wrong idea about our relationship."

She took a bite of the scone and put it down. That counted as breakfast in her book. "Fine is a tick on the tail of the dog.

You need to sell the deal to *La Tigra*, not waste time on the help."

"Fine's the one facing trial this month," Cash said.

"Whose fault is that?" She rose. "Don't sweat the small stuff. I can get an extension for Fine, but *La Tigra* is already living on borrowed time."

"What's that supposed to mean?"

"Judge Ferguson will grant a continuance on Fine's trial date." She sounded confident. "But if you don't deliver *La Tigra* to us by next Friday, it's officially hunting season south of the border, and she's the fox."

Delgado took a latte on the way out, leaving Cash to stew over his next play.

Suddenly Fuck, Marry, Kill wasn't the only game in town.

Three women had darkened his door this morning, but two who hadn't occupied his mind: Eva and *La Tigra*. Tough to save a damsel in distress from one, maybe two cartels, plus one, maybe two governments.

Much less, save two damsels.

CHAPTER THIRTY-FIVE

"I had absolutely no idea that anyone under the age of eighteen advertised on my website." Fine's defiant tone dared Cash to challenge him.

Dare accepted. "Stop bullshitting."

"But I'm not—"

Cash cut him off before he could air another whopper. "You're not very good at lying. Don't feel too bad about that. Most people aren't, which is why even half-assed prosecutors rack up a ninety-five percent conviction rate. It's not like they're going up against a de Niro or a Streep on the stand."

"You don't sound sold on my innocence," Fine said, "much less committed to defending me."

"Like it or not, I'm all in, which is why I have to assess what kind of witness you'd make. The jurors will damn sure want to hear from you. If you don't testify, the judge will tell them not to hold it against you, but no juror in the history of jurisprudence has ever followed that instruction."

"I want to testify," Fine said.

"No, you don't. If I were fool enough to put you on the stand, Delgado would destroy you."

The client opened his mouth, but no words spilled out.

"Even if you were better at the fine art of lying," Cash said, "today's not the time or place for it. This office is your safe space to come clean. Lie to everyone else on the planet. Your parents, spouse, kids, a girlfriend or boyfriend. Just not to your lawyer. Deal?"

Fine nodded.

Not that Cash expected to hear the truth any time soon. That wasn't how most clients rolled. The skinny rarely surfaced on the first round. Nor the second. Some defendants never shot straight, but the vast majority suffered through several brass-knuckle sessions before Cash hammered out a semblance of reality.

"So can we drop the B.S. that you didn't know there were underage kids on the site?" Cash said.

Fine's temples pulsed. "It's not like I had a choice in the matter. Once the cartel sunk its hooks into me, I couldn't say no. You of all people should get that."

Cash did. Fine had inched a little closer to the truth, but not all the way there. With the time of reckoning at hand, Cash hit on a shortcut to the endgame. He buzzed Tina to join them in the office and made the introductions short.

"Tina, meet Fine. My client on this month's trial docket and the owner of the *Backdoor*. Fine, meet Tina, my new girl Friday by day and an escort by night. Twenty-five now, she's been on your website for half her life."

Cash let the intros sink in. "She'd be a great leadoff witness at your trial." He paused before delivering the punch line. "For the government."

Fine and Tina jumped to their feet. He spoke first. "If she's on their side, I want her out of here."

Tina matched his decibel level and outrage. "Hey, I'm not cool with helping the law."

Cash motioned for them to settle down. "I'm talking hypothetically here. It's not this Tina I'm worried about. It's all the other Tinas on your website who are ready, willing, and able to assist the feds in putting you away."

Fine sat. "Why would they do that?"

"A couple of reasons come to mind," Cash said. "For starters, people in Tina's line of work get their asses in a crack all the time. The surest way to slip out of a legal jam is to offer the man a bigger fish."

Tina turned to Fine and said, "Don't look at me. I'm clean."

"More or less," Cash said under his breath but loud enough for both to hear.

She shot him a cross look.

"If someone testifies against me to save her ass," Fine said, "your job is to rip her a new one."

"Then there's always revenge as a motive to join team fed," Cash said. "Fine, you're a perv who preys on kids and profits from their pain and suffering, sometimes even their deaths. Why wouldn't your victims or their friends and families want to draw blood?"

Fine shook his head. "I run a legitimate business."

"You're a cog in a sex trafficking ring," Cash said.

Tina cleared her throat, loud enough to take the floor. "You're both right and both wrong."

"Meaning?" Cash said.

"It's more complicated than that." Her brow furrowed. "The *Backdoor* is called a site for a reason. It's a place, like a bar or a street corner or the backseat of a car, with a good side and a bad side."

"Let's hear the bad first," Cash said.

"My pimp put me on the site when I was thirteen, and I've been on it since."

"And the good?" Fine said.

"When I aged out of my teens, Rocky dropped me. He likes his stable young and fresh."

"After your pimp split, why on earth would you remain on the website?" It came off harsher than Cash intended.

"That's the good part," she said. "Once I was on my own, I could've met potential clients in a bar, on a street corner, or in the backseat of a car. Instead, we hook up online, and I vet them before agreeing to a face-to-face. That's how I stay alive. Same goes for most of the girls."

The germ of an idea sprouted in Cash's imagination. From that seed, a full-blown defense could blossom.

Not how he'd expected the encounter between Tina and Fine to go, but he'd take it. A 9-1-1 text from a familiar number buzzed his cell phone.

Cash rose from behind the desk. "Sorry, but I've got an emergency." He rushed from the office and onto the elevator. Pressed the button for the ground floor.

As the elevator door was closing, a thin arm shot through the gap and tripped the sensors. The door reopened. A Latino in a leather jacket with "13" tattooed on his neck stepped into the compartment. The kid had a bad case of acne and couldn't have been older than fifteen.

Cash flashed back to the meeting at EPIC and the video of the beheading of the police chief's daughter. Not that the image of the young victim and her even younger executioner ever left his scarred psyche.

The teen reached into his jacket. Cash cocked his arm, gambling that an elbow to the face followed by a knee to the groin would give him a shot at surviving the ride down.

The kid pulled a cell phone from his pocket. Cash lowered his arms and started breathing again. Took a little longer for his heart rate to steady.

At the ground floor, the teen went one way. Cash, the other.

Outside the building, he heard a humming and looked up. A small drone hovered overhead. He recalled the old line that just because a person is paranoid doesn't mean the world's not out to get him.

He took off at a brisk pace, making right turns at four street corners, thereby circling the block. The round trip confirmed his suspicion about the drone.

It was tailing him.

What he didn't know was whether he was being tracked by the government or a cartel.

And if by a government, which one?

If by a cartel, the same question.

CHAPTER THIRTY-SIX

The messages arrived a minute apart. Tanaka's first, then Maggie's. Both texts screamed 9-1-1, demanded an ASAP meeting, and rocked Cash's world.

He hadn't heard from Tanaka since the showing of the snuff scene at EPIC. Nor from Maggie, since her banishment to Bismarck.

Putting business before pleasure, he replied to Tanaka first. A bidding war between agencies offered the only shot at landing a deal *La Tigra* would take.

Tanaka and Cash agreed to meet at La Calle Doce at 3:00 p.m., nonpeak time for the popular East Dallas restaurant. She brought along DEA dinosaur Duane Leroy Lee, making it a threesome, but not the fun kind.

Leroy reported for duty wobbly and worthy of the unofficial title of World's Worst Chaperone. The burnout must've started his happy hour around 10:00 a.m.

Jesse, the owner, greeted Leroy with an *abrazo* and offered a round of margaritas on the house. Tanaka vetoed the drinks. "Three iced teas," she said, "and make sure I get the bill." Her tone brooked no debate.

Jesse didn't try to hide his surprise at a fed turning down a free drink. Nor his greater surprise that Leroy settled for tea.

Cash silently awarded another title, this one to Tanaka: World's Tightest Ass.

Though they had the restaurant to themselves, Tanaka made a beeline to the most secluded table and got down to business. "The Mexican government gave *Los Lobos* the green light to make a move on *La Tigra*. Your client has forty-eight hours, seventy-two max, before she's a former client."

Cash took stock of his strengths and weaknesses. His strong suit: reading juries. His Achilles' heel: cutting deals. While plea bargains might be the best course for 90 percent of defendants, they sucked for a stand-up lawyer who came alive in the courtroom.

It wasn't so much that Cash was bad at bargaining. More that he hated the game. In his book, drawing down on an opponent beat dealing, no matter how badly he was outnumbered and outgunned.

Eva had always handled the back and forth of negotiations. As a seasoned paralegal, she could do damn near everything a lawyer could. Everything, that is, except speak in court.

On his own now, Cash stuck to a few simple rules from Plea Bargaining 101. The first and most important being, maneuver the other side into putting the opening offer on the table.

"I get that the clock's ticking," he said, "but what does the DEA propose to do about it?"

"Stop a bloodbath for starters. If the only way to do that is to save *La Tigra* from *Los Lobos*," she said, "we can do that. We can also save her from the FBI. *Los Lobos* will bury her alive in the desert. The Bureau plans to stick her in Supermax. Either way she'll never see the sun again."

"You still haven't told me what your agency has in store for her."

"We'll send her to a prison camp in Alderson, West Virginia, where she'll have her own wing. If some sweet, young inmate happens to catch her eye, she can keep a pet."

"You know what they say about putting lipstick on a pig," he said. "Well, the same goes for prison. You can slap a fresh coat of paint on the walls, but it's still a prison."

Tanaka fished from her purse two packets of sweetener for her iced tea. It surprised Cash that the control freak hadn't brought her own tea bags.

"Don't sell Alderson short," she said. "It got the *Good Housekeeping* seal of approval from no less of an authority than Martha Stewart, who did her time there."

As prisons went, Cash probably couldn't do better than Alderson, but his client wouldn't do backflips over life at club fed. "What happened to your master plan to keep *La Tigra* in the game, as a check on *Los Lobos*?"

Tanaka's eyes narrowed. Her lips pursed. He'd hit a nerve.

"That was Plan A," she said. "Now we're onto Plan B."

Plan A must've been Tanaka's brainchild, but she couldn't sell it to the brass. No wonder. Too much could go wrong and wind up on the front page of the *New York Times*. If the DEA got caught propping up a cartel leader with buckets of blood on her hands, that'd make the "Fast and Furious" gunwalking scandal look like a botched buy-bust of a dime bag.

"Let's revisit A," he said. "*La Tigra* may not be a Girl Scout, but *Los Lobos* are animals."

"We hit too much headwind trying to keep your client afloat. The powers that be turned thumbs down." Tanaka's eyes signaled she had more to say.

Cash gave her the chance. "On which side of the border?"

"Both."

Leroy shook off his stupor. "Which is why it's always better to ask for forgiveness after the fact than seek permission in advance."

Which explains, my friend, why Tanaka's on the fast track, while you're spinning your wheels on the streets.

Cash raised another hurdle. "And the daughter, what happens to her when *La Tigra's* locked away for life?"

Tanaka was slow to answer. When she did, it landed with the thud of a deal-breaker.

*　*　*

Cash left La Calle Doce with the Alderson card in his pocket. Not what he'd been fishing for but not bad as DEA's opening bid, at least the *La Tigra* part.

However, Tanaka's proposal to dump Marisol, the daughter, into the purgatory called witness protection was DOA. WITSEC meant no future contact of any kind between parent and child. No one had bounced the deal off Marisol, and the mother would never go for it.

Nor would Cash try to sell it. He couldn't, not with his backstory.

Business before pleasure turned into business before more business. Not that meeting number two started that way.

At Klyde Warren Park on the cusp of downtown Dallas, Maggie rushed to Cash and locked lips. The kiss caught him off guard, less for its ferocity than for its public nature. PDA was new to her playbook.

Ribbons of intersecting highways not only embraced but also cradled the oasis of green, which rested on an overpass. Scores of kids, parents, and nannies packed the playground on sunny days like today, and a United Nations of food trucks ringed the block.

Maggie wore shorts, sandals, and a sleeveless shirt that bared her waist. J. Edgar was spinning in his grave.

They sat on a bench near the ping pong tables. She took his hand and squeezed.

"Tell me you're back for good," he said.

"Working on it."

"Work faster." He tried to make it sound less desperate than it came off. "How long can you stay?"

She was slow to answer. "That's up in the air. I came back to tie up loose ends."

"Like a proper goodbye to your man."

She squeezed harder. "I hope it's not goodbye."

An errant shot sailed toward them. He pulled his hand free, caught the ping pong ball in midair, and tossed it back. The break loosened his tongue. "The ball's in your court. I can tell that you want to say something. Now is not the time to hold back."

She looked away. "How's the Fine case coming?"

Her attempt to pass off the question as idle chatter backfired. Cash's senses sharpened, as did his tone. "Who wants to know?"

"Who doesn't?" She was a good actor, but not that good. Not when reciting lines fed to her.

"Were you brought back to pump me about Fine?"

The question hung in the air for an eternity. She shook her head. "I'm here to find out what *La Tigra* will do. Specifically, if she'll take the deal we offered. It's her only chance to stay alive."

Cash sighed. Another scripted line that needed work.

"And if you can sell me on selling her?" he said.

"I return to Dallas."

And to me.

"And to you." As if she had read his mind.

"If you can't close the deal...."

"It's back to Bismarck," she said.

While he wondered how far she would go to end her exile, a small drone darted among the kites and Frisbees in the crowded sky. It swooped down and hovered over them.

In the struggle for Maggie's soul, the score now stood: Bureau two, Cash zero.

CHAPTER THIRTY-SEVEN

Uh-oh. *This can't be good.*

Federal Judge Anna Tapia had summoned Cash. His last trip to her chambers had ended with a night in lockup for contempt of court. Not that he looked forward to another visit to the Graybar Hotel, but after two years in a federal prison, he could do twenty-four hours in jail standing on his head.

"Thank you for coming, Cash." She sounded semi-sincere and looked almost happy to see him. Up close and without the black robe, she seemed smaller, more fragile. The lines flaring from the corners of her eyes ran longer and deeper.

His threat alarm spiked. Not only had she called him by his first name, but she had also thanked him. Could the apocalypse be far behind?

The western motif of her chambers reinforced her well-earned nickname: *The Hanging Judge.* A stuffed palomino stood guard by the door. A framed display of cattle brands staked claim to the northern wall. Her black Stetson hung on the top rung of a wooden hat rack, with a coiled rope a peg below.

"Do you know why I asked you to come?" she said.

Funny, it hadn't felt like a request. Never did when coming from a judge with lifetime tenure and the U.S. Marshal under her thumb.

"Let me guess," he said. "To express how much you've missed having me in your courtroom, while I was away in Seagoville."

Laughter shook her to the brink of tears. "Never lose that sense of humor." She paused to catch her breath. "I sent for you because...." Another pause, longer than the first. "Well, it's about Mister Goldberg."

When she fell silent again, Cash filled the void. "He and I are no longer partners."

"That's the problem," she said.

"For whom?"

"Most immediately, Fred Foster."

"Who's he?" Took Cash a few seconds to place the name. He would've snapped immediately if she'd spotted him the alias *Freddy the Forger*.

"He's a defendant going to trial in my court next month," she said, "with Mister Goldberg as his counsel."

"Is Goldy flying solo?"

The judge nodded.

"I see how that could be a problem," Cash said, "but fortunately, not mine."

Tapia fiddled with the pen on her desk. Never before had Cash seen her struggle for words. Forced him to consider the possibility she might be human after all.

"It's definitely an issue for me," she said, "because I have to assure that Foster receives effective representation at trial. Over the past several weeks, Mister Goldberg has been in my court for various hearings, and it hasn't gone well. While I should take him off the case, I fear that would kill him."

Cash couldn't contest that.

She went on. "Did you know that I lost my husband to Parkinson's three years ago?"

Cash's spine stiffened. Tapia was sharing something personal and painful, with him of all people. He nodded. Her husband's descent into dementia had spurred the creation of a charitable foundation that bore his name.

"I watched him slip away, and it broke my heart." She paused until Cash looked at her eyes, welling with tears.

"I see the same symptoms in Mister Goldberg," she said.

Damn. Cash had spent years trying to deny those symptoms. She had shaken his belief that Goldy would live forever, or at least outlive him.

"Simple fix," Cash said. "Appoint someone to assist Goldy. The new lawyer will technically sit second chair but actually take the lead at trial. That way Freddy the...." He caught himself before blurting out the defendant's nickname. "Foster is covered, and Goldy saves face. Problem solved."

"So glad we're on the same page." She took the pen in hand, signed an order, and passed it to him. "Congratulations on your appointment as backup counsel for Foster. You and Mister Goldberg will be a dream team for the defendant and a nightmare for everyone else, including me."

Cash bolted to his feet. "You can't be...." He sat just as abruptly.

He was tempted to spill everything. Go into all the gory details of why it would be dangerous to pair him with Goldy, or with anyone. He was radioactive. But he couldn't think of a way to come clean without dragging Fine through the dirt.

Since resorting to the whole truth was not an option, he settled for a half-truth. "With all due respect, Your Honor, this is a really bad idea. Goldy and I didn't part on the best of terms."

"Never too late for you to apologize."

"Me? Why should I be the one to apologize?"

"When my husband got Parkinson's, it was hard on the whole family. We had to make allowances for him and adjust our lives around his condition. Thank God, I never bailed on him. Couldn't live with myself if I had."

Hard to push back when she got personal, but Cash did his damnedest. "Are you trying to guilt me into going along with this charade?"

She smiled.

"Well, you did a damn good job of it."

"Watch your language in my chambers, Mister McCahill, or I'll be forced to send you to lockup, again."

Eyes dry. Temporary truce over.

* * *

At Goldy's downtown apartment, Eva answered the door. "What are you doing here?"

"Happy to see you too." Cash tossed off the words, as if it was a throwaway line. Truth be told, he was ecstatic to see her. "I came to check on Goldy. And on you."

"We're fine." She didn't sound fine and tried to close the door.

He blocked it with his foot and barged in. Eva was dressed for flight, not fight. She wore sneakers, running shorts, and a sleeveless shirt. Hair in a ponytail. No jewelry to weigh her down.

Because Goldy had a history of losing houses in divorces, his residence at the complex meant he was between mansions and between marriages. He referred to his exes by the order of their appearance in and exit from his life, from G-1 to G-5.

Shambolic: the perfect one-word description of the apartment. Papers, law books, and empty pizza boxes littered the floor. Taped to a wall were two large poster boards of lists: witnesses on the left, exhibits on the right. The odor of burnt popcorn and stale pizza fouled the air.

"Maid's month off?" Cash said.

"We're prepping for trial," she said, "so we don't have time to visit today."

"That's why I'm here. Judge Tapia in her infinite wisdom appointed me to assist you on the case."

"We don't need help," she said, "certainly not from you."

"That's the beauty of being a federal judge. Tapia doesn't have to consult you or me before issuing a decree that throws us together."

She grabbed Cash by the arm and squeezed. "I'm not going to let you hurt him, not any more than you already have."

Her words stung. Her grip, not so much. "Is it so hard for you to believe that I might be here to patch things up?"

"Are you?"

"I figure it's time to get the band together again."

Goldy emerged from the kitchen, beer in one hand, a limp slice of pepperoni pizza in the other. He wore a baggy warmup suit that failed to flatter his lumpy frame. It took a lifetime for him to cross the living room and confront Cash. "What are you doing here?"

"Business is slow at my shop." Not far from the truth. "I came with an offer to sit second chair at the Foster trial." A little farther from it.

Goldy harrumphed. "Figured you'd come crawling back on your belly." He took a bite of pizza, washed it down with beer, and belched. "I guess you can carry my briefcase to and from court."

As the old man limped from the room, he said to Eva, "Put him to work on the jury instructions, but keep an eye on him."

A text pinged Cash's phone. The message gave him twenty-five minutes to get to Love Field. It didn't spell out what would happen if he missed the flight.

Didn't have to.

Cash held off speaking until he trusted his voice not to break. "I'll work on the instructions on the plane."

"Where are you going?" Concern crept into Eva's voice.

"TBD."

"How long will you be gone?"

"Also TBD," he said on the move. At the door he turned back to Eva. "Give Paula a call. She's worried about you."

He left before she could hit him with more questions he couldn't answer. Everything was up in the air. Not only the destination, but also whether the trip would be one-way or round.

CHAPTER THIRTY-EIGHT

Cash made it to Love Field with a minute to spare and boarded the private jet. The Airbus 319 sported a black-and-gold color scheme outside and in, down to the gold-plated seatbelt buckles.

A tricked-out plane fit for a Bond villain or a Saints fan. Hard to tell which was more deranged.

Half of the sixteen black leather seats were empty. Cash recognized none of the passengers, save one.

Cash stopped in the aisle. He had half a mind to wheel around and run like hell for the exit. Instead, he stared at Shorty, the mini-muscle who had met him at the Culiacan Airport for his first face-to-face with *La Tigra*. Cash based the positive I.D. partly on stature—five-five give or take an inch—but mostly on the LeBron jersey.

On the ride to *La Tigra's* compound in the past, Shorty had talked nonstop. Today he didn't have that option. Gagged and strapped to the seat, he blinked out a signal of some sort. A silent message that meant either pull me from this mess or put me out of my misery.

Cash reached the obvious conclusion. *La Tigra* had caught Shorty defecting to *Los Lobos*. According to widespread media reports, she was bleeding support in the countryside and losing her few remaining friends in power.

Not that she ever had an actual friend in government. Public officials were for rent, not sale. On both sides of the border.

If Shorty had been busted switching sides, his fate would serve as a lesson to the rest of *La Tigra's* troops. And to Cash as well.

A flight attendant led Cash to his seat and offered him a drink. He ordered a scotch and soda and made it a double. As the jet took off, a sinking feeling swept over him. He took a long, last look at Dallas.

He had left too much unsaid and undone. His strategy of sparking a bidding war between the agencies for *La Tigra's* snitch services had barely gotten off the ground. The best bad deal on the table was a ticket to a prison camp in West Virginia and the permanent loss of her daughter.

Even that outcome, however, might prove as flimsy as a cloud. Nothing would prevent the feds from checking her into Alderson one day and transferring her to a hellhole the next. Once she went inside, the Bureau of Prisons—BOP for short—owned her body and soul. Not the FBI or DEA. Certainly not the judge.

The current offers wouldn't tempt *La Tigra*, and cartel leaders weren't noted for taking bad news well. Best Cash could hope for would be relaying the bids without losing his head.

He studied his fellow passengers. Two gangbangers wore Beats headphones, lip-syncing the lyrics leeching into their brains. Two others were snorting lines on tray tables.

The lot displayed an array of scars and tatts, including tell-tale teardrops on their temples. Every teardrop told a story. A hit earned the badge of dishonor and an entry-level job in the cartel.

The brute in the last row must've inked a notch for every kill. Tatt Face had a mug awash in rainbow-colored tears. No doubt merely a drop in the ocean of real ones shed by his victims and their families.

Cash faced a wall of stone faces. Not a jury he would've chosen to render a life-or-death verdict. Way too many "M"s for his taste: male, macho, and middle-aged.

Well, middle age in the cartel world, which meant early twenties. Took a miracle for a drug soldier to reach the ripe, old age of thirty.

His sights set on seeing fifty, Cash launched into his defense. Oh, and Shorty's as well. "Where are we going?"

"We are not all going to the same place," Tatt Face said.

"Let me rephrase my question. Where are you going?"

"Veracruz."

"And me?"

Tatt Face smiled, flashing a mouthful of gold teeth. "Remains to be seen."

Cash could take *remains to be seen* two ways. One bad, the other worse. Might indicate that his destination was up in the air. Alternatively, it could mean that regardless of his fate, at least the authorities would find his remains.

In one piece or many.

Shorty jacked his sobbing to a migraine-inducing level, reminding Cash there was another life on the line.

"And him." Cash pointed to Shorty. "Where's he going?"

"For a swim."

Three goons with switchblades pounced on Shorty. They slashed the tape binding him to the seat, sticking him a few times for good measure. Their stabbing was surgical in its precision. The superficial cuts missed major bleeders.

Shorty fought like crazy, but the trio beat and kicked him senseless. Screams muffled through the gag gave way to pleas, all the more piteous for being unintelligible.

They dragged Shorty to a backroom and closed the door behind them. The plane dived toward the water before leveling off low enough to see the white caps of the waves below.

The plane turned as silent as a tomb. Cash assumed the traitor had bled out until a racket in the back erupted. Shorty's screams became full-throated and frantic. The door failed to filter any of the fear from his voice.

A roar like a tornado from the backroom drowned out the screams. The plane shuddered.

"Look out the window," Tatt Face said.

The jet banked hard right. Cash caught sight of Shorty, as he was flushed from the bowels of the beast. He tracked Shorty to splash down in the Gulf of Mexico.

That's what Cash thought he saw, anyway. It happened so fast that he couldn't swear to what had been tossed out like trash. For all he knew, it could've been waste from the shitter. Except the roar had died, along with the screaming and begging, lending weight to his first instinct.

Shorty now slept with the fishes. Remains, not to be seen.

The LeBron jersey also supported the leading theory on Shorty's fate. When the takeout team returned from the backroom, the last in line tossed the blood-soaked jersey to Cash. Like passing a baton. A silent way to say, "You're next, sucker."

Cash held up the jersey. "It won't fit."

"No matter," Tatt Face said.

"You guys had better hope that *La Tigra* doesn't have second thoughts about what you just did to her lieutenant," Cash said.

Tatt Face did a double take. "*La Tigra*! Who gives a flying fuck what that *puta* thinks? *Somos Los Lobos.*"

* * *

Cash never made it to Veracruz.

Two hours out of Dallas, the plane dipped under the cloud cover. Cash stared out the window. Nothing but water below.

Two toughs grabbed him by the arms and yanked him to his feet. They dragged him toward the back, for Cash's turn on the diving board.

He wouldn't go down without a fight. He elbowed one thug in the face, managed to kick the other in the groin. A reinforcement with a baseball bat took a full swing and connected with Cash's gut.

He fell to his knees, puked pure scotch, and fought for breath. The slugger dragged Cash by the hair and dumped him in the seat next to Tatt Face.

Tatt Face handed him a sat phone. "You have a call."

Cash held the phone to his ear. He picked up the sound of steady breathing and recognized the jazz classic in the background. Dave Brubeck's "Take Five."

Excellent advice, which Cash had given to countless clients. "Who is this?" Cash wheezed.

The music died. "The dude who will decide where you get off." The tone marked the speaker as an alpha, accustomed to giving orders. "And how."

A new instrumental played in the background, this one also familiar to Cash. "The Beautiful Maria of My Soul."

"Give the phone back to Carlos."

Cash handed the phone to Tatt Face, who listened for a few seconds before placing it on a tray table and pressing the speaker button. "Carlos, tell Mister McCahill his options."

"You have only two." Carlos sounded matter of fact, almost bored. "You tell us where *La Tigra* is, and we let you walk off the plane in Veracruz and catch the next flight back to the States."

Cash didn't need to hear the second scenario to know what it was.

Carlos continued anyway. "Or you do not tell us where she is, and you join Shorty for a swim with the sharks."

Cash took no pleasure in having guessed what was behind door number two. "What if I don't know where *La Tigra* is?"

Tatt Face snickered. "That is what Shorty said and the option he took."

"It's not really optional," Cash said, "if I don't know."

"If that is the case," Alpha said, "we have no reason to keep you alive."

Cash couldn't argue with the logic and figured he had about thirty seconds to come up with a counter, or at least a stall. That's how long it would take to drag him to the rear and load him into the chute.

Money was off the table. How do you bribe a cartel that burns more in an hour than he'd earn in a lifetime?

So Cash went with a pitch that had clicked before. "If you take over *La Tigra*'s territory—"

Alpha cut him off. "*When* we take over her territory."

Copy that.

"When you do, you'll need a good lawyer in Texas. You're talking to the best. What say I give you a friends-and-family

226

discount on my fees to handle your legal problems north of the border?"

"To save your skin a year ago," Alpha said, "you promised *La Tigra* that you would work for free."

Cash sighed. The bottom line was about to take another hit. Then again, better to drown in debt than in the Gulf of Mexico. "Okay, you can have the same sweetheart deal."

The longest silence of Cash's life robbed years from it.

"I don't think so," Alpha said. "Your services did not work out so well for *La Tigra*."

A shorter silence this time, but it still shaved what little remained of Cash's life. "Mister McCahill, enjoy your swim."

The toughs grabbed Cash by the arms and legs and dragged him toward the back. For every wild punch or kick by Cash, the thugs landed three or four. Cash's blows became feebler. He flirted with a blackout.

They pulled him into the backroom. Though his limbs were limp, his mouth still worked. As the door was closing, he shouted, "You haven't heard my best and final offer."

CHAPTER THIRTY-NINE

The thugs tossed Cash from the jet.

Fortunately, he fell only ten feet onto a private landing strip, where the Airbus had made a pit stop. His wrists and knees absorbed the brunt of the fall. He kissed the baked, brown earth.

It didn't kiss back.

He rolled onto his back and choked on the dust kicked up by the departure of the plane. The sun wrung tears from his eyes. Or that's how he explained the burst of waterworks to himself.

Threatened with a watery grave on the flight, he had kept his cool, more or less. In the solitude of a barren stretch of desert, he could let go, and he did. Took only a couple of minutes to flush the tears from his system and scream himself hoarse.

He struggled to his feet. *Los Lobos* had kept his watch, cell phone, and wallet, leaving him a passport, less than a hundred dollars in cash, a Topo Chico, and no clue of his location.

Well, one clue. He was smack dab in the middle of nowhere and for damn sure closer to hell than heaven. Doomed to wander across a wasteland that might prove to be the boondocks of west Texas or northern Mexico, as if there was a difference.

Given the flight plan and his time in the air, he bet on the latter.

He walked an hour or so along a dirt road, failing to flag down the first three vehicles to pass by. All three had Mexico license plates, confirming his belief of being south of the border.

As dusk descended, an old man in a pickup pulled alongside Cash and stopped. The deep creases in the driver's face almost swallowed his eyes. His leathery skin blended into the landscape. While he looked to be in his seventies, Cash subtracted a decade, based on the toll of a hardscrabble life.

"*Dónde estamos?*" Cash said.

"Coahuila." Phlegm crackled the old man's voice.

"*A dónde vas?*"

"Monterrey."

"*Puedo ir contigo?*"

The driver nodded toward the pickup bed, a silent invitation to join the other passengers. Cash thanked the driver and climbed aboard, sharing the space with a tied goat and two caged chickens. Given a choice of travel companions, he'd pick critters over cartel killers every time.

Cash hopped off in the first city of any size, Saltillo, and boarded a bus for a ten-hour trip to Dallas. Buying a one-way ticket, bottled water, and a day-old cheese sandwich left him with $3.67.

* * *

Dead tired, he made Dallas at 10:00 a.m. and went straight to the office. He expected to find it dark but walked into a hive of activity. Tina was marking trial exhibits at the reception desk.

Wearing a tank top that showcased her latest pair of enhancements, she barely glanced at him before returning to her task.

"You look like shit," she said.

He couldn't argue with that. Much as he needed a shave, shower, and sleep, he didn't have the luxury, not given the looming deadlines imposed by courts and cartels.

"You look...uh...different," Cash said.

"While you were gone and I was holding down the court, I squeezed in a visit to Doctor Katz." She arched her back, accentuating the new bust. "Like them?"

"They'll do in a pinch."

"Please do," she said. "I could use a good harassment lawsuit to pad my bank account."

"Get in line."

She stroked her chin. "Maybe I should make it a class action." She stopped stroking. "Where the hell have you been?"

He ignored the question and asked his own. "What are you doing here?"

"You hired me to temp until I worked off my legal bills."

Not exactly how Cash remembered it. While she had certainly made the offer, he didn't recall accepting.

Eva emerged from an office. Dressed for the down and dirty of trial prep in a Texas Rangers jersey, cutoff jeans, and sneakers. A look of relief gave way to a cold glare. She dumped a stack of documents on the reception desk. The next batch of exhibits for marking.

Goldy approached from another office. He shuffled like a zombie on a bad day. If not at death's door, he was certainly on the porch.

Both acted as if they belonged here, with Cash being the odd man out.

This just keeps getting better and better.

"You don't smell so great either," Eva said.

Cash turned to Tina. "What are *they* doing here?"

"I invited them to set up shop." No trace of an apology. "They're our co-counsel in a case set for trial in two weeks, and they were working out of Goldy's apartment. Not an ideal arrangement."

Cash raised his voice. "And this is?"

"You didn't answer Tina's question," Eva said. "Where have you been?" She sounded more concerned than curious.

"To hell and back," Cash said.

"You should feel right at home there," Goldy said, "along with all your friends."

"The three of you certainly have made yourselves at home, but it's time to pack up and return to the hole you climbed out of."

"Our mutual client will be here at two," Goldy said, "and he expects to find his dream team hard at work. We wouldn't want to disappoint Freddy the Forger."

Cash calibrated how much to divulge of his past twenty-four hours, balancing their need to know against his desire to keep them safe. In the circumstances, knowledge wasn't power. More like poison. He resolved to share next to nothing.

"Walk away," Cash said. "It's for your own good."

Eva shook her head. "Not until you tell us why."

Cash recalibrated, adding a new variable to the equation: Eva's damned stubbornness. The trait made her a great ally, as well as a royal pain in the ass.

Cash led all three to a conference room, where they sat at a round table. Not sure where to begin, he started at the end. "I just had a near-death experience with *Los Lobos*."

"*Los Lobos!*" Goldy said. "Aren't they trying to kill your client?"

"Exactly," Cash said, "and they were prepared to kill me, unless I divulged *La Tigra's* whereabouts."

"So did you?" Goldy said.

The question pissed off Cash. How could his mentor of all people think he would sacrifice a client to save himself? Stoked by anger, Cash threw the challenge back at Goldy. "Would you?"

"Of course not." Goldy spoke with all the certainty of the untested.

"Nor did I," Cash said.

Goldy refused to drop the line of attack. "Do you even know where *La Tigra* is?"

Cash shook his head. Goldy leaned back in the chair, smiling.

Eva piled on. "Did you tell *Los Lobos* that you didn't know where she was?"

Cash nodded.

Her expression said something didn't add up. "If they believed you, why didn't they kill you?"

"I convinced them that I could find out where she is faster than they could track her down."

Cash pinched the bridge of his nose, fighting a headache. No one asked the obvious follow-up, a bad sign. The people who knew him best must've assumed the worst.

"Hey, I would never actually tell them where she is." Anger amped his voice. "I said whatever it took to stay alive."

"I for one am fine with that," Eva said. "If it comes down to a choice between you and *La Tigra*, burn the bitch."

"At least you got *Los Lobos* off your back," Tina said.

"They gave me a one-week stay of execution. Seven days to betray her, unless the bad guys go back on their word and take me out sooner. Which is why none of you should hang around. When the *sicario* comes for me, anyone in the same zip code is at risk of winding up as collateral damage."

Goldy scoffed. "When you reach my age, sonny boy, threats like that don't cut the mustard. Bikers, tweakers, bangers, neo-Nazis, and badasses of all stripes have come gunning for me. None proved half as terrifying as my exes."

Goldy slapped both palms on the table. "But it does make sense to send the womenfolk to safety." He looked from Eva to Tina. "As for myself, I ain't going nowhere."

Cash rolled his eyes. If Goldy hoped to persuade Eva and Tina to play it safe, that wasn't how to do it.

Sure enough, Eva shot from her seat. "Say what, old man? *Womenfolk*? Seriously?"

"Everyone calm down," Cash said, "and hear me out. *Los Lobos* aren't the only wolves at the door. When *La Tigra* hears the best offer I have for her, she won't be happy, and it's not a good career move to make a crime boss unhappy."

Eva crossed her arms, a sign of a closed mind. "Doesn't change my decision to stay."

"In for a penny," Goldy said, "in for two."

"That's not how the saying goes." Cash surrendered to the mother of all migraines. "Never mind that. There's more at stake to consider. I'm playing off the DEA against the FBI to try to get a better deal for *La Tigra*. In the process, I'm sure to fuck over one agency, if not both. Meaning one or both will retaliate by coming after me and anyone fool enough to throw in with me."

Eva took the floor and aborted the meeting. "All in favor of sticking together, raise your hands."

Three hands shot up. Cash slumped. The odds were stacked against saving all three, but at this rate, he'd be lucky to save even one.

Tina's iPhone pinged. She picked it up. Her face turned ashen.

"They found another body," she said.

CHAPTER FORTY

The corpse lay on a metal gurney, covered by a white sheet. The lighting in the morgue burned mercilessly bright. The temperature in the room dipped to meat locker lows.

Cash had come to the viewing of the body with an empty stomach. Not his first field trip to the chop shop. It was a first for Tina, whose tear-streaked face paled. Her breaths escaped in bursts. She teetered on high heels.

Cash sidled away from her. Far enough to avoid a direct hit if she hurled, but close enough to catch her if she fainted.

A detective named Robert Gamez stood over the body. A decade ago, he had seamlessly slid from the Marines to the Dallas Police Department, keeping the same crewcut, combat-ready body, and blind allegiance that made him a good soldier in whatever war the suits blundered into.

Cash had given the cop—then a rookie—a baptism in fire, ripping him a new asshole on cross-examination in what should have been an open-and-shut DUI case. He recalled Gamez's stumbles on the stand and hoped like hell the detective didn't.

Fat chance.

Gamez pinched the sheet at the foot of the gurney and pulled it down slowly, like a magician milking a trick to build tension. He first revealed a forehead, unwrinkled and scrubbed clean of makeup. Eyes closed. Lashes, long and fine.

Everything looked peaceful until the sheet cleared her lips, which had twisted into a rictus grimace. Though death had silenced her screams, the lips don't lie.

When the face came into full view, Tina let out a cry and clutched Cash's arm.

The death had been slow, painful, and prolonged by a sadist. Despite the last hours or days of torment and torture, the face had retained a beauty that was exquisite, partly by nature, mostly by design.

The detective continued to tug on the sheet. It slid past breasts that were larger than Tina's and slowed over the speed bump of a shrunken penis. The cover caressed her thighs before the cop ripped it off and tossed it aside.

Cash focused on a tattoo on the instep of her right foot. A red tongue protruding through black lips. He had seen the tatt before but not on the deceased. Tina sported matching ink. Same design, colors, and spot. Marking them as BFFs.

"Recognize her, Miss Campos?" Gamez said.

Tina nodded. "It's Brandi." The words, more wheezed than spoken. "Brandi Foxx."

Gamez pulled out a notebook. "Do you know her real name?"

"That is her real name." A flash of anger swelled her voice.

Gamez blushed. "I meant her birth name."

Tina shook her head. "She was Brandi when we roomed together. She came from Oklahoma as a teen, after her folks threw her out. I don't think she's talked to them since."

"How long have you known her?" the cop asked.

"Eight years. She took me in when my...when my boyfriend turned me out."

Cash didn't call bullshit on her rewriting of history. Her pimp, not a boyfriend, had tossed her to the curb when she aged out of his fetish for underage flesh. Big difference.

"When did you last talk to her?" the cop said.

"Day before yesterday. She called me."

"What did you two talk about?"

"She has...had been dating a married man. He wanted to keep it on the down low. She didn't."

"Was she a prostitute?"

Tina turned to Cash. He nodded.

"On and off," she said.

Cash didn't bring up his past representation of Brandi, a referral from Tina. He stepped closer to the table and bent over the body. Red welts dotted her torso and thighs. "What made the marks?"

"I'm here to ask questions, not answer them." Gamez delivered the standard line poorly. Despite the military bearing, playing a hard-ass didn't come naturally to him.

"We're here to help," Cash said, "and you can use all the help you can get."

Gamez leaned closer to the civilians. "Keep this to yourselves, and above all, don't share it with the media. We need to hold back some details to weed out the false confessions."

Cash nodded. Tina followed his lead.

"The killer tortured the vic with a cattle prod. There are more marks on her back, buttocks, and the soles of her feet."

Cash examined Brandi's soles. Sure enough, more welts. But there was something else. A second tatt. Actually two more. A die on the left big toe and another on the right. Matching deuces on the dice. The deceased had rolled a four.

He pried Tina's grip from his arm. She didn't need to hear the rest. "Wait outside while I talk to the detective," he said.

She took the cue and left the room. The good news, she hadn't broken down at the sight of her friend. The bad, she was too numb to let go. The numbness would wear off, and he needed to be there when she fell apart.

"How many victims does this make?" Cash said.

"Again, this isn't for public consumption, and I don't want to see it in the press." Gamez waited for Cash to nod before going on. "Four in eighteen months. All attractive transgender women between the ages of eighteen and thirty-five and active in the LGBTQ community. Your friend out there...." The cop clammed up.

Cash filled in the blanks. Tina fit the killer's type. A young trans tempting enough to be a trap and bold enough to speak out.

"Where did you find the body?" Cash said.

"Dumped in an alley in Deep Ellum, like all the others."

"Did the killer take a souvenir?"

Gamez stiffened.

Cash took that as a yes. "What was it?"

"How did you know?"

"Serial killer 101. A sick fuck who tortures before he kills usually takes something from the victims. Something to remember them by."

Something to masturbate over later.

"Take a closer look at her mouth."

Other than the death grimace, nothing seemed unusual about Brandi's mouth. Her lips were full, but so what? It would've been more surprising if they hadn't been pumped with collagen.

"Inside the mouth," Gamez said.

Cash massaged her cheeks. The skin was cold, clammy. He stopped massaging when the lips parted.

Her tongue was gone.

Cash's legs went rubbery. He grabbed the side of the table.

"He took a part of her, like all the others," the detective said. "This detail has been kept out of the media."

"Always the tongue?" Cash said.

Gamez shook his head.

"Did the victims advertise on *Backdoor*?"

"You want to tell me how you know that?"

"Good guess." Cash didn't mention his current representation of Toby Fine. Might put a damper on the detective's cooperation. "What can you tell me about the killer?"

Gamez developed a sudden case of lockjaw. Could be because he'd already said too much. More likely, he didn't have squat to share.

Cash didn't let it go. "Tell me you have something."

"We're looking for a sadist with a dungeon straight out of a Rob Zombie movie."

As Cash turned to leave, Gamez grabbed his arm. "By the way, your boy Clarkson was guilty."

Cash shrugged. So Gamez hadn't forgotten the cross-examination. Nor that Cash's guilty-as-hell client had walked. "Not the way the jury saw it."

The cop squeezed Cash's arm. "I'm still waiting for a rematch."

* * *

Three days later at dawn, Brandi's army of friends descended on Oak Lawn Park for the memorial service. Rainbow-colored kites kissed the sky, and a marijuana haze hugged the earth. Loudspeakers blared the staccato sounds of dueling sitars, lending a festive air to the sendoff.

Cash arrived arm in arm with Tina and in time to catch the release of a white dove from the center of the crowd. A symbol of the ascension of Brandi's spirit to the heavens.

Since the trip to the morgue, Cash had shadowed Tina, even to the point of moving her into his guest bedroom. Though he doubted she would do anything drastic, he couldn't run the risk.

He stuck by her side as she made the rounds among her extended family. She introduced him as her "guardian lawyer." It was all he could do to keep from handing out business cards to the target-rich crowd. Not the time or place for it.

Cash pointed to a petite Asian-American in a black leather vest and pants. No way would he have made her out to be trans, if they had passed on the street. Also, no way would they have passed on the street without him taking a second look, and a third.

"Who is she?"

"That's Faith," Tina said.

"She's passable."

Tina rolled her eyes. "Don't tell her that, not if you're trying to impress her. She's not trying to pass as a woman. She identifies as a woman."

"I meant it as a compliment." He sounded defensive.

"She wouldn't take it as one."

Faith joined a flock of her spiritual sisters surrounding a grandfatherly figure in a white suit. The center of attention had the whitest and waviest hair, beard, and mustache this side of Colonel Sanders.

"Who's Mister Popularity?" Cash said.

"He's someone you definitely need to know." She dragged him over to the mystery man. "Cash, meet Doctor Katz, the top cosmetic surgeon in the southwest. Brandi put me onto him, and in turn I've touted him to half the girls here."

She elbowed Cash. "You're looking a little long in the tooth yourself. Better get his card."

Cash and Doctor Katz shook hands and swapped cards. Not clear which of them would reap the most clients today. Nor who would be the first to need the other's services.

"Based upon how Tina turned out," Cash said, "I second her assessment that you're the best in the field."

Katz stroked his beard. "She says the same about you. But to give credit where it's due, Tina was a beauty when she came to me. A touch here and there, and she became a goddess. You, however, will prove more of a challenge."

"Whoa," Cash said. "Keep that scalpel in your pants, Doc. I'm not in the market for a new look."

"Well, not yet anyway," Katz said.

Cash crossed his hands over his crotch. Pure instinct.

"Relax," Katz said. "Without making any big cuts, I could shave five...ten years off your face."

Cash's arms dropped to his side. "Looking around at the beautiful people gathered here, I don't doubt that you can roll miles off the odometer. My question is whether you can add miles to it."

Katz did a double take. "Sure, but there's not much of a market for that in Dallas."

Cash pocketed the business card and drifted away.

CHAPTER FORTY-ONE

Bettina Biddle had been on Cash's mind when her text pinged his phone. Not really much of a coincidence, because she dominated his thoughts these days.

Her message read more like an FYI than an SOS. A woman had shown up at her house unexpectedly, asking questions about her late husband.

He texted back: *say nothing, on my way.* Pegged the odds at fifty-fifty on whether she would heed his advice. Her husband Marty hadn't been able to keep his mouth shut, not until death sealed his lips. No reason to believe Bettina would do better.

He sped to her address in Richardson, a suburb that straddled Dallas and Plano. The ranch-style house looked depressingly similar to its neighbors on a block that struggled to keep the spirit of the '70s alive. The new place was several rungs below the Southlake showplace, which had been forfeited to the feds to pay down Marty's restitution order.

Without slowing to knock, Cash entered the house and rushed to the living room, where Bettina and Eva sat on opposite ends of a couch. They were drinking tea and sharing a laugh, like old friends. Clearly, Bettina hadn't followed his advice.

Of the two women, Bettina seemed more rattled by his arrival. Her hand shook as she put down the clattering cup and saucer.

In contrast, Eva calmly sipped away. Cash chalked up their different reactions to experience. While Eva had a long history of flouting his orders, Bettina was just getting started.

"What are you doing here?" Cash said to Eva.

He had expected to find a Latina in the house. Just not this one. Regina Delgado of the Justice Department had been his prime suspect. She always found an opponent's pressure point, and Cash had a fresh one: the grieving widow, single mother, and *pro bono* client, all rolled into the small frame on the couch.

The prosecutor had a ton of leverage over Bettina, who had paid down but not paid off her husband's debt to the government. That gave Gina a leg up on Cash as well.

Eva placed her empty cup on the coffee table. "I'm enjoying a drink and conversation with my new friend, who doesn't need your protection from me. Whether she needs my protection from you, well, that's a different story."

Cash turned to Bettina. "Eva worked for the law firm that set up your husband to take the fall."

Bettina went ashen-faced. "Is that true?"

"I quit two weeks ago," Eva said, "and he knows that."

"What I don't know is whether you quit for good or whether you'll crawl back to the firm and your girlfriend there," Cash said. "Either way, you haven't explained what you're doing here."

Color flooded Bettina's face. "There's obviously a lot of history between you two. What I need to know is whether you're on the same side and, more important, whether you're both on my side."

Not sure where he and Eva stood, Cash struggled to answer without bogging down in the backstory.

Eva showed no such hesitation. "We *were* on the same side, until he fired me for doing my job."

Cash steered clear of the past. Bettina didn't know the whole truth about her husband's hell in prison. If Cash had his way, she never would. He resorted to as much truth as the widow could bear. "I don't believe Marty killed himself, and I'm all in to prove it."

Eva said, "I'm the one who pushed Cash to take you on as a client."

Bettina leaned back on the couch. "Then we're all on the same page about Marty. That being the case, can you two work together?"

* * *

The business portion of the meeting done, Cash hung around Bettina's house, hoping to wind up alone with her. Never happened. Eva ignored the hundred or so hints he dropped and stayed.

Bettina showed both of them the door when her daughters returned from school. Cash made it to the Porsche before extending an olive branch. Well, more like a twig. "Hungry?"

"Famished," Eva said.

"I'll buy."

"The least you can do."

Same old Eva. Had to get in the last word.

He took her to Fernando's in northwest Dallas, his favorite place to order breakfast for dinner. That meant migas, refried beans, corn tortillas, and the second best frozen margaritas in the city.

They were two top-shelfs into the meal before she brought up business. "So what's the deal? Are we together again?"

"With cartels circling me like sharks, it's still too dangerous for you to come back as my secretary."

"Assistant," she said.

"That's what you took from my warning? Not the part about the clear and present danger of torture and death, but my use of a title that offends your eggshell ego?"

"Your warning comes a little late." She raised the decibel level of the debate. "We're already working together on Freddy the Forger's defense."

He lowered it. "First, let's stop calling our innocent-until-proven-guilty client Freddy the Forger. Second, the court ordered me to work with Goldberg on Foster's defense, not with you."

"Which means we both wind up working for Goldy. Just like old times. As for Freddy, he's already been convicted twice for forgery, so I think he's earned the nickname."

She had him there, on both counts. "I suppose we can collaborate on Bettina's behalf," he said, "as long as we're not too open about it."

"You've certainly had lots of practice carrying on relationships with women on the down low." She made it sound like a bad thing.

He ordered a third round of drinks, which would be one past his limit and two over hers. "You never told me what you were doing at Bettina's house."

"What you should've already done." Tequila turned her into an attack Chihuahua, high-pitched, yapping, and almost comically combative for her size. "I was looking for documents related to her husband's trial."

"Did she have any?"

Eva shook her head. "After the trial, Rocket took everything. Claimed he needed it for the appeal."

"Since Rhoden got himself killed, it looks like we're at a dead end."

"Not exactly," she said. "I did a little sleuthing at Paula's law firm before being fired. Well, technically I resigned, but—"

He cut her off. "You did what?"

"I stayed late one night to search the computer archives for the files on Longhorn Investments."

"Are you insane?" He caught himself mid-sentence and lowered the volume. "You took a helluva risk."

She leaned in, drawing Cash closer. "Turns out that Powell, Ingram & Gardner handled the internal investigation of Longhorn that led to Biddle's indictment and conviction."

Suddenly three drinks didn't seem like enough. "Right off the bat, I see two big problems with that," Cash said. "First, if the Powell firm served as general corporate counsel to Longhorn Investments—"

Her turn to cut him off. "Which they did and still do."

He continued. "Then the internal investigation of the company should've been handled by truly independent counsel, not its go-to law firm. Second, U.S. Attorney Jenna Powell should've recused herself from any involvement in Biddle's case. Her father's law firm gave the feds a road map of who to indict."

"And who not to," Eva said. "Jenna didn't recuse herself. She's neck-deep in the swamp."

"So the law firm protected its gold chip client by offering the feds a sacrificial lamb named Martin Biddle, and the U.S. Attorney played along with it."

She nodded. "And that leads to another question. Why would a white-shoe firm like Powell, Ingram & Gardner get in bed with a bottom feeder like Rocket?"

Cash had a ready answer for that. "The firm hired Rhoden to protect Longhorn, not Biddle. His job was to make sure the lamb went silently to slaughter."

"Which is the same reason cartels hired him to represent mules," she said. "No matter how fat a carrot a prosecutor dangled in return for cooperation, Rocket made sure the mule didn't bite."

"Did you get a copy of the firm's files on the investigation?"

"I had just gotten into the archives when IT cut off my computer access. Before I could flee the building, security grabbed me and locked me in a conference room. An hour later, the HR lady showed up. She gave me a choice: resign on the spot or be fired for cause and prosecuted for hacking."

"Probably a good thing you got busted before seeing the files," he said.

"Why?"

"Up to this point, I assumed a cartel killed Rhoden. Now I'm not so sure."

CHAPTER FORTY-TWO

Cash left the office late and counted only three cars on level two of the underground lot, including his Porsche. The flickering lights on P2 were hit or miss, with about every third bulb a burnout. Leakage from vehicles and pipes made the garage a slip-and-fall case waiting to happen.

As soon as Cash slid into the driver's seat, an alarm sounded in his head. Someone had tilted the steering wheel toward his crotch, too close for comfort. A steady ticking shattered the silence of the enclosed space.

His first instinct was to bolt from the car, but he checked that. Clicks to the right and left made him jump. A remote control had locked the doors. He was a sinner in the hands of an angry goddess.

He froze, fearful the slightest twitch would trigger an explosion. His breaths were short, shallow. His mood darkened by the tick.

Fuck this shit.

Done with inaction, he patted down the seats, console, floor, and dashboard. A wire dangled from the underbelly of the dashboard. It hadn't been there this morning, or so he thought.

Attached to the wire was a post-it note. He peeled it loose and read:

> *Turn on the car, and you die.*
> *Open the glove compartment, and you might live.*

He reached for the glove compartment but stopped short. The ticking grew louder, either in fact or in his imagination.

He fought through fear and removed a burner phone and another post-it from the compartment. The note read:

> *Hit the callback number.*
> *If no one answers, I am already dead.*
> *And so are you.*

A shaky finger pressed the callback button. The ring tone went on and on. Cash braced for a blast.

"You had better not bill me for this call." *La Tigra's* tone was playful, almost flirtatious.

He smelled a reprieve and kept the conversation light. "A deal's a deal. No charge, period."

"Good. You won't have time to spend what you already have."

The reprieve might prove short-lived. "How much time have I got?"

"That depends on this conversation."

He threw his whole energy into keeping her talking. "Where are you?"

"That is not a topic for discussion. What I want to hear from you is where I will be tomorrow and the day after. Have you found a haven for my daughter and me?"

The conversation had turned tricky. The short answer was no. A cell in a minimum-security prison in West Virginia for her and a new identity for the kid was still the best deal on the table.

He pulled a country from the air. "How does Cuba sound?"

In the silence that followed, he whipsawed between hope and despair. He went into full sales mode. "Cuba has beautiful beaches, politicians with greasy palms, and no extradition treaty with the U.S."

He stayed mum on the negatives. Only ninety miles separated Cuba from Florida, which might prove too close for her comfort. A bigger problem, corruptible leaders cut both ways. Just as *La Tigra* could bribe them to provide safe harbor, *Los Lobos* might pony up a dollar more to turn her over.

The silence finally broke Cash. "How do I get out of this jam in one piece?"

"By convincing me that you have a real offer in hand. How close are you to making Cuba happen and how much will it cost to stay there?"

She had asked the right questions. That was bad news, because the straight skinny was not close at all and every *peso* she had. He tap-danced around the truth. "All I needed was the green light from you."

During a longer silence, sweat beads raced down his forehead and stung his eyes. "It's stuffy in here," he said. "Is it safe to open the door?"

No response.

"Or crack a window?"

Still no response.

Maybe he had lost her with the choice of Cuba as a landing spot. He racked his brain for runner-up sanctuaries.

The beaches and climate would've made Panama a perfect paradise, but the release of the *Panama Papers* had trained an international spotlight on the tax haven. In the circumstances, too much heat for *La Tigra* to fade.

Australia boasted great beaches, but the drawbacks included close ties with the U.S. and a tight-as-a-tick extradition treaty between the countries. Russia had no extradition treaty but rocky beaches and chilly weather. Maybe Cyprus or one of the Greek Islands would fit the bill.

"Pursue the Cuba option," she said. "Nail down how much it will cost us to live there."

"The Cuban authorities will want proof it's worth their while to take you in." Spoken as if he knew what he was talking about.

"A down payment?" she said.

"A big one, and it had better come from accounts that can't be seized by the U.S. or Mexican governments. Where is your money parked?"

"Also not a topic for discussion. My money is safe. That is all you need to know."

"In addition to an up-front sum," he said, "you will need to make payments from time to time, as leaders come and go. If the flow of funds were to stop, so would your protection."

"I understand." She sounded resigned to life as a fugitive, dependent not on the kindness of strangers, but on the avarice of officeholders. "It is not so different in my country and the way I live now."

He couldn't contain any longer the pressing issue of his personal safety. "Any chance you can disarm the device in my car, or at least tell me how to get out of this death trap alive?"

"Your car is clear." She reverted to a lighter tone. "The wire was planted to demonstrate how easy it would be to get to you."

"And the ticking?"

"An alarm clock under your seat," she said.

He breathed easier. "A simple verbal warning would've done the trick."

"I will be the judge of that."

He pressed his luck, asking a question that had been eating at him for weeks. "Did you order the hit on Rhoden?"

La Tigra tortured him with an extended silence. "No."

Decades of experience had conditioned him to doubt a client's denial of wrongdoing, but he bought hers. Partly because there were other suspects for the murder, but mostly because she didn't give a damn whether he believed her.

A double click spooked him again. This time it unlocked his cage.

Out of the frying pan....

CHAPTER FORTY-THREE

Cash killed the afternoon setting up tomorrow's showdown at his office. It took an hour to browbeat DEA agent Duane Leroy Lee, a zombie from the graveyard shift, into agreeing to an 8:00 a.m. meeting and even longer to lure Regina Delgado of the DOJ onto enemy turf.

FBI agent Maggie Burns, the final member of the four-some, proved the hardest to corral. Cash finally wrangled her promise to participate by phone from Bismarck.

Cash baited the hook differently for each fish. A chance to parlay the meeting into a place at the heavy hitters' table in D.C. netted Gina the barracuda. He tempted Maggie the goldfish with a shot to come in from the cold. Good ole Leroy the flounder drooled at the prospect of chocolate croissants and fresh coffee.

Ever the hard bargainer, Leroy held out for Irish coffee.

The next morning Gina arrived late at Cash's office. The prosecutor on a perpetual power trip wore a dark blue suit. One look at Leroy, unshaven and disheveled, and she said, "What's the help doing here?" Her way of starting conversations had a tendency to end them.

"Look, lady, don't give me any shit." Leroy mumbled through a mouthful of dough. "I've been on my feet for eight hours, and this circle jerk sure as hell ain't my idea of a fun morning."

"Nor mine," Maggie said over the phone. "Whatever scam McCahill has in mind, the mess will not land in my lap. Not my case, not my jurisdiction, not my problem." She sounded resigned to her exile.

Cash already regretted his damn fool decision to bring the three together in a summit that marked the end of his efforts at shuttle diplomacy. The strategy to spark a bidding war between the DEA and FBI for *La Tigra*'s services as a snitch, though sound in theory, had dragged on too long.

It might take weeks, even months to wheedle a decent offer, and he didn't have the luxury of time. *Los Lobos* had laid down an ultimatum: turn over *La Tigra* or turn up dead, with four days to the deadline.

For all Cash knew, *La Tigra* could've shortened his fuse. As her clock wound down, so did his.

In danger of losing the audience, Cash rushed the pitch. "With the appropriate safeguards in place and adequate assurances from all three governments with a dog in this fight, my client is willing to lay down her arms, retire from the business, and relocate herself and her daughter to Cuba."

The silence that followed meant one of two things. Either the feds were mulling it over, or they were in shock.

"Cuba!" Leroy exploded with laughter. "Why don't you ask for two tickets to the moon? That'd be an easier sale."

"Make it three tickets," Delgado said to Cash, "and we'll send you into space with them."

"While you're booking your client's getaway, arrange a dream vacation in Havana for me." Maggie sounded amused by the offer. "My tan's fading up here, and I have a wicked thirst for Cuba Libres."

Roger that. In the not-so-distant past, Cash had witnessed Maggie's weakness for rum—even counted on it to loosen her up.

He kicked himself for thinking the trio could work together on anything, much less on a high-risk gamble that threatened their careers. Good chance that come fish-or-cut-bait time, no one would want his or her fingerprints on this folly.

"Hail Mary" time.

"This is a win-win-win," Cash said. "The U.S. and Mexico avoid an all-out war that will leave rivers of blood and red ink on both sides of the border, and the Cubans benefit from the company of a very generous visitor, with the deepest of pockets and the strongest of incentives to keep her hosts fat, dumb, and happy."

"And how exactly does this help me?" Maggie said. "Or any of us?"

"You three take credit for a strategy that saves thousands of lives and billions of dollars."

Gina scoffed. "Even if your crazy plan had a snowball's chance of success, you've shot way too low by bringing it to us. This would have to be approved at the highest levels in D.C., Havana, and Mexico City."

Cash had anticipated the pushback. "I'm starting with you three, but I sure as hell hope it doesn't end here."

"Any higher-ups with the *cojones* to green light this disaster in the making," Gina said, "would have to be in a position to deny any knowledge of it, if things went south. Make that, *when* things go south."

Cash perked up at the first positive sign of the morning. Gina had made the telltale leap from trashing his plan to tweaking it.

Leroy belched. "Got any more chocolate croissants?"

Okay, with Leroy, maybe Cash had shot too low.

* * *

Cash ended the meeting without a clue whether the "Great Cuban Getaway" had legs. He ended the day still up in the air, this time literally. The lone passenger on the FBI's private jet, bound for Quantico—the bound part, not literal.

The next morning, he sat across the table from FBI Director Danfield. Scores of photos featuring Danfield with a rogues' gallery of politicians plastered the office walls, confirming Cash's worst fears about the director and the pols.

Danfield's eyes bounced between Cash and the bank of TVs bracketed to the wall, each muted and tuned to a cable news station. His back to the TVs, Cash caught the reflection of Wolf Blitzer in the director's reading glasses.

"Been to Quantico before?" Danfield said.

"Once. When I was an AUSA, four of us front-line prosecutors were flown here to play the hostages in a rescue scenario."

"How did that go?"

"Not well," Cash said. "When the HRT commander heard that the hostages were lawyers, he said 'fuck it' and left us up shit creek."

Bureau humor. Danfield cracked a rare smile.

"When is the A.G. getting here?" Cash said.

Danfield stopped smiling. "You deal with me."

Cash had a bad feeling about doing business with the director but didn't have time to hold out for the boss lady. "I take it that you've heard my offer."

"More of a joke than an offer," Danfield said. "Why would we reward a mass murderer with a Cuban vacation?"

"For starters," Cash said, "the offer on the table involves safe passage and a soft landing for my client and her daughter. And question number one is, can you make it happen?"

Cash's gambit banked on Danfield's god complex. No way would he admit there was anything beyond his powers.

"I can make it happen," the director said.

"Then we have something to talk about."

Danfield's eyes locked on the TVs. The color drained from his face. "If this is your idea of bringing more leverage to the bargaining table, I'll see to it that you spend the rest of your sorry life in Leavenworth."

Cash wheeled around. All four screens carried the "Breaking News" banner, with a crawl below that read: Bombings on the Border.

Danfield unmuted CNN, catching Blitzer mid-story. "... rocking El Paso and Juárez. There are twenty-nine confirmed deaths so far, with hundreds missing. We will bring you more details as they develop."

Cash turned away from the TVs. The bombings couldn't have come at a worse time.

Nor a better one.

CHAPTER FORTY-FOUR

The fog of war obscured who had fired the first shot. Or in this case, who had detonated the first bomb.

According to CNN, neither cartel claimed credit for a cross-border body count that had climbed into triple digits. Both governments vowed a crackdown, as if they meant it.

Danfield aborted the meeting and booted Cash from Quantico. In a close call, the director decided against holding him for questioning. Bigger fish in the cesspool.

Danfield commandeered the Bureau jet, forcing Cash to fly home on his own nickel. He returned to Dallas more uncertain than ever, not knowing whether the bombings helped or hurt *La Tigra's* chances of relocating to Cuba.

Time ticking, he was torn over whether to devote his final days to working on the queenpin's great escape or cracking the mystery of Martin Biddle's hanging. Odds were stacked against doing either, much less both.

Before it was too late, he owed it to Bettina Biddle to share his suspicions with her. After he was gone, perhaps she could persuade another knight to take up the quest.

He tracked down Bettina at the Chuck E. Cheese on Mortfort Drive in North Dallas, where her twins were on a sugar high, celebrating one of the dozen or so birthday parties rocking the place. With kids running wild from table to table and game to game, it was impossible to tell where one party ended and the next began.

The decibel level in the madhouse induced migraines. It had to be quieter on the border, bombings and all.

Bettina held court among a cluster of women. She looked relaxed in sandals, shorts, and a t-shirt that read: *World's Okayest Mom*. She rushed to Cash and gave him an awkward hug.

"What are you doing here?" She broke the embrace. "Poor boy, you're wasting away. How about a slice of pizza?"

Lip reading allowed him to catch her every other word. He shouted over the tumult. "Let's go outside."

She nodded and handed him a slice of pepperoni pizza on a paper plate. Grease soaked through to his palm. "Can they legally call this pizza?" he said. On the way out, he took a bite and trashed the rest.

The hum of traffic on Montfort settled his nerves, though his ears still rang and the cardboard taste lingered. "Do you actually like the food here?"

"I wouldn't know. Despite coming to countless parties here, I've never had the courage to try it. You're my guinea pig." She laughed. "But if you weren't a confirmed bachelor before, I'm sure you are now."

He looked her in the eye. "You might be surprised."

She blushed. "Why are you here?" Her tone turned serious. "Did you find out something about Marty?"

He nodded but held off speaking until a gaggle of incoming kids moved out of earshot. "Rhoden sold your husband down the river."

"I never trusted him."

"For good reason," Cash said. "But I'm no longer sure that a cartel took Rhoden out."

Her brow furrowed. The wheels were turning in her head. "Do you think his murder had some connection to Marty?"

"I don't know," he said, "but one thing is clear. Rhoden's not the only bent lawyer in the picture."

Bettina's eyes darted back and forth between him and the restaurant entrance. "I want to hear it all, but my girls are bouncing off the walls in there. Do we have to do this now? Why don't you come over for dinner tonight? We can talk after I put the girls to bed."

Hard as it was to resist the invitation, he shook his head. Just as he didn't know when the hit would take place, he didn't know where. He couldn't risk putting Bettina and the girls in the crossfire.

"If it's more money you need—"

He cut her off. "It's not money. It's time."

"I thought that time *was* money for lawyers."

"Funny, but I always feared I'd run out of money before running out of time. Looks like it will be the other way around."

"You're scaring me," she said.

"Good. Stay scared."

"If you need a place to crash," she said, "we've got a guest bedroom. It's nothing fancy, but you can stay as long as you like."

He shook his head, more forcefully this time. When the end came, her home was the last place on the planet he wanted to be. "I'll make this quick and give you the condensed version of what I know."

She nodded.

"All roads to and from Marty's death lead to the law firm of Powell, Ingram & Gardner." He stopped as more groups flocked to and from the building. "Let's finish this in my car."

They sat in the Porsche, overshadowed by the SUVs parked on three sides. He kept the windows up and his voice down. "The Powell firm has represented Longhorn Investments from the beginning. Over the past two decades, it has billed the hedge fund tens of millions in fees."

Her eyes widened. "Mister Powell recommended that we hire Rhoden and said the company would pay our legal fees."

Must've sounded like a good deal at the time. Now, not so much.

"A pillar of the bar like Stewart Powell wouldn't share the same elevator with a bottom feeder like Rhoden. That is, unless Mister High-and-Mighty needed an ethically challenged attorney to sit on your husband and send him to prison as a sacrificial lamb."

Her eyes brimmed with tears. "Are you saying Marty wasn't guilty?"

Cash faced a fork in what could be his final conversation with her. The safe path was to continue coddling the widow. The risky road involved taking a first step toward the truth. He took the risk. "Longhorn couldn't have fudged the books without your husband's knowledge and involvement. After all, he was the CFO."

That brought tears but no protest from her. He plowed on, trusting that she'd prove tougher than her petite frame suggested. "But there's no way he carried out a fraud of this magnitude by himself, which is how the law firm pitched the criminal case to the feds and how things played out in court."

Her mouth dropped open, but no words fell out. He filled the silence. "Federal prosecutors charge conspiracy at the drop of a hat. Why no conspiracy count here? Why didn't the feds indict others with your husband? Why did he fade the heat alone?"

She shook her head. Tears flowed freely now.

"Here's how I think it went down," he said. "Powell's firm handled the internal investigation of Longhorn, which conveniently pointed the finger at Marty but cleared everyone else of wrongdoing. The whitewash worked because Powell's daughter happens to be the United States Attorney in Dallas, putting her in a perfect position to rubber-stamp the findings of Daddy's firm."

She grabbed his arm. "Can you prove this?"

He shook his head. "Not yet."

Maybe not ever.

He went on. "Step one would be getting our hands on the report Powell's firm prepared and turned over to the feds. Dollars to donuts, I could blow holes in it. I almost had it, but my mole inside the firm got caught and fired."

She squeezed his arm. He couldn't have broken her grip. Not that he wanted to.

"You will keep trying?" Her voice cracked. "My girls will grow up knowing their father died in prison. They shouldn't be tortured by the belief he took his own life."

"I'll see this through to the end." He didn't say what end.

Or whose.

CHAPTER FORTY-FIVE

ash's farewell tour moved to a private dining room at Ocean Prime in Uptown Dallas, where he gathered the trial team. Goldy, Eva, and Tina arrived in that order and in varying moods, like three of the seven dwarfs: Grumpy, Sleepy, and Happy.

Not that anyone would confuse Cash with Snow White.

He lifted his wine glass. "To my mentor and the finest standup lawyer I've ever known, Gary Goldberg. A good gunslinger wins a string of shootouts, but when you're one of the greats, like Goldy, the bad guys don't dare draw on you."

Goldy looked around the room. "What the hell's going on here? Whenever you say something nice about me...." He paused. "Hey, wait a sec. You've never said anything nice about me."

"That's not true." Cash rummaged through his memory for an example of public praise but found none. "I've complimented you countless times. Granted, in the past it's always been out of your earshot. Tonight I'm saying it to your face."

"About time," Eva said. "And speaking of time, why are we wasting ours here, when we should be at the office prepping for trial?"

"Glad you brought that up," Cash said. "It's one of the things we're celebrating tonight. While we still have Freddy the Forger on the docket, Fine is on the verge of receiving pretrial diversion."

"Is that like probation?" Tina said.

"Better." Cash killed a bottle of an excellent Hall Cabernet on three glasses at the table. He bypassed Goldy's glass, which Eva had filled with Perrier. "Probation means either you pled guilty or were found guilty by a jury. With pretrial diversion, however, if Fine keeps his nose clean a year or so, the feds flush the indictment. No conviction, no prison time, no supervised release. Bottom line, it's a no brainer."

"You're delusional if you think Fine will get a walk" Goldy said. "Pretrial diversion is reserved for pissants who commit pissant offenses, not co-conspirators to major crimes like sex trafficking and money laundering."

"First time for everything." Cash sipped the cab. No one followed his lead. "And all we have to do to secure a sweetheart deal for Fine is to end a cartel war, by whisking *La Tigra* to safety in Cuba."

That got Goldy drinking. He killed the glass in three gulps. "I'm going to need something stronger."

Eva slapped the table with both palms, rattling the dishes. "I've been busting my ass to get us ready for back-to-back trials, working twenty-four seven." The bags under her eyes backed up her claim. "This is information I could've used weeks ago."

"I didn't have the offer nailed down then," Cash said. "Didn't get the client's signoff until yesterday."

"Is she in Cuba now?" Goldy's tone suggested he knew the answer.

Cash shook his head. "Still waiting for the green light from the feds."

"Then tonight's celebration is premature," Eva said. "How many great deals have we put together for clients, only to see them fall apart at the eleventh hour?"

Cash couldn't dispute that. Nor could he level with them on why he had jumped the gun on the closing dinner. The deadline imposed by *Los Lobos* to turn over *La Tigra* loomed, now only two days away. There were loose ends to tie up, and he might not be around to finish the job.

Make that, the jobs.

Solving the mystery of Biddle's death topped Cash's to do list. He couldn't shake the belief that if only he'd filed Marty's appeal sooner....

"I owe it to Biddle's family to look into how he died," Cash said, "and why."

"I'm in," Eva said.

Tina nodded.

Goldy pushed away from the table. "As the lone adult in the room, allow me to remind everyone that we can't afford to get sucked into another one of Cash's charity cases."

"What's the matter, old man?" Cash said. "You afraid to tangle with a highflying hedge fund, the most powerful law firm in Texas, and the United States Attorney in Dallas?"

"Son, at my age, the only things left to fear are—"

Cash interrupted him, having heard the line a thousand times. "Are losing your car keys and running into a coven of your exes."

Still, it was a good line.

Cash shared with the team his suspicions about Biddle's death. He detailed everything. Stewart Powell's hiring of the sleazebag Rhoden to represent the sacrificial CFO. Jenna Powell's failure to recuse herself from the case and complicity in the cover-up. The whole father-daughter connection stank to the heavens.

Goldy's scowl signaled that he wasn't sold. "Do you have any proof of this wild-ass theory?"

Eva beat Cash to the punch. "How about the fact that Powell's firm fired me for trying to get my hands on the report of its internal investigation of Longhorn Investments?"

Goldy turned to Eva. "Did you actually see the report?"

She shook her head.

"Which means we don't know what's in it or even who saw it." Goldy crossed his arms at his chest. "For all we know, the feds might've sent it straight to the shredder, where it probably belonged."

Cash waved down the waiter and ordered another bottle of the 2015 Kathryn Hall cab. "The reason I summoned you here...." After a long pause, he resumed in a softer voice. "If something were to happen to me—"

It was Goldy's turn to cut him off. "Nothing's going to happen to you."

Good old Goldy. In his world, no one gets to predecease him.

"But say I were to be hit by a bus or develop an incurable case of amnesia," Cash said, "I don't want to take my suspicions to the grave."

Eva stood, wine glass raised high. "All in favor of getting to the bottom of Biddle's death, say aye."

On the first ballot, Goldy got outvoted three to one. The old man was on a losing streak.

* * *

Goldy, Eva, and Tina left the private dining room at Ocean Prime in the same order as their arrival. While Cash nursed an after-dinner drink, Tina circled back and closed the door behind her.

"Forget something?" he said.

"No, but you did. The official ruling on Biddle's death was suicide, right?"

He nodded.

"Tonight you laid out the case for murder, but you failed to present the evidence for suicide."

The cognac left a bitter aftertaste. "There's something about Biddle I haven't told the others. Not even his widow. Especially not her." He closed his eyes. "My other cellmate at Seagoville, a brute called Big Black, terrorized Marty. When the mood hit, he forced the poor boy to wear a wig, makeup, and lingerie. He made Marty his bitch."

"And you're sharing this with me and not the others because...?"

Her question caught Cash off guard. He thought the answer obvious. "Well, you being transgender and him being... more or less in the same boat...sort of."

She sighed loudly. "What you don't know about the trans-gender community could fill the Grand Canyon. For starters, based on what you've told me, Biddle wasn't transgender. I'm a trans woman, which means I identify as a woman. In contrast, a predator forced Biddle to cross-dress. But unless you know something about him that I don't, he never stopped identifying as a man."

"Big Black robbed him of that identity."

"So your alternative theory is that Biddle hung himself, because he couldn't handle the abuse and shame."

He nodded.

She picked up his glass and polished off the cognac. Her hand shook as she put down the glass. "Remember the first time you represented me for soliciting?"

"Sure."

"There's something I held back from you then." She stared at the table. "When I got booked into the Dallas County Jail, I demanded to be locked up in the women's wing. The guards refused and decided to teach me a lesson. They stripped me to my panties and bra and paraded me up and down the men's cellblocks. To this day, I can still hear the whistles and catcalls. Still wake up in a cold sweat over that night."

"Were you raped?"

She shook her head. "Humiliated and scared shitless, but not raped. When the guards tired of teasing the caged men, they tossed me into my own cell, naked. Threatened to send in gangbangers to keep me company." She shuddered. "Suicide seemed like the only option, and I came close to ending it all. No one entered my cell that night, but the thought of suicide stayed with me for months."

"Why didn't you tell me?"

"Because Brandi saved me. She was always there for me until...." She didn't spell it out. Didn't have to.

"Like I was there for Marty," Cash said, "until my release. Then he had no one. If we dig up the truth, I fear it won't comfort Bettina, but make things worse."

"You tell me," Tina said. "Your mother either left you or was taken from you. If it turns out she left of her own accord, are you better off not knowing?"

Cash had been asking himself the same question for thirty-five years.

CHAPTER FORTY-SIX

Bam.

The knock on the front door jolted Cash.

Bam. Bam.

He froze at the kitchen table, midway through the first paragraph of an online article with the all-caps headline: CARTEL WAR ESCALATES. Another day, another round of bombs rocked the border, leaving body parts piled high on both sides. The casualty count for the week ran deep into four digits.

Bad news from the border fed Cash's fear over who or what loomed on the other side of the door. A harbinger that more blood would soon flow closer to home.

His home. His blood.

The knocking stopped, allowing Cash to catch his breath. Today's unexpected visitor came on the deadline to betray *La Tigra* or become a blip on the rising body count, a drop in a raging red river.

Then again, maybe the visit was expected. *Los Lobos* hadn't specified the hour of his execution. Was checkout time at noon? Did he have until sundown? Midnight?

Whoever waited at the door might hold the answer, along with an automatic weapon.

The extended silence gave Cash hope. Maybe it had been a salesman. Or someone with the wrong address.

Bam. Bam. Bam.

His peace of mind shattered, Cash clung to another thin reed of hope. Surely *Los Lobos* would be a no-knock cartel. The barbarians would barge in without warning. Show no mercy. Offer no chance to talk his way out of the fix. Refuse even to wait for his last words.

The banging on the door grew louder. Cash quelled an instinct to bolt through the back door and flee down the alley. If *Los Lobos* had come for him, he'd never make it to the fence.

Besides, it could be the cavalry to the rescue. If so, he bet with himself that DEA would be his salvation.

He voted Dani Tanaka the girl most likely to score a late inning save. She played the game a step faster than the competition. The drug agency would likely tap her to do its dirty work. She had enough clout in the hierarchy to be taken seriously by Cash but remained sufficiently subordinate to be sacrificed if necessary.

Cash peered through the peephole and got his first surprise of the morning. He lost the private bet. Right gender but wrong government agency.

Maggie Burns of the FBI fidgeted on the porch. She looked paler than usual.

He pulled her into the house and locked the door behind them. "Stay away from the windows. I'm expecting company."

She patted the Glock in her shoulder-holster, probably meant to reassure him. It didn't.

"What company?" she said.

"Bad company."

They faced each other in the foyer for what seemed an eternity. He struggled for an ice breaker. Every time he buried her in the past, she popped into the present and scrambled his future.

She filled the void. "I hear you had a stormy meeting with my boss at Quantico."

No long overdue kiss. No "I missed you, darling." Not even a greeting. Right down to business.

"I've missed you too." Said with heavy doses of pain and sarcasm. He stepped forward to hug her.

She leaned back, out of reach.

He got the message the second time around. Strictly a business meeting. No touchy feely.

Maggie's outfit reinforced the ground rules. She wore the standard blue blazer, starched white blouse, blue skirt, black pumps. All regulation cut and color.

Her eyes warned him not to bring up their history. Cash made another bet with himself—double or nothing. The Bureau was recording their conversation. Only way to explain the stick up Maggie's ass.

Cash should've been pissed and called her out on the covert taping, but he let it slide. She must be down to her last shot to come in from the cold—literally and figuratively.

He played ball, for her sake. "Agent Burns, what brings you back to Dallas?"

"I came to deliver the best and final offer your client will get from the government."

Cash noted the omission. She hadn't mentioned the client's name. More evidence a tape was rolling. A recording that might surface later.

Or not.

"I've been dealing with the A.G. and the FBI director on this," he said. "Are they too busy to give me a call?"

"I don't know anything about that." She delivered the line without an ounce of conviction, nowhere close to selling it.

Cash still didn't call bullshit. She was simply a go-between, a convenient fall girl, if the need arose. One bad headline away from shipment to a shithole that would make her nostalgic for Bismarck. The cockroaches in power would keep their prints off any deal this dicey and dangerous.

He moved the bargaining session to the kitchen, where he poured her a cup of coffee the way she liked it. Black with one Splenda.

"Okay," he said, "I'll bite. What's behind door number one?"

"You asked for a beach, and we found you one." She pulled out her iPhone and showed him a shot of a stretch of sand.

"Where is this?"

She pocketed the phone. "A stone's throw from San Juan, Puerto Rico. The Bureau of Prisons recently built a camp for female inmates outside the city."

"Can you actually *see* the ocean from the camp?"

She hesitated too long to lie. "You can smell it, and we can arrange a work detail for your client that involves keeping the beach pristine." She reached out her hand to shake. "Do we have a deal?"

He extended his hand but stopped short of hers. "We're so close that I can smell a deal, but I still don't see one."

She took a deep breath and resumed the negotiations. "What if we were to—"

A knock on the door startled Cash. Maggie drew her Glock.

Cash calmed down first. "Hold that thought, while I see what's behind door number two."

* * *

Cash whisked Dani Tanaka off the porch and into the kitchen. After he introduced her to Maggie, the temperature in the room fell ten degrees. Having one armed agent in the house made him feel safer. Two armed agents, less safe.

He handicapped which agent would come out on top in a brawl. Maggie had the edge in reach, but Tanaka looked as if she could take more punches. He decided it would be a bloody draw.

And a monster draw on pay-per-view.

"Can we talk in private?" Dani said to Cash.

"You got something to hide?" Maggie's tone ratcheted up the tension.

The women squared off jaw to jaw. Or more like jaw to breast, given Maggie's height advantage.

Cash stepped between them and immediately regretted putting his body at risk. "Now hold on a hot second, Maggie. You made the Bureau's bid in private. It wouldn't be fair to deny Dani the same opportunity."

He snapped his fingers. "Hey, I've got a solution. We give Maggie a choice. She can stay for DEA's pitch, if we disclose FBI's offer to Dani. Or Maggie can take her leave now, and both agencies shield their bids from the competition."

He turned to Maggie. "What's it going to be? Do you stay or go?"

Maggie looked flummoxed. The Bureau must not have prepped her for this. She opted to stay, so Cash shared with Dani the bid to beat.

Dani's smile hinted that she had the upper hand. "If your client is tempted by the Bureau's offer, ask her one question. How long can she tread water? I give it six months before the next hurricane barrels into PR."

"Big talk," Maggie said, "for someone who hasn't put an offer on the table."

Dani dropped a brochure on the table. Cash scooped it up. Studied it front and back, before looking at Dani. "Cuba?"

She nodded.

Cash's heart raced, but he kept a poker face. DEA had come through on the country of choice. "Where in Cuba?"

"Guantanamo Bay."

Maggie laughed. Cash slumped. His disappointment gave way to anger. "Do you really expect me to send my client to a living hell with terrorists, who have nothing to lose?"

"Of course not," Dani said. "She would have her own place on the beach and enjoy paradise under the fulltime protection of the United States Navy."

Cash stroked his chin. The presence of military muscle cut both ways. Might keep the cartels at bay but would definitely cramp *La Tigra*'s style.

Another knock on the door prompted both agents to pull their pistols. Cash settled them down. "Maybe the third time's the charm."

* * *

Eva remained on the porch. She came to deliver a message and balked at joining Maggie and Dani in the house.

"Two's company," she said, "three's a crowd, and four's more than you can handle on your best day. And this isn't your best day."

Just as well that Eva stayed put. For Cash, a day that had dawned with news of a tragedy threatened to turn into a French farce.

"There's been another killing here," she said. "Another trans woman."

"Does Tina know the vic?"

Eva winced.

It was all the answer Cash needed. "Sorry, but I don't have time today to comfort Tina or browbeat the cops into finding the serial killer. Those are your jobs now." He looked over his shoulder to make sure his guests weren't killing each other. "You could've called and saved yourself a trip."

"We have a meeting downtown in thirty minutes," Eva said. "I came to pick you up and make sure you got there on time."

"A meeting with whom?"

"The devil in the flesh."

CHAPTER FORTY-SEVEN

Cash and Eva met with not the devil himself but his advocate.

Cash stared hard at Stewart Powell. Casual Friday be damned, the founding partner of Powell, Ingram & Gardner sported a two-thousand-dollar Canali suit. As befits the state bar president, a heavyweight bundler for GOP candidates up and down the ballot, and the father of the U.S. Attorney in Dallas.

The suit was charcoal gray, matching his eyes, hair, and ethics. Gray was definitely his color.

More dangerous than meeting a lion of the bar like Powell on a neutral site was doing so on his turf. Everything in the corner office on the top floor of Dallas' tallest building reinforced the power imbalance at play.

Attesting to the occupant's clout were rows of framed photos of him with every living president, plus the dearly departed Reagan and Bush I and minus Obama and Biden. A picture of his daughter Jenna at her swearing-in as the U.S. Attorney dominated the rosewood desk.

Powell stood behind the desk to greet the visitors but made no move to shake hands. "Eva, so good to see you again."

She snickered. The *bullshit* was silent.

"How about me?" Cash said. "You excited to see me too?"

"Sure, sport, as excited as you are to see me." Skilled a liar as Powell was, he couldn't fake even a smidgen of warmth for his daughter's ex-fiancé and worst mistake.

"Much as I'd love to chat about the good old days," Cash said, "I don't have time today. If you have business with us, spit it out. If not, do you validate parking?"

"Don't be in such a hurry to piss away your last chance to put your lives back on track," Powell said.

Eva's eyes flashed. "Who said our lives are off track?"

Powell laughed. Stopped abruptly. "Oh, you were being serious. Hmmm, where do I start?" He looked from Eva to Cash and back again. "Ladies first. You had a job at one of the most prestigious and lucrative law firms in the world. We have paralegals who make more than junior partners at Brand X shops."

Powell shook his head slowly. "And you threw it away to work for this pillar of the profession." He nailed sarcasm like a pro. "A lawyer who has been convicted, disbarred, and disgraced."

"Hey," she said, "don't forget that I also proudly work side by side with Gary Goldberg."

"A has-been with one foot in bankruptcy court," Powell said, "and the other in the grave."

"Goldy and Cash are the top criminal defense lawyers in Dallas," she said. "They actually go to trial. You should try it sometime."

Powell picked up a document on his desk and thumbed through it. "We haven't filled your job, Eva."

"Meaning?" Cash said.

"She can have it back." Powell looked up from the document and into her eyes.

"I'll pass," Eva said.

"You haven't heard the rest of the offer." Powell drummed his fingers on the desk. Stopped. "With a nice raise and a five-year, no-cut contract."

"Make it ten years," Cash said, "and whatever raise you have in mind, double it."

Eva elbowed Cash harder than necessary to shut him up. "You can make it a hundred years," she said, "and it won't move the needle. I'm never coming back here."

"Give me the contract," Cash said. "Eva and I will review it and get back to you." He stood and reached for the document.

She intercepted the pages and ripped them up. "I'm sticking with you and Goldy."

Cash bit his lower lip. Not the time or place to remind her that the cartel would dictate his future, assuming he had one, and that Goldy was hanging on by sheer cussedness.

"That wasn't your contract that you tore up," Powell said to Eva.

Cash reassembled the document on the desk and skimmed over the boilerplate, focusing on two key provisions. First, the compensation clause offered Bettina Biddle twenty-five thousand dollars a month for ten years. It described the payments as "a gesture of goodwill for the benefit of the widow and children who, like Longhorn Investments, have been victimized by Martin Biddle's fraud."

So much more civilized than calling it what it was: hush money.

The *quid pro quo* lurked in a non-disparagement clause. In return for the stipend, neither Bettina nor her heirs, assigns, agents, attorneys, so on and so forth would bad mouth the company, its officers, directors, employees, agents, and attorneys. A violation resulted in the forfeiture of future payments and a clawback of funds already disbursed.

In short: no gag, no green.

If executed, the contract would abort the investigation into Marty's death, while bailing out Bettina, financially if not emotionally. The ten-year payout silenced the widow until the statute of limitations ran.

"As Bettina's attorney," Powell said, "you have an ethical obligation to relay this very generous offer to her."

"I don't need an ethics lesson from a lawyer who crawled in bed with Rhoden." Cash leaned back in the chair. "Besides, three million dollars doesn't come close to making reparations to Bettina for sacrificing her husband to save your biggest client."

Powell's jaw tensed. He pulled copies of two contracts from a drawer and slid them to Cash. "The offers to Bettina and Eva expire in forty-eight hours. We look forward to bringing both ladies back into the fold."

Cash didn't push back on the tight time frame. Odds were he'd expire sooner.

He and Eva didn't say a word until they were alone in the elevator. "Are you going to see Bettina now?" she said.

"Yes."

"Want me to come along?"

"No."

"Are you going to recommend that she take the deal?"

"I don't know."

The elevator reached the ground floor. "Shit," Cash said.

"What's wrong?"

"Forgot to get my parking ticket validated."

* * *

Cash ambushed Bettina in the carpool lane of Doctor Michael Hinojosa Elementary School, slipping onto the shotgun seat of her SUV. In the wake of Marty's death, she had downgraded from an Escalade to a Ford Explorer and from Hockaday to a public grade school.

She caught her breath. "You scared the holy shit out of me."

"A friendly reminder to keep your doors locked at all times."

The SUV lurched forward, its progress to the pickup point measured in car-lengths. With a couple of minutes to make his pitch outside the twins' presence, Cash went straight to the bottom line. "Longhorn Investments will pay you twenty-five thousand dollars a month for ten years."

She stiffened. "For what?"

"Dropping the investigation into Marty's death and keeping your mouth shut."

"Tell them to fuck themselves," she said.

The next three car-lengths rolled by in silence. "Sleep on the offer and call me in the morning."

"My answer won't change."

"The *only* reason I ask you to consider the deal," Cash said, "is for the sake of your little girls."

"They're the reason my answer won't change."

The twins in sight, he bailed from the SUV, leaving the contract on the seat.

CHAPTER FORTY-EIGHT

On route to Love Field Airport the next day, Cash woke Bettina Biddle with a 6:00 a.m. call. Her answer to Stewart Powell's offer had hardened from a firm *no* to an emphatic *hell no*.

Her final decision left him with mixed feelings. On the one hand, it proved him right about her mettle.

On the other, it proved him wrong. Yesterday he believed he had maxed out on pain over the prospect of losing her. Today it turned out he could hurt more.

While Bettina's mind hadn't changed, Cash's plans had. On what could be his last day in the office, he had intended to tie up loose ends and update Goldy and Eva on pending matters. Bid goodbye to both, without actually saying the word. Exit with a hug for his mentor and surrogate father. A farewell kiss for his girl Friday and best friend.

Instead, *La Tigra* diverted him to a private hangar at Love Field for wheels up at 6:30 a.m. No hint of the duration or destination of the flight, beyond her instruction to pack light. In Cash's book, that meant a toothbrush, a change of socks and underwear, and the Michael Connelly paperback of the month.

The part about packing light sounded ominous. Might indicate he wouldn't make the full flight. Perhaps not even enough time to finish the paperback.

Fine leather and polished wood gave the Gulfstream G-550 a new plane smell. The skeleton crew on board—only a pilot, a co-pilot, and a flight attendant—offered Cash the coldest of greetings.

With the passenger cabin to himself, Cash passed by eight seats and landed on the longer of two couches. The attendant ignored his attempts to flag her down, as she made her way to the cockpit with the seductive sway of a runway model.

As the plane lifted off, Cash stared out the window at what was likely his last look at Dallas. The ever-changing skyline reminded him why he had sunk roots here twenty years ago. Big D constantly reinvented itself, much like the strivers lured by the clarion call of cranes, concrete mixers, and construction crews, whose labors kept the city from sitting back and catching its breath.

The jet banked hard left, leaving Dallas behind. Cash grieved, as if he had lost a loved one.

More like, loved ones.

"Where are we going?" he shouted to the attendant, her back to him.

She stopped flirting with the pilot and turned toward Cash. "Would you like a drink?"

"Why not?" He ordered champagne. If this was to be his final flight, might as well go out with a buzz.

The Moët & Chandon Imperial Brut smoothed out the bumpy flight. Three hours and four flutes later, the plane touched down on a private landing strip. The flight attendant wouldn't disclose the location, and the view from the window didn't narrow the field much.

As far as Cash could see stretched a desert populated by cacti and tumbleweeds. A desolate scene in sunbaked shades of brown. A good place to bury a body, where it would stay buried.

La Tigra, her daughter Marisol, and six henchmen boarded the jet. It was the first time Cash had seen Marisol, but he didn't need a formal introduction to make her as the prodigal daughter. The eyes gave her away. Black, bottomless pits that could suck the soul from an enemy.

Or a friend.

The daughter had a good four inches on the mother. She was lithe, lanky. A larger and possibly more lethal version of *La Tigra*.

Scary as the soldiers were, the daughter shook Cash more. Her frown could kill. He'd seen the look before. On jurors, right before they were about to return a death sentence.

He gave the girl a pass on the attitude. Must suck to be yanked from the bosom of NYU and forced into what could be permanent exile. Doomed to pay for the sins of the mother.

Marisol walked past Cash without a word, flashing a dismissive smirk that put him in his place. He was the help, no more than a glorified gofer. She staked out the entire back row for herself.

La Tigra sat next to Cash on the couch. The white leather pantsuit accentuated her mocha complexion. She looked relaxed, like a typical tourist. That is, if a typical tourist could afford a sixty-million-dollar jet.

"Where are we going?" he said.

La Tigra smiled, in no hurry to answer.

The attendant served a round of champagne to the passengers. *La Tigra* clinked Cash's glass. "Enjoy the bubbly. We will be drinking rum tonight."

Cash's heart went into overdrive. Finally, he had something to celebrate and a shot to survive the flight. The feds must've come through on Cuba. God bless the good ole U-S-of-A.

He killed the flute. "Great news about Cuba, but why am I on this flight?"

"If your government decides to shoot down my plane," she said, "I want them to know a U.S. citizen dies with us."

Cash couldn't help smiling.

"What is so funny?" she said.

"Having me on board makes it *more* likely that my government will take us out."

* * *

Three limos met *La Tigra* and her retinue at the José Martí International Airport in Havana, and headed east on the Via Blanca Highway. *La Tigra*, Marisol, and Cash rode in one limo, sandwiched between the vehicles loaded with soldiers.

No one spoke during the three-hour ride. Marisol retreated into her private hell, insulated by an iPad and ear buds. Amazing how long she could hold a scowl.

La Tigra stared out a window, giving Cash the chance to do the same. The highway narrowed to a single lane that connected the mainland to the tip of a peninsula.

He held his pent-up questions until a pristine beach came into view. Figured the scenery might settle any waves he was about to make. "Where's Fine?"

"Sadly, he did not make it," *La Tigra* said.

"Make it to the plane or...." Cash didn't complete the sentence.

"Make it to today."

"Who took him out? You or *Los Lobos*?"

"Does it matter?"

Cash thought for a moment. "It does to me. He was a client. Not a good client or even a paying one, but still...."

"*Los Lobos* made him the same offer they made you," she said. "Deliver me or die."

He didn't call her on the non-answer and dropped the line of inquiry. Fine belonged to the past. Besides, the revelation that she knew Cash had received the same ultimatum from *Los Lobos* rattled him. Revived his fear that he would soon share Fine's fate.

"Stop the car," she shouted.

The driver braked and pulled onto the shoulder. She kicked off her sandals, shot from the limo, and ran across the whitest beach Cash had ever seen. Soldiers poured from their vehicles and secured the stretch of road. Marisol didn't budge from the limo.

Cash followed *La Tigra* to the water's edge. The turquoise tide licked her feet. The sun kissed her face. She looked radiant, like a golden goddess.

"I am home." She sounded like a new woman. Younger and freer than before.

"Where are we?" he said.

"Varadero Beach."

"Never heard of it."

"The most beautiful beach in Cuba," she said. "Your most famous gangster, Al Capone, stayed here almost one hundred years ago."

"Then you *should* feel right at home."

She turned to him. "It can be your home too."

The offer blindsided Cash. Left him speechless.

No way could he live with her. It'd be like riding a tigress. On the other hand, it wasn't clear he could live without her either. After all, he had ridden the tigress all the way to the tropics. How could he get off and survive?

"You should not go back to Dallas." Sweat beads crowned her forehead. "*Los Lobos* will be waiting for you there."

He nodded.

She took his hand. "Are you not better off with the devil you know?"

Her touch jolted him, stirring something deep and dangerous inside. He weighed her offer.

"I can protect you here," she said. "If you leave, they will hunt you down wherever you go. There will be no place to hide."

He regained his senses and his hand. "Except in plain sight."

CHAPTER FORTY-NINE

L a *Tigra* ordered the pilot to take Cash anywhere in the world, and he picked the most dangerous place on the planet. For him, anyway.

Dallas, Texas.

Then again, he had nowhere else to go and no time left on the clock. *Los Lobos'* deadline had passed yesterday.

Back in Big D, he couldn't decide on the next stop in his farewell tour, but it wouldn't be his home or office. Those would be the first venues staked out by the cartel. If he had reached the end of the line, he'd exit alone and not risk the lives of old and new friends.

At Love Field Airport, he stewed in the parked Porsche, surrounded on three sides by SUVs. Too claustrophobic to stay still, he slowly backed up. An unmarked van pulled behind his Carrera, pinning it in.

Cash crouched into a smaller target and hit the horn. Its blare drowned out his cries for help. He went silent before the horn did.

A SWAT team in tactical gear poured from the van and stormed the convertible. Cash resisted the urge to reach for his phone, a move that might prove too threatening to trigger-happy troops. Instead, his hands clamped onto the steering wheel at eleven and one o'clock, held high enough to be visible.

His palms sweat. Knuckles turned white. Mind raced a million miles to nowhere.

Frozen in the seat and facing forward, Cash tracked the assault in the mirrors. D-E-A emblazoned in large, white letters on the team's black vests comforted him a bit but not much. Cartels had a history of impersonating law enforcement. Plus, there was plenty of precedent for cops to play both sides of the drug wars.

A stocky agent, either real or counterfeit, opened the driver's door. The plastic face shield of the helmet hid his eyes. His right hand held a Sig Sauer P220, the weapon of choice for both DEA and the bad guys.

With his left hand, the agent motioned for Cash to ease from the car. No words spoken meant no chance for Cash to detect a foreign accent.

"Am I under arrest?" Cash said.

The agent pulled him from the car. "Let's call it protective custody." He had an East Texas twang. "For now."

* * *

"You should've stayed in Cuba," Dani Tanaka said.

"I'm happy to see you too." Cash sat across a pockmarked table from her and Agent Duane Leroy Lee. Dani seemed hyper this morning. A haggard Leroy binged on a box of donuts.

The interrogation room at DEA headquarters was windowless and ten degrees too hot. "You didn't need to send a SWAT team to pick me up," Cash said. "A simple invitation would've done the trick."

Tanaka's dark eyes narrowed. "There was concern on our part that we wouldn't be the only ones at the airport to greet you. Even if you've ruled out Cuba, you shouldn't have come back to Dallas. We can't protect you here."

He made a show of looking around the cramped room. "Not even in the bowels of your own building?"

"Don't be a wiseass," she said.

He couldn't help it, not with no-nonsense Dani as a foil. "Protect me from what?"

"Don't play dumb," she said, "because you're not very good at it."

"I'll take that as a compliment."

"Don't." She killed a cup of coffee, clearly not her first of the morning. "We know all about the threat from *Los Lobos*."

Cash's spine stiffened. "Who told you?"

Dani looked at Leroy, whose shrug gave her the green light to burn his source. She turned back to Cash. "Eva freaked out when she couldn't reach you yesterday. She contacted Leroy, and he called me. She told us about the ultimatum."

"She shouldn't have done that," Cash said.

Leroy shook off his stupor and mumbled through a mouthful of donut. "Eva has more sense than you do."

"Seems to be the consensus," Cash said.

Dani slapped the table. "Either you're not taking the threat all that seriously, or you have a death wish."

"Definitely no death wish," Cash said.

"Well, we can't protect you from a cartel," she said, "not if you're going to tool around town in a red Porsche that screams asshole attorney."

"Asshole attorney is redundant." Not the first time Leroy had used that line.

Her glare silenced the street agent. She shifted her sights to Cash. "You've got one chance to survive, and that's to disappear into witness protection immediately." She pushed a pile of papers toward him.

He thumbed through the two-inch stack. No need to waste time reading the fine print. He'd seen the forms before, not that any of his clients had been foolish enough to sign away their souls to Uncle Sam.

The contract would be ironclad and impossible to honor. Kiss his old life goodbye and embrace a fresh start as a greeter at Walmart in Bumfuck, Idaho. Or a bellboy at End-of-the-World, Indiana. A checkout clerk in Nowheresville, Nebraska.

"No thanks." He pushed the pile back to her. "I'll take my chances on my own."

"Once you step outside the building, you become the next unsolved murder on some burnt-out cop's desk." She sounded almost sad.

Cash was touched. He didn't know she had it in her to give a shit.

"Before you make the biggest mistake of your life," she said, "you need to know that Fine was gunned down thirty-six hours ago."

"Old news," Cash said. Though he didn't know which cartel claimed or deserved credit for the hit, he decided not to ask.

"And *La Tigra*," Dani said, "is also dead."

The new news gut-punched Cash. For several beats, he couldn't muster even an inner voice. He finally managed the faintest of whispers. "That can't be true." He regretted the words as soon as they left his lips. Of course, it could. The reality of cartel life is that anyone can die at any time. Aloud, he added, "I saw her last night."

Again, so what?

Dani poured him a glass of water. "She was killed while you were in the air."

Cash bowed his head, lost not in prayer but in second-guessing the call on Cuba. "All the work we did to find her a safe place to land, and the fucking Cubans give her up just like that." He snapped his fingers.

"The Cubans didn't do her in," Dani said. "It was her daughter."

The hits kept coming. Another pause while Cash collected his thoughts. "Why? How?"

"The 'how' part is easy," Dani said. "The daughter stabbed her to death."

She took a deep breath and went on. "The 'why' is more complicated, but start with the fact that Marisol never wanted to go with her mother. The girl had a life and a lover here in the States. She hated her mother for forcing her to flee to Cuba. After you left, they argued. *La Tigra* slapped Marisol, who grabbed a knife, took a swipe, and hit the jugular. The mother bled out in minutes."

Cash fell silent. It wasn't the first client he'd lost. Not even the first this week. It still hurt, as if the fates didn't trust him to balance the scales of justice. Plus, he'd put together the deal of a lifetime, only for it to fall apart in twenty-four hours.

"What will happen to Marisol?" Cash said.

She shook her head. "That's out of our hands. Just like you will be, if you turn down WITSEC."

The offer tempted Cash, for a nanosecond. He came to his senses. "The program's not for me."

True that. Witness protection had a thousand picayune rules, and Cash had trouble following a few simple ones. In the end, he couldn't close the door permanently on Eva, Goldy, and Bettina.

Dani looked to Leroy. "You're his friend. Maybe you can talk some sense into him."

Cash expected Leroy to deny the friendship. Instead, he pushed the box of donuts toward Cash. "You look like you haven't eaten for days. Take one, but not the chocolate-glazed."

Famished as Cash was, he passed.

"Is there anything I can do for you?" Leroy said.

Cash nodded. "Give me my phone back and fifteen minutes alone in the room."

Dani stood, followed by Leroy. They exited the room. She left behind the paperwork for WITSEC. Leroy took the box of donuts.

CHAPTER FIFTY

"Where the hell have you been, son?" Goldy sounded older and crankier over the phone than he did face-to-face, if that was possible.

Alone in the DEA interrogation room, Cash stuck to the game plan for throwing Goldy off his trail, permanently. Resort to the big lie. Spring the whopper on the old man first. Fine tune the falsehood before laying it on Eva, who had a better ear for detecting his bullshit.

"I'm entering witness protection," Cash said.

Goldy's wheezing sounded perilously close to death rattles. Given the state of the old man's ticker, this conversation could be their last. Both knew the rules of WITSEC, the chief one being no contact with anyone from a past life.

"Want me to look over the paperwork?" Goldy said.

Cash had expected the old man to trash the program and try to talk him out of vanishing into it. Goldy didn't go there, which showed a healthy respect for the long, lethal tentacles of the cartel.

"Too late for that," Cash said. "I've already signed up."

Another pause. Labored breathing on both ends now.

"When do you go in?" Goldy said.

"After my next call...to Eva."

Goldy groaned. "Much as I hate to lose that gal, she'll want to go with you."

Cash gripped the phone tighter. "We both know that can't happen. She supports a mother and more relatives in Mexico than I can count. She can't cut them off."

Plus, she has to take care of you, old fella.

"Your call with Eva won't go well," Goldy said, "and things between you two will end badly. Want me to break the news to her?"

"Tempting," Cash said, "but she needs to hear it from me."

The next silence proved longer and more painful than the prior ones. It broke when both blurted out, "I'm sorry."

Cash recovered from shock first. "Never heard you say that before."

"I could say the same about you." Goldy had developed a catch in his voice.

"Sorry about what?" Cash said.

"Driving you away. We were one helluva trial team, until I started taking you for granted. Remember what I always said about our partnership?"

Cash smiled. "Yeah. The only thing that could stop us, was us. Don't beat yourself up. You didn't drive me off. I lost my temper, said some things I didn't mean, and had too much damn pride to ask for my job back."

"Pride got the better of me too," Goldy said. "I picked up the phone a hundred times to ask you to come back, but never managed to make the call."

Cash blinked back tears. Good thing the conversation had played out over the phone. If he couldn't wade through this call without waterworks, no way would he dam the flow of tears during the next one.

* * *

"I've been worried sick about you." Eva had a voice for the phone. A perfect pitch that could soothe or sting on command. So far today, more sting than soothe.

"I took a quick trip," Cash said, "and I'm about to take another."

"Where are you going?"

"TBD."

"How long will you be gone?"

"Also TBD."

A click on the line interrupted the call.

"Are we being bugged?" she said.

"Almost certainly."

"We have to talk face-to-face."

For a host of reasons, that was the last thing he wanted to do. "It's not a good time for us to get together. Some very bad people are out for my blood. That's why I'm entering the witness protection program."

It proved surprisingly easy to lie to Eva. After all, it was for her own good.

"That's insane." The sting in her voice spiked.

"It's my only shot at staying alive."

"If you go in, I go with you." It didn't come off as a threat. More like a statement of the obvious. A law of nature.

"This is goodbye." Cash choked up, the strain of holding back tears proving too great.

"We're not doing this over the phone." Her voice quivered.

"It's too dangerous for us to meet," he said. "This isn't up for debate."

Like hell it wasn't. Eva turned everything into a negotiation.

"I know a safe place," she said.

* * *

Though the courtroom lights were dim, Cash could make out Eva. She sat in the jury box in the chair reserved for the foreperson. Judging from the look on her face, Cash didn't expect the verdict to cut in his favor.

The high ceiling room was empty, except for the two of them. Lining the walls were oil paintings of the succession of judges who had ruled over this courtroom.

The court painter had flattered the current occupant, Anna Tapia, by erasing a decade's worth of worry lines and softening her angular features. She looked good, actually better than good. Not the first time Cash had fantasized that under different circumstances....

He instinctively sat at the defense table, the one farther from the jury box. "Persuading the judge to open her courtroom for us was no small feat. Do you have pictures of her with a dead chicken?"

"Those weren't nearly as embarrassing as the one shot I had of her with you. Seriously, when I told her that Freddy the Forger's case could be dropped from Monday's docket, she would've offered her house to us. Amazing how accommodating a judge can be, when she gets back three weeks of her life."

She walked to Cash. He stood. Had a clear escape path behind him, but his legs wouldn't move.

She put her arms around him and held on tight. He couldn't muster the strength to break her grip. Instead, he hugged back.

She buried her face in his chest. Her tears soaked through his shirt, burning his heart.

"You have to let me go." His voice shook. It came off more like a plea than a command.

"I can't."

"Your mother needs you. The family needs you. Most of all, Goldy needs you."

"And you don't?"

He had no comeback for that. He finally broke her grip and held her at arm's length. "The sooner I leave, the better the odds that both of us stay alive."

"Will you ever come back?"

"I'll be gone forever or until *Los Lobos* get wiped off the map, whichever happens first. Pray that another cartel comes along and clears out the competition."

"And your clients," she said, "how can you desert them?"

He had thought that through. "Bettina Biddle is the only loose end that'll haunt me, but I've got a plan there. The key to helping her lies in the archives of the Powell law firm. To find that key, we need a mole inside the firm."

"Don't look at me," Eva said. "They won't take me back, not after we turned down the deal Stewart Powell offered."

"We'd never accept a deal that required Bettina to drop the investigation into her husband's death, so I've found another candidate to infiltrate the firm."

"Who?"

"A player to be named later," he said.

"You realize that you'll probably end up in the frozen tundra or worse."

"We'll see." He released her arms and walked away. At the door he turned back to her. "Leave the courthouse through the back door. I'll walk out the front."

"What are you going to do now?" she said.

"Remember what you used to tell me whenever we faced an impossible task?"

She nodded. "Never send a man to do a woman's job."

* * *

After a dozen aborted calls, Cash gave up on phoning Bettina. He rolled onto her block at 9:15 p.m. and parked across the street and two houses down from her place. Close enough to catch a glimpse if she popped outside. Far enough to keep her safe if he were followed.

At ten sharp the porch light came on, the door opened, and Nuisance bolted onto the yard. The chocolate lab had grown so large that Cash barely recognized him. The pup dashed to a flowerbed to do his business.

Bettina stepped onto the porch, barefoot and wrapped in a scarlet robe from her neck to her knees. It took all of Cash's self-control not to call out to her and superhuman strength not to run to her.

Bettina clapped her hands and yelled, "Come on, Sport. Time to turn in for the night."

Sport?

Cash could live with a name change for the pet. Just not sure he could live with one that sounded like something Stewart Powell had come up with.

Bettina followed the pup into the house. The porch went dark, and Cash saw her in a different light.

CHAPTER FIFTY-ONE

Six months later....

Cash listed starboard while shuffling into the Ritz lobby. He leaned heavily on a cane, a black staff capped with a silver-coated lion's head for a grip.

He stuffed a twenty into the tip jar on the baby grand piano. The pianist obliged the request for an up-tempo version of "Send in the Clowns."

Cash tapped out the beat with his cane, before moving slowly to a barstool. He stared into the full-length mirror behind the bar. An old man stared back, disapprovingly.

Cash blinked first.

The old man in the mirror had a new face, courtesy of the incredible Doctor Katz. The cosmetic surgeon had flipped the script by designing a flatter nose, a deeply-furrowed forehead, and sagging jowls. Padding here, cutting there. Adding twenty-five years on a good day. Thirty on a bad.

The transformation had started with a scalpel but hadn't ended there. Contact lenses changed the eye color to a dusky brown, fitting for the autumn of a man's life. Likewise, the complexion had darkened to a beige hue that hinted at hot climate ancestry. The salt-and-pepper hair featured more salt than pepper, and the right ear hosted a hearing aid.

Or what passed as a hearing aid.

Cash's own mother wouldn't recognize him. Then again, since she hadn't seen him since he was eight, that wasn't much of a test.

"Another scotch and soda?" the bearded bartender said.

Cash green lit round three of his go-to drink. The mixed drink reflected his mixed feelings about being here. The site of his highest highs and lowest low. His mood swung between hyper and haunted.

In a past life, the Ritz had been his happy hunting ground. The intersection of cheaters' corner and lust lane. However, his arrest for jury tampering had gone down here, landing him behind bars for two years and without a law license for three. Had kind of put him off the place.

From his perch, Cash could take in the entire room, confident that he remained unseen. In a bar packed with the glam and glitterati, the only thing more invisible than a forty-year-old woman is a seventy-year-old man.

Cash reached for the drink but stopped short of the glass, mesmerized by the counterfeit liver spots on the back of his hand. They seemed to have multiplied overnight.

DEA agent Duane Leroy Lee appeared in the mirror and landed at a table, the first of the party to arrive. Like Cash, Leroy sported a new look. Clean-shaven and in a suit, he looked more like an arrester than an arrestee. For a change.

Eva placed second and joined Leroy at the table. From the barstool, Cash couldn't make out what was being said, but clearly both were stumped as to why they had been summoned.

Next to claim a seat at the table was Detective Robert Gamez of the Dallas Police Department. Despite being in plain clothes, the ex-soldier with the Marine Corps crewcut and a baton up his ass couldn't have looked more like a cop, even if he'd worn dress blues and pinned a badge to his forehead.

Tina Campos completed the quartet and step one of Cash's game plan. Assemble the team for their assignments.

Tina placed a purse on the table. Cash fine-tuned the fake hearing aid. The bug in her purse allowed him to eavesdrop on the conversation at the table, while the mirror behind the bar offered him a panoramic view of the room.

Eva looked to each of her tablemates in turn. "Will someone explain why I'm here?"

"Same goes for me." Detective Gamez sounded beat.

"I brought you here because we have something in common," Tina said. "A desire to help someone we care about: Cash McCahill."

Gamez snorted. "I met the guy only once. Twice, if you count the time he cross-examined me."

Eva winced. "Let's not."

Cash recalled the cross of Gamez, then a rookie on the force and a virgin on the witness stand. It had been the biggest meltdown since Three Mile Island and a major reason a guilty-as-hell client walked from the courtroom.

"It's time folks accepted the facts of life and death in cartel world." Gamez's tone turned harsh. "We'll never find McCahill's body. *Los Lobos* will make sure of that."

"Not so fast," Tina said. "Leroy, is there still a contract out on Cash?"

Leroy nodded. "My snitches swear it's still open, and last month the jackpot jumped to five million U.S. dollars for proof of death."

Cash choked on the figure. Five million bucks! He ordered another scotch and soda.

Leroy loosened his tie. "Who do I have to fuck to get a drink around here?"

After a waitress took their orders, Tina got back to business. "Why would *Los Lobos* keep open the contract, if Cash were already dead?"

"To throw everyone off their trail," Gamez said.

Leroy shook his head. "That ain't how cartels roll. When they take out someone, they generally want the world to know about it. Tends to keep the living in line."

"If Cash has stayed alive," Eva said, "it's because he's burrowed deep into a hole in the middle of nowhere. Long as he's underground and safe, we shouldn't try to find him. Odds are we'd lead the *sicario* straight to his door."

"True," Tina said, "unless someone were to remove *Los Lobos* as a threat." She turned to Leroy. "I've read that the cartel wars are heating up south of the border."

"North of the border too," Leroy said. "The peace both governments brokered by siding with *Los Lobos* over *La Tigra* lasted all of six months. The new kids on the block call themselves *Los Asesinos*. Subtle fuckers. They make *Los Lobos* look like a kindergarten class."

Cash was glad he'd ordered another drink.

"What if *Los Asesinos* were to do the world a favor by wiping out *Los Lobos*?" Tina said.

"The new apex predators wouldn't give two shits about an old contract on our boy," Leroy said, "and they sure as hell wouldn't pay off on it."

Cash drank to that.

The waitress returned to the table with four drinks. While Gamez had passed on booze, like a good Boy Scout, Leroy made up the slack with a whiskey and a beer chaser.

Gamez stood. "You three can war game this out all night, but I've got better things to do with my time."

"Better than catching a serial killer?" Tina said.

Gamez froze for a beat before sitting. As the lead detective in the murders of six trans women, he was drawing heat from higher-ups and the LGBTQ community. The strain showed in his face, where premature lines bracketed his hangdog eyes.

"And me?" Eva said. "What am I doing here?"

Tina nudged her purse closer to the center of the table. "Have you talked to Bettina Biddle lately?" The conversation came in louder and clearer on Cash's end.

Eva blushed. Odds were she owed Bettina a call.

"We talk from time to time," Eva said, "mostly about Cash. She doesn't believe he's dead either."

"Are you still looking for someone to infiltrate the Powell law firm?" Tina said.

Eva leaned forward and nodded.

Tina smiled. "Because I know the perfect girl for the job."

* * *

LIFO. Last in, first out. Described Leroy's office hours during the dregs of a career marked by more downs than ups. Standard nonoperating procedure for a beer-guzzling burnout.

FILO. First in, last out. Leroy's schedule at the Ritz tonight. After the others left the hotel with their assignments from Tina, he relocated to the bar, two stools down from Cash.

Cash almost gagged on the agent's buy-by-the-gallon aftershave. Leroy must've bathed in the swill. "Looks like your friends deserted you."

The agent glanced at Cash. "They're not my friends." He ordered a Jim Beam Black.

"I would've guessed you were more of a beer drinker," Cash said. "A Tecate guy."

"Busted." He changed his order to a Tecate. "Figured I had to up my game to mingle with the beautiful people."

"I sensed that this wasn't your usual watering hole, and that's not a putdown. I'm a fish out of water here too."

"So what else can you tell just by looking at me?" Leroy said.

Cash leaned back and took in the full measure of the man. "You a cop?"

Leroy did a double take. "What gave me away? Is it my trim but powerful physique?"

Cash laughed. "Yeah, that for sure. Plus your suit is too snug to hide the shoulder-holster."

Leroy patted the bulge at his left ribs. "For an old-timer, you've got good eyes. Say, back in the day, were you a cop?"

"Guilty as charged," Cash said. "Twenty plus keeping the peace in Buffalo."

Leroy gave Cash another look, longer this time. "There's something familiar about you." He frowned. "Have we met before?"

"Not in this life."

Tina doubled back to the bar and put her hand on Cash's shoulder. "PawPaw, I told you to wait in the car."

"This is your father?" Leroy said.

"*Mi abuelo*, but most of the time, he acts more like *mi tontito*." She eased Cash from the barstool and held on until his balance steadied. "I hope he wasn't bothering you."

"Not at all," Leroy said. "Sharp as the old fella is, we could probably use him in the agency."

Tina laughed. "That'll be the day."

Cash shuffled from the bar, listing port. She kicked his instep, a warning to shift the cane to the other hand.

"A mistake like that can get you killed," she whispered.

On the way out, he tipped the pianist another twenty, made his parting request, and exited to "I Fought the Law."

THE END

ACKNOWLEDGMENTS

A t the head of a long line of people to thank are my parents, from whom I inherited a precious gift: a love of reading and writing. I am blessed to have in my life a wife, Regina, and daughter, Jessica, both writers themselves, who are infinitely patient and supportive.

I am eternally grateful to super-agents Jan Miller, Austin Miller and Nena Oshman at Dupree Miller & Associates. Jan is more than an agent to my family and me. She is a longtime friend, a confidant, and most importantly, the godmother of our only child.

It also takes a village to produce a book, and I had a great team at Savio Republic and Post Hill Press, including the talented trio of Debra Englander, Heather King, and Anika Claire.

I have the good fortune of being a small cog in a group of talented writers who break bread on Wednesdays and critique each other's works. The "Wednesday Night Writers' Conspiracy" includes: Jan Blankenship, Victoria Calder, Will Clarke, Peggy Fleming, Harry Hunsicker, Brent Jones, Fanchon Knott, Brooke Malouf, Ellijzah Manuel, Clif Nixon, David Norman, Glenna Whitley and Max Wright.

Finally, my belated and wholly inadequate thanks to lawyer and friend, Jim Blume, and my Austin angel, Erin Brown, both of whom love mysteries as much as I do and who have read every word I have written. My trusty sidekick, Veronica Long, who is my Della Street, makes working at a law firm fun.

ABOUT THE AUTHOR

Paul Coggins is a nationally prominent criminal defense attorney, whose clients have included A-list entertainers, powerful politicians, Fortune 500 executives, professional athletes, nonprofit organizations, and government bodies. He is the former United States Attorney for the Northern District of Texas and is currently the immediate past president of the National Association of Former U.S. Attorneys.

His most recent novel, *Sting Like A Butterfly*, introduced Cash McCahill and his journey to reclaiming his license and his life.

·